Lisa Lang is a Melbourne writer. She is the author of the non-fiction title *E W Cole: Chasing the Rainbow*, and was selected in 2007 for the Australian Society of Authors' mentorship program. *Utopian Man*, her first novel, was the co-winner of *The Australian*/Vogel Literary Award in 2009.

UTOPIAN MAN

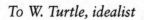

To W. Turtle, idealist

Prologue

EARLSBRAE HALL, ESSENDON, 1918

The marmoset runs through the grass, straight towards the old man in the black suit and top hat. It climbs up his leg, swings from his coat and settles on his shoulder, muttering in his ear. The man strokes its chest.

The day is winding down, the sun is low, and bees fly drunken circles around the lavender. Soon the birds will come to roost in the palm trees, singing wild songs to ward off the night. Shadows stealing colour from their bodies and wings. Soon the night will come, and stay for hours, days. And he will lay the usual traps for sleep: books, warmed milk, lavender beneath the pillow.

The marmoset breathes its warm breath on his neck. They are waiting for him in the house.

He turns, stumbles, and the monkey dips earthwards, grips his ear to keep from falling. It happens, since the stroke. Cut down the middle like a figure in a medical book. Hard to change the gait of decades. He adjusts his step, moves closer to the house. It still makes him smile: a mansion, plate glass windows, white columns aglow in the last of the sun. Corinthian. The marmosets come running across the grass towards him, and his bulldog, Alfred, rises slowly from the mat, shaking bugs from his coat. Edward lifts the monkey from his shoulder and places it with the others.

'I'd invite you in, but the last time you ate all the pâté.'

The monkey cries out, a short, sharp sound, and the others begin to chatter softly. He goes inside without hearing their complaints.

...

He limps through the hallway, parquetry glossy as honey on the floor. Fine materials used throughout this place, which was built by a man who made his money on the goldfields. Edward wonders if they might have crossed paths, if they ever tipped their dusty hats in passing. No doubt he would have heard of him, back then. The men who found gold, their names were well known, legendary. A few syllables, more intoxicating than all the liquor in the camp.

'There you are,' says his daughter from the doorway, moving towards him.

And he sees the slight frown, realises he is standing in the middle of the hallway. He hands her his hat and she takes it to the hatstand—what passes for a hatstand here. A stuffed polar bear in a nickel-plated cage, bought long before she was born, fur yellowing and gaze still fierce. As if the image of a man and a gun is forever trapped behind glass eyes. Eyes that have seen his children grow to adults and seen him grow old.

'The fire is lit, and there's a fresh pot of tea,' she says, as if to entice him, unable to see that he is not reluctant, only living with a different sense of time.

...

The fire burns almost red against the bluestone. Steam rises from the dragon's-head teapot. His daughter pours, all collarbone and long, white neck above a dark fox stole. Her brother sits beside her. A little fleshy in the jowls, his coat buttoned high as if to hide the fact.

Once, Edward knew, precisely, how to make them laugh, or squirm with excitement. He knew their fears. He knew that Valentine had a horror of slugs, would scream blue murder at the sight of their wet and primal bodies, while Ivy was repulsed by velvet and would not touch it with bare skin. Young Eddy, his namesake, had worshipped sculling champion Henry Searle, and Ruby had been fond of the smell of ripe cheese. But as they had grown, they had somehow grown strange to him, and now he knew them less well than he did when they were nine or ten. How could that be? At no point was he aware that his knowledge of them had stalled, or moved in reverse.

The tea, an oolong, tastes of dust and berries. In Japan, the teas were dense mysterious pools in rounded cups, flavours shifting on the tongue, on the roof of the mouth. Impossible to find tea like that now.

'You look tired, Pa. Do you feel tired?' His daughter refills his cup. She had been a serious child, eager to please. The sort one could give a locket and chain. Never overtaken by high spirits, as Ivy was, or easily distracted, like the boys.

'Well, I have been busy. Resting, reposing, lolling about. A little idling, when I can fit it in.' He smiles. But not sleeping, hardly sleeping.

'They say you've been wandering about the grounds.' His son's voice is careful, neutral. 'Talking to yourself.'

Edward turns his head to face the fire. Wavering coppery flames. He remembers all the fuss one summer, of having to rescue, time and again, this same son's imaginary friend: from drowning in the sea or a foot caught in the railway tracks. A pigmy, daunted and bamboozled by the civilised world—what *was* his name? Edward touches the wisp ends of his beard. 'Heard from Kuku lately?' Ah, Kuku. The name has arrived like a gift. It isn't always the case these days: names, words can be elusive. His daughter laughs, then stops herself, tea rolling down her chin.

'I was eight, a child! It's normal for children to imagine things.' His son flushes and unbuttons the collar on his coat.

So the gardener has told tales on him. Or maybe the cook. Mostly he talks to D'Ama and Eliza, and sometimes, lately, to Beaver. No harm in it, no harm.

His son runs a tongue over straight front teeth. 'I think—all of us think—the time has come to put your affairs in order.'

Before he loses his mind. And leaves his Arcade to the monkeys, or worse, to the scheming Joy Endicott. To the polar bear in his nickel-plated cage.

'You do seem restless, Pa, thoroughly out of sorts. If you settled everything, you might be able to relax,' says his daughter. Leaning forward to brush monkey hair from his suit. Her soft perfume, like freesias.

If only he could settle everything! Publish all the work cooked up by his eager brain. Promise a long and satisfying life to each of his children. Ensure the future of the Arcade. His fear is that they will divide the Arcade and, like dividing a rainbow, end up with nothing. His singular, beloved life's work.

He lowers his empty cup to the table, dismayed by the sound it makes rattling on its saucer. 'Well,' he says, looking around, smiling at them both. Pressing his hands to his knees. 'It's been delightful. But I must get back to it.'

...

It takes time to climb the stairs to the second floor.

They had tried to move him downstairs, on account of the stroke. They had lectured, pleaded, begged. But there is no good view of the gardens from the downstairs bedrooms. You will be lying in bed, they argued, you won't see them anyway. He instructed the gardener to plant a seventy-foot floral rainbow, a sweeping curve of petunias, marigolds and pansies. When it was finished, he asked Eddy to construct a series of mirrors, like a periscope, so he could see the coloured flowers from his bed. Every day he wakes to find himself alive the flowers are there, cheering him on.

With the door closed, the room is cool and silent. He sits on the end of the bed and removes his shoes. He sniffs the air. Lately, the room has smelled of eucalyptus. It might be a real smell, something used in cleaning, or a memory. Clean as pine, but with Mallee heat at its heart.

And he wonders how it is that in all these years he never went to Adelaide to see Beaver.

Sleepiness, that rare thing, is settling behind his eyes. Time to pull back the covers and take off his coat. Eyes on the mirrors, he sees his white head nearing the white pillow. Then the flowers, lines of pink and indigo, happy corridor to his dreams.

Chapter One

MELBOURNE CUP DAY
1883

Edward stands on the third floor watching clouds drift above the city. Below him, on the street, a thick caterpillar of people is forming. The race is finished. Earlier in the day the city was desolate as thousands of people made their way to Flemington, to watch those sweat-lacquered beasts in motion. To cheer, and throw paper to the wind, and drink. Now they are returning, buoyed and restless, to the city's heart. In perfect time for the grand opening of Cole's Book Arcade, Bourke Street. Edward smiles to think how he has piggybacked on this day, how he will ride its rough energy, he who never drinks and never gambles.

He glances down at the street, as the feathers in their hats sway left in the breeze and right themselves.

He turns his back on the window and crosses the empty room. Soon it will be filled with their furniture, all the rugs and cosies and trinkets of home life. Home. This is not how he had pictured it. It is not the paradise of children, dogs and flowerbeds he had imagined return-ing to each evening, lawns scattered with fallen apples and shoes. But his wife claims that the suburbs make her sluggish. She had pressed for them to keep living in the city, and suggested they make the Arcade's top floor their own. This was not straightforward. Edward had already designed a ceiling—a hundred-foot-long centrepiece of iron rosettes, flanked by rows of glass panelling on either side—which was to flood the ground floor with the sun's own light. And this meant pushing rooms on the second and third floors to the periphery, keeping the central space empty to allow the light through. Which left no room for a standard rectangular flat. But they could, he conceded, design the flat in a horseshoe shape. That settled it, as far as Eliza was concerned: what could be luckier than living inside a horseshoe? And besides, she had added, it would save them a good deal of money.

Edward closes the door on their soon-to-be flat. He walks towards the interior balcony, leans into its pol-ished wood, and surveys the main room of his Arcade, two floors below. Sun streaming through the glass ceil-ing, the whole thing, at this angle, blanched into near whiteness. The red jackets of his staff in brilliant con-trast. He is rather proud of the jackets. The idea is to give them a little confidence, the younger ones, with their thin necks, their bad skin and fear of getting it wrong. Dress a man in red velvet and he is equal to anything. He watches them moving through the aisles, straightening books that have yet to be pulled from the shelves, and chairs that have yet to be sat on. Twelve red figures, all in motion for fear of looking idle. But the brass columns have already been shined to a state of perfect reflection. And the shelves have been wiped clean of dust. Four hundred feet of cedar shelving. Seven hundred thousand books. Everything from geology to gladiators, Persian myths to phrenology, Buddhism to pigeon breeding. Too many books for a city this size; he may have got carried away. But that is the point. Let them see for themselves how wide the world is. Let them see what it can hold.

He was twenty-five the first time he entered a large public library, and was almost flattened by the weight of his own ignorance. There was just so much there. He had hoped to find a book on carpentry; there were more than a dozen. He chose one at random, his hands grey against the paper despite the cake of good soap the library provided. He was sleeping in the street then, living in a world of dark and narrow lanes, and the sudden excess of light and space and knowledge was brutal. He felt exposed in its glare, grubby and uncouth. He slid the volume back. There was shame in the way he dropped his head, his hand trailing columns on his way out. But by looking down he saw a simple plaque, missed on entering, which read: *For the people of the city*. It stopped him in his tracks. The people of the city—wasn't that him? It was true he was grimy, ignorant and all the rest, but that library was there for *him*. He could read any book he liked. He could read all day, every day, if he chose. Nothing was stopping him. Nothing! The power of this thought was dizzying: the world spread before him.

Now he hopes, more than anything, that the Arcade will be a place of wonder, of generosity and small revelations. And if he has cheated a little—exaggerating the number of books, both in his ads and in the careful placement of mirrors—then it is all for the cause.

One floor below he sees his wife, Eliza, leaning on the opposite balcony. Swaddled in a shawl, ballooned in late pregnancy, she looks up and catches his eye. Smiles her true smile: small teeth and excitement. He blows her a kiss, and another for the baby that will be their fifth. Every penny now sunk in this one venture. Their future bound up in ton of paper and the whims of public taste. But what is the point of nerves? Building the Arcade was like trying to dream the same dream every night: holding the vision clear while details twisted and changed. Glaziers refused to tackle his design, builders quit and the cost of timber soared. But here it is. He grips the balustrade. Right here in his hand.

By the time he reaches the bottom of the stairs, his staff have turned to stare at him with the blank, expectant look of newborn chicks. He realises he should have prepared a few words to mark the occasion. He rubs his hands together and offers them a grin. 'What do you say we throw these doors open, and see what happens?'

...

There is a long moment when nothing happens. The doors are opened wide, and a crowd stands bunched at the entrance. Faces peer inside and Edward smiles back at them. Beside him stand the Little Men, a pair of foot-high sailor dolls, rotating a bar that flips a series of tin signs: *Cole's Book Arcade*; *One Million Books*; *The Reign of Knowledge and Humanity Is Coming*; *Read*. The clang of tin hitting tin marks the passing seconds, with Edward's heart thumping in the off-beat. *Let the World Be Your Country*; *All Men Are Brothers*; *Cole's Book Arcade*; *Read*. He looks out at the crowd, eager faces flecked with uncertainty, and touches his beard, feeling for its coarse comfort. And then the band starts up. Big, brassy notes crashing over them, as bodies begin pouring through the doorway on a current of powder, beer, sweat, tobacco and hair oil. Voices calling out—*Look, look at that!*—above the jangling piano. Faces filmed in sweat, and women pausing to adjust their hats in the mirrors. Bodies colliding as people walk, heads tipped back, to view the sky-lit roof. Young men sprawl in cane-bottomed chairs for the novelty of it. Pretending to be engrossed in a book one moment, calling out to friends the next. Book after book being slid from the shelves. And a new sound joining the band: the clear tones of the cash register bells.

As more people swarm through the doorway, Edward notices that the crowd's momentum is pushing people over the threshold, making them stumble or lose their balance. And while they mostly seem to laugh it off, some clearly look alarmed. One man even turns and pushes back. Beneath the broad goodwill lies a hint of violence.

Edward looks around until he spies his manager, Owens, a short man with a concertina brow. He is sweating freely, sidestepping and ducking his way through the throng towards Edward.

'The medals,' calls Edward. 'Quickly, bring the medals!'

Button-sized and made of copper, he has planned the medals as a gift for his first customers. Each one bears the image of a tree and its own uplifting message: *Dare to Do Right*; *All Men Are Brothers*; *Reading and Thinking Bring Wisdom*; *The First Book Arcade in the World*. When they were freshly minted, he had shown them to his friend, the import magnate D'Ama Drew, who shook his head and warned Edward not to scare people before they'd bought something. But now there is no time to play it safe. Edward is thinking on his feet, waving over two long-limbed youths in scarlet jackets. He uses them to form a barricade at the door, to stop the flow of people, which brings shouts and boos from those on the verge of entering.

'Ladies and gentlemen!' He waits until the booing dies off. 'Due to the popularity of the Arcade,' he calls through his cupped hands, 'an admission of threepence will be charged for entry, and a rare commemorative medal issued, which may be kept or spent at the Arcade as valid currency.' This will at least slow them down, if it doesn't drive them away altogether. Edward reaches his hand out to Owens, who has just worked his way back through the crowd, and takes the small hessian bag from him. He grabs a couple of the tokens—bright as new coins—and holds them up for the people to see.

At which point they begin to cheer. Raw, spirited, big-throated cheering. He is charging them admittance, and they, in their festive fervour, are cheering him for it. Just wait until he tells D'Ama that.

Edward dips his hand into the bag of cold medals and laughs.

...

That night, Edward is too elated to sleep. He lies in bed beside Eliza, who is also restless, the life within her demanding space and movement. They repeat their happy inventory of the day: the barely contained crowd, the brilliance of the band, the thrilling atmosphere. They turn their pillows over, seeking the cooler side.

'It was like a cathedral,' she says. 'Do you know what I mean? Before you opened the doors. There was that stillness, and the high ceiling. I felt small and light, and in the grip of a great optimism.' Edward reaches beneath the sheets to pat her hand. 'But those chairs, Edward! They'll be ruined. You need something sturdier.'

Edward smiles in the dark. The chairs can end up as kindling, for all he cares. So long as people come, and use them, and wear them out reading.

He drifts, and wakes each time she hauls herself up to use the chamber pot. He sees a figure sitting on the bed in the semi-dark. It is his old friend Lucky Cho, thin, in threadbare clothes. He leans in, touching Edward lightly on the wrist. 'I see you made good use of our money.'

Edward wakes with a jolt that rocks the mattress. His skin is prickly hot.

I see you made good use of our money. He turns the words over, trying to decipher the exact tone. *Good use.* Could it be approval, a kind of blessing? *Our money.* More likely an accusation, a reminder that the dead do not easily forget.

Maybe it is nothing at all: overexcitement, a dream of a ghost.

...

The evening is warm and the children run outside to see their father off. Eddy and Vally make for the gutter with its murky, forbidden water. Linda stands on the steps, all angles and soft hair, bouncing her baby sister on her hip.

'It smells!' says Vally, crouching with his hands pressed against his nose.

'Keep out of the gutter!' calls Eliza.

'I saw a rat, and it was swimming and had cheese in its mouth.' Vally paddles his arms, miming a swimming action. Eddy, the older of the boys at five, clicks his tongue in disbelief.

'Now, make sure you go to bed when your mother tells you. And don't forget to kiss your sisters goodnight.' Edward uses his mock-stern voice, the closest he comes to paternal authority. At fifty-one, he is too enamoured of his family, too grateful, to play the fearsome patriarch. In eight short years he has gone from bachelorhood to this: a wife, four children with another on the way, and a tenderness that flows from him, towards them all.

Eliza stands in the doorway, plump and placid, with her hands folded across her belly. Ruby squeals loudly and begins to kick at Linda like a mad jockey. The late sun sends out hazy peach rays, enfolding them all, and Edward is suddenly nostalgic for this moment, even as it's happening. They grow quickly; he loses them with every moment.

He hopes D'Ama will be late. But he sees Linda is already lifting her hand, pointing. 'Look, it's D'Ama's carriage.'

And the boys are running to meet it, chanting, 'D'Ama, D'Ama, D'Ama.'

Edward moves towards Eliza, placing a kiss on her talcum-scented cheek. 'Don't have the baby before I get back.'

Eliza smiles, puff-eyed and sleepy. 'You go on now and enjoy yourself. Say hello to D'Ama for me.'

Inside the carriage, D'Ama smokes relentlessly, and Edward pushes open the small window. Neat terrace houses appear framed for a moment before sliding from view.

'I hope this debate isn't about cremation,' says Edward, crossing his arms.

'I agree. Tempers flaring, arguments going up in smoke.'

'And I hope it's not about anarchy either.'

Ash falls from D'Ama's pipe, soft as down. None of it lands on his striped suit pants. 'Alright, why is that?'

'They're always getting out of control.'

D'Ama's long, curled moustache lifts slightly, the only sign that he's amused. Edward is buoyed. They haven't been out together in months. It was too draining, that endless round of architects, lawyers, glaziers and builders. Edward had drawn the Arcade plans himself—cramped, crooked sketches—then taken them to professionals to have them redrawn, and this had earned him a good deal of scorn. One builder grumbled that the work was too finicky, worse than his last job—a grand brothel in the legal district—and for what, a heap of dusty books?

'They won't touch spiritualism, I know that for a fact,' says D'Ama, pipe gripped between his teeth.

'No, why is that?'

'Last time they tried it, not a soul turned up.'

...

They file through the doorway, past a paper sign (*Secularism vs Christianity, tonight*) and into the busy hall, where they find seats on a bench in the last row. Edward's neck prickles. He is both drawn to and fearful of crowds: the volatility, the body heat and tang, the noise. Tonight the noise is mostly men's voices and their boots crossing the floor, and it drops a notch when the chairman introduces the debate, the last few men taking their places against the back wall.

The first speaker is a short man with strictly parted hair.

'The principles of secularism are to use your time, intellect and strength for the improvement of life, and to bring the greatest good to the greatest number of people.'

A quick, pink tongue wets his lips. 'Unlike Christianity, it permits the culling of good from all sources. Imagine you stumble upon a magnificent orchard, with apples, pears, cherries, plums and many more fruits, and you are told you can only eat the fruit off one tree. Well, the world is like that orchard, and Christianity is only one tree. As a secularist you can sample the best fruit from all trees: Christianity, Buddhism, Brahmanism, and so forth. Your diet is varied and your mind grows strong.'

Edward loves the structure of debates, their careful order. Logical minds working at the knot of existence.

'But just as importantly, secularism allows us to reject the fruits that are rotten. When I read a story that says Jesus Christ was born of the Virgin Mary by the power of the Holy Ghost, then I say, this is of no use to secularism because it is clearly untrue.' He pauses, eyes directly on his audience. 'Virgins do not give birth to children, nor are ghosts the father of them.'

The room erupts in hissing, booing and scattered laughter. A stocky, red-faced man gets to his feet and shakes his fist at the man on the podium. D'Ama leans closer to Edward. 'That Hugh Browne is always leaping out of his chair over something. An ape in fine clothes. Look at his son-in-law—wishing the ground would open up. Poor Deakin. I hope his pretty wife is worth it.'

Edward only loosely follows D'Ama's talk. He is caught up in the emotion, its sudden surge. It's amazing to him that in this sweat-soured auditorium full of men, ideas matter. At the first debate he ever saw, in Castle-maine, the diggers stood in a tin shack, mud-cast to the knee. *Standing*—after a full day of dredging the earth. Edward was astounded. He followed the arguments, the rough interruptions, in a state of near elation. This was not money-making, carousing, fighting—everything he knew of the goldfields. This was something else. Edward could feel energy moving through the room like a secret currency and understood, at twenty-two, that words were power too.

Another short man takes the stage, motioning for quiet in the crowd. 'Before he chose to insult the Virgin mother—'

The noise, which had subsided, rises up again. He speaks loudly, right over the top of it.

'Before the insult which I will not repeat, our opponent told us the moral code of secularism is this: the greatest good to the greatest number.' The man scratches his head in an exaggerated gesture. 'I must ask him, then, how it is possible to ascertain the greatest good? Does he decide on the greatest good? Does the government? Do I?'

The man smiles, a rueful, put-on smile, and shakes his head. 'The strongest instinct of human nature is that the highest good is my own good. We are, at heart, selfish beings. Without a belief in higher judgement, or a supreme being, am I not justified in believing I serve the highest good by helping myself? And what is there to stop me helping myself to the property of my neighbours and friends?'

D'Ama whispers in Edward's ear, 'Word has it he's helping himself to his brother's wife.'

The short man pounds his chest with his fist. 'If I, as an individual, am to be the judge of what is the greatest good and who forms the greatest number—and remember, some people say that one is the greatest number—private property could very well be threatened, and society as we know it would fall to pieces and be destroyed.'

Fierce clapping breaks out across the room. After a moment, Edward joins in. Not in agreement—he sides with the first speaker—but in acknowledgement of the evening, its very existence. Men grappling with how best to live. The more he claps, the more he wants to clap. He claps with gusto until his palms start to burn, until it almost seems peculiar to him, this bringing together of flesh-covered bone, a foreign act, a disembodiment.

Then he settles back to listen some more.

Chapter Two

1886

Edward walks the corridors in his socks so as not to wake the household. Summer mornings he wakes hours before he needs to, a soaring feeling high in his chest. It strikes him this is the feeling he had as a boy in summer. Waking to the day's possibilities: the discovery of a wild patch of blackberries or a strange stray dog. The whole summer tasting of anticipation, when in fact vast tracts of it were spent in farm chores, bible studies or tending to brothers and sisters. He didn't mind the games of hide-and-seek, the wheelbarrow rides which so amused his young entourage. But if he got the chance he would tear off on his own, through country lanes and woods, convinced that wondrous things could happen to him only in solitude. One time he saw a powerful white falcon lifting skyward with a mouse in its talon, and it seemed to hover for a moment, eyeing him, as though they were the only two creatures on earth.

These days the feeling is connected to the Arcade, which is proving to be its own rich world. Today it is getting a fernery. Twelve months ago he acquired a building adjoining the back of his Arcade through a disused walkway, and was pleased to be expanding, though he viewed the walkway itself as dingy and drab. But it soon occurred to him to treat that space—technically city property—as his own. Within a month he had built a glass canopy to tie in with the Arcade's glass ceiling and to protect his customers from wind and rain. And today he is installing the masterstroke: giant tree ferns from Mount Dandenong. The Arcade will have its own lush hideaway where city people can seek nature, and solitude.

Edward can hardly wait. It is all he can do not to hum as he steps through the corridor's cool green shadows and into the kitchen. The hanging copper pots gleam gently. The white marble bench glows, coolly, like a slab of polar ice. It is a clean, bright room, smelling of lemons and lye. It is not a place spilling over with food; they live close to the markets and make regular visits. Living above the Arcade is, after all, convenient. It has its charms. The front rooms enjoy large windows where he can watch the changing panorama of sky above a patchwork of rooftops. A view he finds calming, even distancing, as if it puts him beyond the everyday concerns of men. But the kitchen, which runs down the right-hand side of the Arcade, butting up against another building, has skylights instead of windows. This, to Edward, gives it a feeling of energy and purpose.

He takes a bag of plums from the cupboard and steps back into the corridor. Then he follows the U-shaped passage around to the building's left, past the drawing room and his bedroom, to the children's rooms. Ah, the sound of singing—someone is awake! He opens the door to the girls' room: heavy curtains edged with sunlight, three walnut beds with white lace spreads. But the three girls lie sleeping, Linda's face covered by the dark seaweed of her hair, and Pearl partly buried beneath the bedclothes. He sees Ruby with her fists curled beneath her chin, her face blank, and realises she is singing in her sleep. Sweet, wordless faerie song. He stands there, breathing in the milky, intimate, sweet-sour smell of the room.

Then he takes out a plum. Made of darkest purple, it seems lit from within. He places it gently on the frilled lap of a porcelain doll, and hides the rest of the plums around the room.

'Somebody's taken my Limburger cheese!' he says, loud enough to wake them, watching as Ruby's eyes fly open, and Linda sighs and rolls over, tugging hair from her eyes. Several beats later, Pearl emerges from the bedclothes.

'I've been searching this whole house, following the trail with my nose,' he says, loudly sniffing the air. He bends to sniff the bedspread, then sniffs his way up Pearl's arm to her hot little ear, making her squeal with laughter. 'I think it's somewhere in this room. Oh, who has taken my lovely old ripe smelly cheese?'

Ruby giggles, clambering out of bed, while Linda is already up on her long, lean legs, searching the room.

'No, Linda, wait,' cries Pearl. But Linda simply uses her height to point out plums to the younger children— on a windowsill, on the dresser—then hoists them up to collect their prizes for themselves. Soon they are all sitting on Linda's bed. Ruby tackles her plum with intent, juice splattering her white gown, while Pearl cradles hers gently in her palm. Edward knows she will save it for an hour, perhaps a whole day. At three and four years of age they are remarkably, perfectly themselves.

'Remember how you gave Mother a bag of plums on the day you met?' says Linda, licking juice from her fingers. Edward smiles, knowing what comes next.

'Will you tell us again how you met?' she asks hopefully.

Edward sits himself down on the bed and the girls shuffle closer. Ruby rests her head in his lap and he touches her hair, warm as new bread.

'Well, it was during the wife shortage of seventy-five,' he begins. 'A bad year, a terrible year, for the finding of wives. Worse, some say, than the bachelor plague of thirty years ago, but that's just opinion. Anyway, times were certainly tough.' Edward rubs his palms together. 'What was a man to do? I went down to the *Herald*'s office to place my regular ad for the shop, and instead I decided to place an ad for a wife.'

'With a twenty-pound reward!' adds Linda.

'Well, I didn't think I should like a *cheap* wife.'

Edward laughs, but can still recall, with disturbing precision, the editor's face: eyes cased in fat, the coarse, speckled skin, the way he leaned in to check Edward's breath for whiskey. The office reeking of tobacco and sweat, and a potted palm dead in the corner. Having to trust this slovenly editor with his deepest desire—like dropping a pearl into mud.

And it was his deepest desire.

By forty-three, he had learned to live with periodic bouts of sexual desire. Thrilled and dismayed by their sudden, sweeping intensity, he found them, in the end, easy enough to control. But something else had begun to happen in his forty-third year. Vivid images and memories of boyhood were plaguing his waking hours. A pudding cooling on the windowsill of his childhood home. A baby blackbird, fallen from its nest, frenzied in its death throes. The bitter, cloying smell of hop fields. His newborn brother, swaddled in sheepskin, sucking on his finger. They came upon him without warning or purpose, but with a ruthless domesticity at their core.

Was he dying? Or was it just unnatural, in an evolutionary sense, living on his own for so long?

And then there were the dreams. Almost every night he took part in some epic, full-colour dream with twisting plots. In one, he tried to cross a river in a boat made of straw. Crocodiles snapped at the flimsy craft, which was slowly filling with water, and he pelted them with hard lemons he had found on board. In the same dream, or maybe a different one, he was back at the goldfields, and he'd fallen down a deep mineshaft. There was water up to his neck, and his feet were slowly sinking into the soft mud bottom.

By some inner logic he no longer recalls, he felt that everything would settle down if only he got married.

Linda chews on a knuckle. 'And the man thought you were playing a joke,' she prompts.

'He most certainly did.'

For this was Edward's style: to place outrageous advertisements, to draw attention to his shop in unusual ways. He had once run a story in the same paper claiming that a new race of men with tails had been discovered in the jungles of New Guinea. Every day for a week he placed another instalment of the story, in which he described tail fashion, tail hygiene, tail manners, tail sport and even tail fortune tellers. In the final instalment he concluded that men were happier with than without tails, and that all kinds of *tales* could be bought from his bookstall at the Eastern Market.

So he had not been taken seriously, he understood that.

But he was absolutely serious. More serious, certainly, than the average man, who seems content to find a wife through some accident of timing or acquaintanceship. This struck Edward as risky and absurd. He did not believe in fate, or holy intervention. He believed in words. And he trusted that the right words would conjure the right woman for him.

To his surprise, he received dozens of replies. Some of them were angry, accusing him of using the sacred rite of marriage as a publicity stunt. Some were genuine and probing, sent by the relatives and friends of spinster women. Only one was penned by a woman herself, and this was the only one he replied to.

He was shocked when he saw her. She was so plain: short, dark-haired, with something of the seal in her body and face. He had not expected beauty, that wasn't it, but some quality that shone through, a beauty of the soul. When she spoke she was direct and confident. She believed in loyalty, in following her husband to the ends of the earth. He warned her that his views were not conventional, that he believed all religions were essentially the same, that all races of men were equal.

'That's all well and good,' she had said. 'But how do you treat a man who works for you? How do you treat your friends?'

And he had noticed then the colour of her eyes, not brown or gold, but the colour of a lion's coat.

This is not how he tells it to the children. He does not mention his hesitation or his dreams of death, or the way the city laughed at him for seeking love in a newspaper. He looks at Linda, her thin features grafted from Eliza's, and wonders if time will flesh them out.

'Then we were married, in a beautiful, small church, with D'Ama there to cheer us on. And then came a bunch of naughty children: Linda, Eddy, Vally, Ruby, Pearl and baby Ivy. With every child we thought: Oh dear, this is a very naughty child, we'd better ask for another one. But each child was naughtier than the last!'

Ruby and Pearl clap madly at this, their favourite part. Linda's eyes are wide and glazed with emotion. It is time now to go downstairs and open the shutters, or he will be late. Lifting Ruby's head from his lap, he is surprised by its unexpected weight; a small flesh-and-blood anchor mooring his heart.

...

Edward stands on Little Collins, waiting for the delivery cart. It is a dirty street, backing onto factories, and Edward hears the clank and thud of nearby industry. A breeze blows through, acrid and chemical, whipping up rubbish. It is the kind of street so devoid of life even the rats ignore it.

As he reaches for his fob watch, the sound of hooves breaks into his awareness. The horses come into view, their heads lowered. Behind them, at more than twice their height, are the tree ferns: wavering, fragile, intensely green. Gliding past the factories, a dream of the forest in the city's heart.

Edward is spellbound. As though some other agency has planned all this. He watches the horses: stout and spotted and rough of coat, but with the dignity of thoroughbreds. He watches the ferns, a trembling mirage, barely credible in the grey landscape. Apart from the drivers, he is alone on the street. The whole event coloured by the rare, singular quality of his boyhood adventures.

'You Mr Cole?' calls one of the drivers. Skinny and freckled, he looks no older than fourteen. Beside him, the second driver appears a little meatier. Still, Edward wonders how they will manage to shift their large and awkward cargo. They jump from the cart, and Edward points them to the walkway where the ferns are to be placed.

The boys move swiftly. They carry the plants between them, grunting, cursing, but careful not to damage the tender fronds. When they are finished, Edward tips them generously, thinking all the while of his own two boys.

'Thanks, mister, have yourself a champion day,' calls the freckled one, climbing up into the cart. Edward basks in this rough blessing. He will have a champion day.

...

But by four o'clock he is red and sweating and his tail-bone hurts, as he sits on the hardwood bench at the Turkish baths. On the wall facing him is a gold mosaic of a Moorish castle; the other three walls are covered in white and aqua tiles. The air is dry and filled with astringent forest smells. Edward's towel is tucked in a neat origami around his waist, while D'Ama wears his loosely draped on lean hips. D'Ama does not look hot. He looks like he could live here, sustained by grapes from the hand of an Eastern beauty.

For that is what the baths are supposed to invoke: foreign customs, indolence, the erotic East. Edward understands this. But he is hot. Sweat pours from him and catches on his beard. Beneath his towel, his legs are pale and knobbed. His feet are large, the toes white like bulbs dug from the ground. His posterior pains him. He thinks of the ferns swaying in the laneway, cool and breezy. Fresh lemonade, rolling down his throat.

'How much longer do you want to stay in here?' he asks.

D'Ama lifts his arm and rests his head in the crook of his elbow. 'Oh, I don't know.' He closes his eyes. 'I saw James Endicott in the corridor, and with any luck he'll stop in here and you can meet him. *Fascinatingly* wealthy.'

Edward groans. No. No. They are supposed to be relaxing, leaving the cares of working life behind. But now he suspects D'Ama has really brought him here to mix with certain people. For if D'Ama believes in anything, he believes in connections.

When they met—more than twenty years ago—they were working stalls, side by side, at the Eastern Market. A crazy carnival of a market, open night and day, with a shooting gallery, tattooist and lady wrestler alongside the fruit and vegetables and bundles of hay. Edward sold used books and D'Ama sold curiosities—fossils, skulls, masks, carvings and taxidermy—and it was hectic, exhausting, honest work.

Then one day D'Ama was offered the chance to buy an unusual specimen: a red bird of paradise from the Malay Archipelago. Smooth yellow body, decadent red plumage, and so rare most believed it to be a myth. It was expensive, too, more than either of them could make in a month. When D'Ama calmly packed up the entire contents of his stall and took it to several pawnbrokers to raise the funds, Edward thought he'd lost his mind. He feared D'Ama had been swayed by its beauty and its rarity, and had made a ruinous mistake. His stall stood desolate; even the display cases were gone. But D'Ama laughed and promised to take Edward to dinner that night if he would lend him the final few shillings, which Edward did. As soon as he got hold of the bird, D'Ama took it to the new museum and sold it for an astronomical profit. He had, it turned out, a contact, who kept him informed of what the museum might want, and what it would pay. D'Ama never returned to his market stall; he had made enough in that one transaction to lease an entire warehouse.

So if D'Ama believes in connections, it is not without reason. He has built his fortune on them, his import business one long chain of connections from port to port, country to country. But Edward prefers to trust his own vision, nothing more.

The heat wraps around Edward, tight as a bandage. 'Listen, D'Ama, I have no interest in meeting your Mr Endicott. I have nothing to say to him. I suggest we make our way to the pool and cool ourselves down.'

D'Ama stretches, ribs standing out against his narrow torso. 'Fine, fine. I had too much Château d'Yquem last night. Allow me a few more minutes to rid myself of the effects.' D'Ama yawns, one hand loosely covering his mouth. 'But there is one topic you might speak to James about. He's on the board of the City Corporation. You know, the chaps who own that walkway where you put your trees today? A word from him could make that enterprise rather more . . . legal.' D'Ama rubs his heavy black eyebrows, and Edward cannot help but marvel. His ways are not Edward's ways, but he holds to them with the passion of a believer.

It takes them another hour to plunge into the cold pool, submit to their massages and change back into their clothes, and in that time Edward does exchange a passing word with James Endicott. Turns out he is a fan of Cole's Book Arcade, and not as dull a fellow as one might think.

...

It is dusk by the time Edward returns to the Arcade. He strolls down Bourke Street, loose-limbed and hungry, and pauses at the main entrance: white façade, shop name in black and a coloured rainbow arching over it. Bright as new, for he has it repainted every six months. Then he moves to enter right at the moment when the lights come on: a dazzling arc, tracing the rainbow, lighting it up for the evening trade. It feels lucky to be passing beneath it at just this instant.

The gaslights are already burning inside, giving off their mellow glow. Edward tips his hat to the Little Men, who tell him: *The people everywhere who we do not know are as nice as the ones we do*. Edward couldn't agree more! What a pleasant individual James Endicott was, calling the Arcade a 'feather in this fine city's cap'. What a great sight to see almost every chair in the book section taken up by sprawling young men, or the few ladies game to sit among them. Edward walks through the aisle, the shelves on either side showing coloured spines packed tight as bricks. How wonderful, he thinks, that trees should live a second life as books.

He moves through the stationery section, with its rows of bottled ink and crisp envelopes, and towards the stairs at the back of the room, where he finds Owens is waiting, blocking his path.

'Mr Cole, may I draw your attention to this latest disaster?' He stands on the first step, a full head shorter than

Edward, waving a piece of paper in the air. It is fair to say they have had their disagreements. Mostly over Edward's policy that no one be pushed to buy, moved along or made to vacate a chair. A paradise for thieves, as Owens likes to point out. But Edward cannot bear the thought that a single customer be turned away, intimidated or made to feel out of place when he has come with intentions of reading and learning. So he absorbs the thefts and, even when he catches the thieves red-handed, rarely prosecutes.

'Alright, Owens. How many books have we lost this month?'

'Oh,' says Owens, pursing his lips. 'It's not about *that*; I'd rather given up on that. It's the new fellow, Benson. These are his stock orders, and they're all over the place. He doesn't seem to know what it is he's doing.'

Edward takes the paper from his hand. 'Take a look around, Owens. It's Wednesday evening and the Arcade is full of people. We have three cashiers on duty, and dozens of people reading. Where is the disaster? All I see is a simple matter that needs to be sorted out.'

Owens continues standing, stiff-jawed, in Edward's way. Edward rubs his ear.

'What say I take these orders and correct them myself? And if you have the time, you could show Benson how to do it properly. I'm sure that would help matters a great deal.'

Owens nods and steps neatly off the stair. 'Very good, Mr Cole. I'll see to it at once.'

Edward takes the stairs, wondering how it is that Owens always spots him so quickly. Sometimes he will strike up conversations with random customers, simply to delay Owens swooping on him. Once he held up a baby and kissed it.

Inside his office, tucked into a corner of the second floor, Edward feels blissfully cut off from the world. He sits behind his elaborate Indian desk: monkeys and elephants carved in relief on three sides, with topaz beads for eyes. The top is inlaid with alternating squares: icy jade, and smooth mother-of-pearl like silk turned to stone. He rubs the surface with his thumb, never tiring of its feel. The perimeter of the desk is stacked with columns of paper, and Edward drops the sheet of stock orders onto the nearest pile. He will leave the paperwork for now, his mood too soft and inward-looking. Settling deep into his leather chair, he breathes its warm-blooded smell.

His wife will come to call him soon for dinner, returning him to the warm chaos of family life. But for now it's just him, his space, his thoughts. He slides open the right-hand drawer and takes out a good pen. Finds the page he wants from a pile on the desk. It is headed *By The Year 2000* and already contains several lines in his jagged scrawl. A kind of joy comes over him as he begins to write: *The world will be one federated country, with one religion and one language. Flying machines will be in general use. A network of railways, telegraphs, telephones and later inventions will connect the entire earth.* No love letter was ever more sincere, no poem more heartfelt. *Human disease and suffering will be diminished one half. The average length of life will be nearly doubled.*

If the spiritualists are right, he might one day look down upon this future world and know for himself how things have turned out. Wouldn't that be something?

Men will feel that eating, drinking, sleeping, playing and money-making are not the sole purposes of life, but that they are destined for something higher and nobler.

He smiles to think of showing this to D'Ama. Or to Owens.

He writes: *Cole's Book Arcade, Bourke Street, will be*—and stops to think a moment. What kind of city will emerge by then? Will there be five million, ten million people? Will they come from every corner of the earth? And what about the books themselves—handsome, compact, self-contained—could they change in any fundamental way? A moth appears, circling the unlit lamp on his desk. Drawn to its future light. A muscle cramps up deep in his shoulder. He puts down the pen and takes a moment to rub the tender spot. The room has grown dim and he can smell his body's own slight earthiness.

He is sitting in the dark when his wife knocks on the door, her hand firm and unmistakeable. The room has turned cold, the moth is gone and he cannot recall his thoughts. His mind has gone blank.

Chapter Three

1889

Why do certain memories lodge, sharp-edged, in the mind? Edward is in his office, in shirtsleeves, on a warm spring morning. Windows thrown open to the breeze. On his desk are the cloth-bound volumes he uses for scrapbooks. He is sourcing material for the second edition of *Cole's Funny Picture Book*, a job he adores. Rewriting the captions on cartoons he has clipped from the newspaper. Sorting through rhymes and sentimental poems. Making long lists of riddles. *What ties two people together yet touches one? A ring. What should you keep after you have given it away? Your word.*

Head down in this light, amusing work, when all of a sudden he thinks, *rice with ginger*, and even tastes its back-of-throat burn. Rice with ginger, what on earth? He pushes it away, sensing a trail he doesn't wish to follow. But it niggles at him—rice with ginger, rice with ginger—so he lets it carry him, back to where he knows it must be heading, to the goldfields. Feels the tight-skinned fear of the place. No order, no real governance, just men with shovels, men with guns, exhausting the same small patch of earth.

He was twenty, alone, didn't even have a digging partner. Didn't talk to anyone. Lived in fear of being robbed, being beaten, killed, and no one to notice or to care. Didn't think of getting sick, but that's what happened. Speared by cramps that left him doubled up and gasping, and he guessed, from what he'd heard, that it was dysentery. That he would soon recover, or else die. This should have frightened him, but the delirium was so very good. He lay down by the creek bank, in the ripe gut-stench of his own evacuations, believing he was back home in Kent, dozing in paddocks dug with fresh manure. Smiling. Happy for the first time in weeks. When the fever broke and he realised where he was, how weak, how he stank, he had whimpered like a pup.

Then—a boot tap to the ribs. 'Get up.'

Robbery. At last. He teared up in relief at finally getting it over with.

But when he sat he was handed a bowl and told to eat. Edward saw then that the man was Chinese, and thought, how do I feel about that? Realised he didn't feel any way, apart from filthy, hollowed out. Scooped up the rice with ginger and stuck it in his rank, sulphurous mouth.

'My son loved the whipping machine best,' says the man with the copper hair and beard—and this back in the present, in Edward's office, so that he must try to think who the man is, what he's doing there. Edward rubs his eyes, the bridge of his nose, and looks at the mess of clippings on his desk, as though a tree has shed its black and white leaves.

'I only mention it because I hope you'll keep it in the new edition,' says the man into the growing silence.

Of course he'll keep it. It's probably his favourite cartoon: four boys in stocks, bottoms raised in the air, while behind them spins a steam-powered cylinder with hundreds of sticks attached, giving each bottom a non-stop round of whacks. He'd named it *Cole's Patent Whipping Machine: The Gentle Persuader*, had choked up laughing over that. Claimed it could flog two thousand boys per hour.

The man rubs his jaw uncertainly, and Edward sees his solid fingers, capped with ink. Of course, thinks Edward, it's Benson from the print department. And makes an effort to be more friendly, to shake his goldfields gloom.

'My sons loved it, too,' he says. Eddy, who has never had so much as a slap on the wrist, thought it the greatest joke. Only Ivy worried for a moment that it might be true. 'I should have all this ready for you by tomorrow. Did I tell you today? Is that why you've come?'

Benson nods and offers a small shrug. He is a stocky man, compact, with powerful shoulders and strong hands. Too young, of course, to have been on the goldfields, but the kind of man who would have held his own there. How Edward used to envy those men with a pure physical presence, the best defence. He was all too aware of his own shortcomings—scrawny build, green, jumping at shadows—a victim in waiting. Who knows what would have happened if Lucky Cho had not befriended him.

'If you need me to, I could stay back a little later, make a start on it tonight,' adds Benson, making Edward pause to consider him. Something likeable about him, a way of putting himself forward without fuss. The offer pleases Edward; he'll remember it.

'That won't be necessary, Benson. Thanks all the same. But tell me, what's your son's name? I could put him in the book, write him into one of the rhymes. You know, *Andrew Grace for not washing his face*, et cetera.'

Benson suddenly grins, his face puckering and boyish. 'Thank *you*, Mr Cole, that's really very kind. His name is Ulysses Gideon.'

...

Edward sits down beneath a lazy arching fern, shadows like zebra markings on his hands, across his pants. The air cool as morning grass. He has come from his humid office to meet Eliza, but he is early and knows she won't be there yet. He sighs, glad at least for the change of scenery. It churns him up, thinking about the goldfields, inhabiting the skin of that scared, skinny kid. He makes a point of never dwelling on it, and months will pass when he doesn't give it a thought. But the memories always return, fear having fixed some detail in his brain the way certain chemicals fix a photograph. Thirty-seven years and he can still taste the way the ginger caught the back of his throat.

He runs his hand along the rough log bench, liking the way splinters catch and nearly break the skin, taking his mind in another direction. There is plenty of distraction in the fernery. Take the young couple in the corner, side by side, their heads near to touching, the man polishing his glasses with a handkerchief. See the way the woman takes them from him, gently, as if to say, let me do that, to save him the trouble, but really wanting only to touch his hand. So intimate that Edward looks away, then laughs to think how many people surround them—a dozen at least—sitting on benches in two parallel rows, reading, or eating their lunch. He turns back to the woman, her profile perfect like the face on a coin, the man looking owlish with his glasses on. Some slight nostalgia stirring now in Edward, though he can't think why.

It's not as though he and Eliza ever posed romantically in shady nooks, gazing coyly at one another. They were older when they met—Eliza thirty, and he was forty-three—and they agreed straightaway that they would marry. Trading romance for cold certainty; they both considered the deal more than fair. They would embark on marriage the way gulls dive for fish—swift, determined, bold—not as lovebirds cooing nonsense to each other. So it had come as a shock, after they were married and Edward put his arms around her for the first time, to feel his heart leaping from his chest, towards hers. To feel love, where he thought there was simply goodwill and logic.

'Pa! Pa!' The voices of his children; he would know them from a thousand others. He turns to see Ruby and Vally running down the wide corridor between the benches, their faces stretched with excitement.

'Tom is dead!' yells Vally, and Ruby nods, tears dropping from her eyes. Eliza stands behind them, calm. She holds the basket with Edward's lunch. Tom: the family cat, that ageless beast. Striped and vicious and beloved of the children.

'What happened?' he asks, circling Ruby with his arm.

'Oh, it was very sudden. I think he may have eaten poison,' says Eliza, taking a seat next to Edward. 'I don't think he would have suffered at all.'

Ruby leans against Edward's knees, stroking his beard like a pet. 'I think he'll be reincarnated,' she whispers, looking up at Edward. 'Maybe as a prince!' At seven, her face is already marked for beauty, her lips and cheeks and brows all perfect arcs.

'Is that what you think?' Edward smiles. He has been taking them through world religions: karma, martyrs, angels and demi-gods, and while Eliza complains that it's too rich a fare for bedtime, the children gobble it up.

Vally taps his foot against the floorboards. 'Pa, you haven't even noticed my costume!' He frowns, arms crossed high on his chest. He wears a string of green glass beads, and a towel wrapped turban-style around his head.

'Oh! I'm terribly sorry.' Edward cups his mouth with his hand. 'I thought for a minute you were my son Vally, but you're clearly the Sultan of . . . Fernland.'

Vally bows; pink ears stick out from the old bath towel. His face so round and soft and freckled. Edward bows in return, and Vally perks up. 'I have come to purchase some camels, six of your finest, please. And any books you have on the desert, and a gold pen with silver ink.'

'And what will you do with the camels?'

'I need the camels so I can travel to the desert and look for buried treasure.'

'I see. And what about the pen and ink?'

'That's to draw the map. If you find the treasure, and it's too big, you need a map so you can go back again later.'

'And how, may I ask, will you pay for it all?'

Vally scoops up the beads that hang at mid-chest, holding them towards Edward. 'With my emeralds.'

Edward laughs. He enjoys Vally's performances, his mania for dressing up, the imaginary friends, but worries there is something pleading, almost desperate, beneath them. Some gaping need that life has yet to fulfil. And Edward thinks he might recognise this from his own childhood, his own impassioned flights into solitude, though they seem the very opposite of Vally's posturing. For they have this much in common: imagination, sensitivity, a longing for the extraordinary. Both have come from large close-knit, loving families, yet found themselves, at a young age, craving more. Needing something extra, while their siblings seem perfectly content within the realm of family life.

He wishes he could translate this flash of insight, to let the boy know he is understood, as well as loved.

'I do have a lovely volume on the deserts of the Australian interior,' says Edward, tapping his lip. 'I might be willing to trade for emeralds.'

Vally nods, fingering his beads, wanting, Edward suspects, to say something clever, to keep the performance alive. But Eliza is already opening the basket, releasing meat smells into the air.

'Lunchtime for sultans,' she says, handing Vally a drumstick.

The food is good, the chicken warm and well-salted. Edward has a small bone in his mouth, sucking the last of the bird-flesh, teeth coated in grease, when suddenly he stops. Almost spits it all out. He has remembered a dream. A dream he had in the early hours and forgot on waking. A dream so full of foreboding he wants to fling the bone from his hands.

It starts with him standing on the third-floor landing, studying a handprint on a pane of glass. Eight feet high—however did it get there? But even as he puzzles over it, it begins to fade, and soon there is no trace of it. He hears a noise, a soft-bodied thud, coming from above, and he looks up through the glass ceiling to the blue sky: nothing. It is several seconds before he sees the bird. Bone-white, it flies from the light well to the ceiling, throwing itself against the glass, trying to break out. Edward feels the blood drain from him, a sense of horror. The sky darkens, fills with heavy clouds. But they are not clouds, because they drop suddenly towards the Arcade's roof, and Edward raises his hands instinctively towards his face. Just before the dark mass hits the glass, it splits into pieces, into hundreds of white birds. They wheel away from the glass, cawing, flying to safety. Edward drops his hands to his side, shaking his head in relief. But the birds immediately regroup. Flying in formation, they turn a perfect circle, heading once more towards the Arcade. Edward closes his eyes just as their bodies begin to hit the glass.

'Are you done with that bone?' asks Eliza, holding out the empty basket. He would like to tell her about the dream. He would love nothing more than for her plain good sense to drive away its eerie presence. But he won't mention it now. Not with Ruby slouched against his leg, and Vally—making a show of unwrapping the towel from his head to use as a napkin—glancing at him for approval.

Ruby climbs up beside Edward. She stands on the bench and makes her hands into crabs, walking them across his hair.

'There's something I'd like you to do for me,' says Eliza.

Edward leans over and takes the towel from Vally. 'Well, you know I'm powerless to deny you anything,' he says, wiping his hands clean and winking at Ruby. The couple he'd watched earlier walk past, arm in arm, and the woman looks back over her shoulder to smile at Ruby. The same indulgent smile that is always given to Ruby.

'I'd like you to take me to a party tonight. At the Endicotts'.' Eliza tilts her head, smiling.

Edward swallows, tugging at his collar. 'A party? Tonight? Well, you know how I feel about parties, dear.'

Ruby dabs at his forehead like a nurse with a cold cloth.

'I do, I do. But it's been weeks since we've had an evening out. I'm getting that sluggish feeling. I need to socialise, sharpen up the brain!'

...

Edward is standing against the wall, not so much smiling as flashing a monkey's white grimace. His suit rubs against the velvet wallpaper; it goes against his instincts to move further into the crowd. Smoke drifts through the room, thin and ghostly. He will never remember all these names, these faces. He can hear a piano playing, light and effortless, beneath the rumble of voices. The women wear their finest gowns, jewels shining on skin like pirates' loot. Edward thinks of the thousands of silkworms spinning, of the cotton fields of Egypt, of all the oysters in the South Pacific polishing their hidden pearls.

'Mr Edward Cole, where on earth is your drink?'

Her smell is blissful: gardens at dusk. He turns to see a tall woman in her mid-twenties, her wheat-coloured hair pinned high on her head and woven with jasmine.

'I like to see the world through sober eyes.'

She smiles and raises her glass to him. 'Good for you. I hope you like what you see.'

Edward, who can see an alarming amount of her bosom, says nothing.

'But come,' she continues, sliding a bare arm through his. 'There is someone waiting to meet you.'

The walk across the room takes some time. Mrs Endicott is drawn into several groups of people, Edward standing awkwardly beside her. He realises it is no longer a gold crowd: those hard, self-made men he once met at all the gatherings. The kind of men who, on striking it rich, had stuffed banknotes into sandwiches and eaten them, or hung gold nuggets from their earlobes. These people are soft-skinned types in suits: land speculators, investors, the paper rich. Compared with these people, gold is old money.

When the discussion shifts to Edward, he tells them he would rather invest in rainbows than sink a single penny into land. This helps keep conversations brief. He doesn't trust this latest craze for buying up land that one has no intention of using, in the hope of selling it off at inflated values. Why should he feign any interest in it? To trap himself in hours of tedious talk?

He keeps an eye out for Eliza, hoping to be waved to safety by her plump hands, her sympathetic smile. So much so that he almost steps on a poodle, which glares at him beneath a curled and manicured fringe. Edward thinks he glimpses diamonds in its fur. Joy Endicott frowns.

'I can't understand it, he said he would wait right here.' She bites her lip. 'Will you wait here for me, while I go and get him?'

Edward nods sadly. Trapped between the punchbowl and the wall, he finds plenty of time to regret D'Ama's absence. If D'Ama were here, he might point out the man he had once found drunk and shirtless, embracing the statue of Redmond Barry, planting kisses on its cold bronze nose. Or the woman who had been at a charity ball when she stood on the host's pet lorikeet and, believing she'd killed it, had hidden it in her bodice until it started squawking during the speeches.

If D'Ama were here he, too, would be stationed at the punchbowl, and Edward would not be left alone to twiddle his thumbs. He glances over at the bowl, a cut-crystal basin the size of a cannonball, then blinks, moving in for a closer look. The fruit appears to be swimming. Edward rubs his neck and leans in for another look. No, not fruit, but yellow seahorses, with eyes like tiny black pips.

'They'll be dead by the end of the night,' says a man, his voice so deep it warps the air around them. He holds out his hand. 'Deakin—Alfred Deakin. And I believe you're Mr Cole, of the famous Arcade?'

So this is the man Joy Endicott has sent to torture him. Edward slowly takes his hand. He is young, Edward sees. His eyelashes are too long.

'Mr Deakin. How is it they will die? Attempting to get into land?'

'A deadly business, if you happen to be a fish,' laughs Deakin. 'But don't worry, I'm not here to sell you land. Mrs Endicott tells me you're a man of ideas, and I thought we might talk.' Deakin glances around the room. 'I won't keep you from the festivities for long, I promise.'

Edward also looks around the room, swollen with people now, all bunched together in distinct tribes. They are also getting louder, noise pressing like a thumb against his eardrum. The women tip their heads back to laugh, and the men half shout at each other. Some have the boneless look of the drunk.

'I suppose I could,' he says, squaring his shoulders, 'spare a few moments.'

They find a small room with a single lamp burning. The air is stale and cold, and the party noises faint. They sit on a couch which rustles like newsprint beneath them. There's a ringing in Edward's ears, dull and sustained.

Deakin leans forward, elbow on knee. 'They get a bit much, these parties.'

'Yes. So why did you come?'

'Ah,' says Deakin. 'The wife rather insisted.'

Edward smiles and tries to remember what he knows of Deakin. Something odd about his wife—writes poetry or acts on the stage. Meanwhile, Deakin is singing the Arcade's praises: the perfect marriage of commerce and philanthropy, a boon for Melbourne, jewel of the city.

Did he actually say jewel?

'So, as you can see, I know something of your business, though you may be wondering about mine.'

Politics. Edward's memory connects just in time. Alfred Deakin: chief secretary and leader of the Liberals. But Deakin is quick to brush it all aside. He wants to talk of the big picture, the future: federation. And here he becomes animated, bouncing off the couch, lashes moving rapidly.

'Wage protection, pensions, disease prevention—let's face it, these are the things this country needs to look to, and there's no use Victoria doing them unless New South Wales also does them, and Queensland, and Tasmania.'

Edward nods and listens.

'We need to get the children out of factories and into schools. But it has to be federal, otherwise the factories will simply up and move cities.'

Edward suddenly pictures his own children: Vally and his bony, vulnerable knees; Ivy Diamond with her babyish lisp. How could you put them in a factory, with no fresh air or sunlight, just the constant indifference of metal, crushing and punching and pounding? Not to mention the accidents. The damage done to soft-boned hands. Like the birds in his dream. His throat fills with bile and he quickly swallows it down. 'You need to change the law, to protect these children.'

'I agree. But that's just the start. You have to tackle the poverty that puts them there in the first place.'

And as Deakin expounds on poverty and its causes, his eyes taking on the sheen of wet stone, Edward realises: this man actually *cares*. He might have noticed sooner, if the party hadn't put him in a mood.

'What is it you want me to do?' he asks.

Deakin stops dead. 'Do? Oh no. I just wanted to get your thoughts on this, you know, as a *thinking* man.'

And as Deakin continues to speak, sitting back with his long, bloodless hands in his lap, Edward tells himself: it's only flattery. But he cannot ignore the little buzz this flattery gives him. A thinking man. Edward Cole, former gold-seeker, as poor and desperate a man as ever lived in this city. And along with the ridiculous buzz, another feeling, warm and diffuse, that feels almost like the start of friendship.

It is much later when Deakin seems to shake himself and declare it's time to go. 'My wife will probably be looking for me.'

Only then does Edward remember: Deakin's wife is a spirit medium. Surely if she can find long-dead spirits, she can find her husband at a party? 'One last question, if I may,' he says, stroking his full, coarse beard.

Deakin, already standing, nods his assent.

'Can you tell me what rhymes with Ulysses Gideon?'

Chapter Four

LATE SUMMER 1890

They lie together in bed, his body rounding hers, casting her shape in his flesh. He tries to catch his breath, watches her chest rise and fall, the brass sheen of sweat on her face. She sighs and the candle flame flickers, looping them in shadows.

A bottle rolls across the flagstones, three floors below.

His breathing slows. A state like sinking into sand has him pinned to the bed. Beneath him the sheets are twisted and damp, they smell of salt marsh and hot buttered pastry. Unless it is a dream smell, a memory, for it's just like the smell of the pies he used to sell on Russell Street. Working nights to feed the red-eyed drunks and prostitutes who tore at the pies with their teeth, burning their mouths in the rush for the meat. He remembers those mouths: red as poppies, slick with grease. How he dreamed of those mouths. Dreams crowded with trees and bushes and vines, set deep in forests and overgrown orchards; they would end with him pressing a woman's

45

soft flesh into the dark earth. Waking guilty and soiled in the bed beneath his pie cart.

'I should wash.' Eliza lifts herself onto one elbow.

'No, not yet.' Edward takes hold of her arm, lowers it to the bed. He runs his hand down her side and onto her stomach. He feels for the raised ribbons of skin, marks from pregnancies and birthing, an album of lives brought into the world. He feels the ribs beneath the soft flesh. Her nightgown is draped on the bedframe above them, and Edward remembers how she did not take it off on their wedding night but held it raised to her belly, hands shaking in the firelight.

And he had stood on the cold floorboards, filmed in sweat. Feeling like a predator, a wolf. They had known each other one month.

'Why don't we warm ourselves by the fire,' he had said. So they had sat side by side and, as the wood darkened and fell to ash, she had told him about her home in Hobart. She told him of the cold nights that silvered the leaves and grass with frost, and of giant trees vanishing into cloud, their trunks so wide that ten men could not surround them. She could not wait to leave, had always dreamed of cities and bustle and noise. She said, The land is quiet but it is not peaceful. There is tension in its silence.

And Edward, liking this honesty, told her about the goldfields. He did his best to tell her how it really was. The terrible sound made by thousands of men at work in the same place: rumbling, loud, like herds of horses storming the land. How it unnerved him, a country boy, to be surrounded by this. And what was worse: it was *never* quiet. Not for a second. For as the workday came to an end, and men dropped their pans and picks and left their cradles, the night sounds would begin. A voice raised in song. Accordion music. Voices raised in drunkenness or anger. With darkness came the barking of dogs, which set off other dogs: deep-throated and sometimes vicious beasts, kept as protection. But the sound he dreaded most was the nightly barrage of gunfire. Starting around eleven with one or two shots fired, it would build until the whole camp shook with blasts from hundreds of weapons. Like being dropped, suddenly, into some deranged war. What possessed these men to fire their guns every evening? Edward thought it was partly a warning, to let robbers know they were armed, and partly bravado, whistling in the dark. But even though it was ritual, expected, it left him unable to relax, let alone sleep, until the small hours. And even then he might be woken by drunken voices a few feet from his head.

He had paused in the telling, and she leaned in to kiss him, a slow, deliberate kiss, full of teeth and intent. And he had wanted to tell her then about Lucky Cho: the shelter of his friendship, his tranquillity, his shameful death, but with their bodies close and her mouth on his he had wanted her more.

A knock at the door brings Edward back to their bedroom, with Eliza pulling the covers up over her shoulders. 'Come in,' she says, her voice slow with sleep.

Linda stands in the doorway. She is a dim shape in the candlelight, but Edward recognises her stance, the awkward tilt of her shoulder. She stands on the threshold, as if to enter the room is to breathe water or some unknown atmosphere.

'Ma? Sorry. I think you had better come.'

Eliza enters the girls' room first, holding the lamp, followed by Edward and Linda. Shadows leap to the walls, arched and thin as cats. The room smells of rosewater, acid night sweat. Eliza moves to check on Ivy, her baby, sleeping sprawled and open-mouthed, but it's Ruby who is fretful now, groaning into her pillow. Edward walks towards her, but his legs feel mud-bound, slow. He has seen her face in the lamplight: a dull red-brown, the colour of terracotta. That can't be right, he tells himself, touching his palm to her forehead. Finding it hot, dry, rough as stone. That cannot be right. What has happened to her silky young skin? What has happened to his precious, carefree girl? He stands there a moment, blinking in the lamplight, gripping the end of his beard.

Eliza takes a look at Ruby, one quick touch of her face. 'You did well to come and get us, Linda. Now go telephone to Dr Fry. Ask him to come at once.'

...

Edward sits alone in the breakfast parlour. He rolls an orange along the tabletop, back and forth beneath his palm, his thoughts on Ruby's skin. He cannot get the feel of it out of his head. He once met some fishermen who had caught a shark, a long, sleek, slippery-looking creature, and when they invited him to touch it, was shocked to find the skin as harsh as sandpaper. That was nothing compared to the shock of touching Ruby's skin. To find his girl besieged by vile disease. Scarlet fever: this is what the doctor has told them, assuring them that she will soon recover. He believes the man; it's not that he doesn't believe him. But something buzzes inside him now, an anxiety he cannot simply switch off. Danger has come into his home, and found his child. Just like that.

'I have made us some tea, but I do draw the line at making scones,' says D'Ama, standing in the doorway.

He carries a silver tray with the dragon's-head teapot and sets it on the table.

It is only then that Edward realises he has been clenching his jaw, his whole face tight and aching. 'You've heard about Ruby?' he asks, rubbing some life back into his face.

D'Ama nods and takes a seat, glancing at the sideboard, the newspaper lying unread. 'Yes, I spoke to your cook. She told me Eliza has gone to lie down. What about you, have you had any sleep? Do you need to go downstairs today?'

Edward shakes his head. He pours the tea, wanting only to hold the cup, to feel the heat pass from ceramic to flesh. 'I've leased another building on Little Collins. I was going to go and take a look at it.' He shrugs. 'Nothing that can't wait.'

D'Ama presses his lips to his teeth, staring into his cup. 'I'm not going to talk business with you today. But I do need to tell you something.' He looks straight at Edward. 'James Endicott has declared bankruptcy. All that land he bought: it's worthless.'

Edward sees that D'Ama's moustache, though still black, is tinged with grey. As though the ends have been dipped in milk. He slowly nods his head. 'Well, that *is* bad news. For the Endicotts.' His mind flicks back to Ruby, her flushed and sleeping face, the pale circle of skin around her mouth. A thin crust of sleep on her dark lashes.

D'Ama snaps his fingers with impatience. 'Think, Edward, think. It's not just James. If he has lost his money on land speculation, then thousands of men are heading the same way. The implications are widespread and very serious. What I'm saying is that now is not the time to be taking out commercial leases and trying to expand your business.'

Edward smooths the creases in the tablecloth, a plain, plum-coloured linen. 'That has nothing to do with me. Do you realise how much I owe the banks? Not a thing. No mortgage, not even an overdraft. I don't believe in debt, D'Ama. I own, or else I lease. I live entirely within my means. It's a simple practice, and it keeps me out of trouble. And I certainly haven't thrown my money into get-rich-quickly-without-doing-the-work investments.'

D'Ama sighs. He reaches into his coat, toying with the pipe inside his pocket. 'Nothing to do with you? How can you say that when your business relies on the wealth of this city? For this is surely going to affect the whole city, if not the entire country. Nobody will be immune. I don't know how much clearer I can be.'

D'Ama stands and marches across the room, snatching up the crisp-edged newspaper. 'Maybe you should take a look at this,' he says, dropping it onto the table in front of Edward. 'See here? The government has been made to resign. Goodbye Gillies, goodbye Deakin. They probably thought they were immune too. Everything is about to change, Edward; I cannot put it more plainly than that. *Everything.*'

...

Edward paces the room as grey dust rises all around him. Wanting to relive the moment when he first saw it: the pure, clear notes of excitement, like a bell tone in his chest. But today it is simply a room: square, utilitarian, empty. With grainy light coming through the dirty windowpanes. Still, he tells himself, it will be something wonderful: the Arcade's own music department. Violins, trumpets, sheet music, free concerts: a whole new dimension to the Arcade experience. He pictures factory workers, grim and exhausted, coming past in their lunch hour, their surprise at hearing a band play in the middle of the afternoon. Discovering that the performance is free, and deciding to stay and listen. Being swept beyond their ordinary lives for ten or twenty or thirty minutes, and returning to work refreshed, lighter, their lives that fraction better. And with better lives, won't they make better citizens? More inclined to kindness, to hopefulness, to doing good themselves?

All it needs is to be cleaned up, painted, wired for electricity, and it will be such a fine space: bright, cheery, inviting, with music spilling out into the lane to draw the passersby.

But he cannot feel the magic, not today. He slings the tape measure over his shoulder and walks from the room to sit on the brickwork steps, gazing down into the narrow street, the gutters full of sludge.

James Endicott. Now, he can understand that, was expecting it, in a way. The lavish parties, the heedless borrowing, the greed; what good could ever come of that? While it's not his habit to rejoice in another's misfortune, he feels the sly backslap of satisfaction all the same. But Deakin—Deakin is another story. A rare human being, with the pure ability to see new worlds. Most people cannot do that. They see only the here-and-now, think nothing of the future, are astonished, even frightened, by the giant leaps that transform our world. Mutations turning ape to man; a round and spinning Earth; electricity; the printing press. A man, sleeping beneath a pie cart, dreaming up the Book Arcade.

Deakin has been greatly undervalued.

And what of his own children, what kind of people will they be? The kind to startle the world, or be startled by it? At twelve, Eddy possesses a rare and compelling grace, turning heads whenever he steps onto the cricket pitch. Moving as naturally as any animal in the wild, his body fluid, free of stress. Beside him, other boys look awkward, lacking in poise, and no one feels this more than Vally Cole. Poor Vally! Always running in Eddy's slipstream, never catching up. Clowning for the attention that Eddy accepts as his due. But Vally has a good mind, a broad and searching intelligence, qualities enough for him to shine someday in his own right.

Is it possible they will run the Arcade one day? Is it something they could enjoy?

He thinks of Linda, so shy, as if words alone might bruise her. Finds it hard to imagine her giving orders or taking a stand. But she is already helping to run their busy household, with a diligence impressive for her age. Pearl, the little lady, most private of his children. Who knows what fantasies are kept inside her clamshell mind. And Ruby, wonderful Ruby. Taking delight in the smallest of things: a ladybird on a leaf, a piece of sky reflected in a puddle. Rescuer of strays, maker of friends, adored by all.

Edward swallows, and drops his head into his hands. They must, of course, choose their own paths; he would never risk making them unhappy. Just imagine if his own father had insisted he become a minister, attending to his small flock of farmers in the hop fields of Kent. The narrow, scrubbed church, the codes of country life, the set-in-stone routine. Writing the Sunday sermon—the highlight of his week, sole outlet of a roving, hungry mind.

As Edward walks back through the Arcade he glimpses his mottled suit in one of the mirrors. Like a dark animal that has got into the flour. He frowns and begins to slap the dust away, not wanting to look a mess in front of his staff. Glancing up at the mirror, he sees a tall man striding directly towards him.

'Mr Cole. I have found myself with some unexpected free time.'

The two men walk through the fernery, with Deakin quick to downplay his disappointment. 'Governments will always be blamed for bad times,' he admits. 'It is natural, inevitable, all part of the democratic process.' His face is hard to read, the ferns casting shadows across his skin, or letting through rippling worms of light.

'Much easier when we could blame it all on God,' Edward tells him, and is warmed by his sudden laugh. He wonders if it's true, remembering his own deep immersion in religion as a simple time. But then, he was only a child, and maybe what he remembers is the flavour of childhood itself. Holding in his mind a clear picture of Jesus: soft brown beard, sad and knowing eyes, the unyielding sandals. How he loved to plan the kind of ark he would build, avoiding the mistakes made by Noah, such as saving snakes and wasps. Edward tries to mention this, but Deakin has already veered off, saying he is done with state politics—the back-scratching, the pettiness, the endless tit-for-tat. Everybody knows there are bigger fish to fry. They have done him a service, really, freeing up his time for the federal cause.

'Federation by decade's end,' he insists, wagging a playful finger. 'Mark my words.'

His tone is light, almost flippant, but Edward senses the effort involved, the will to stay positive, even as his own mind drifts upstairs to where Ruby lies, her hair on the pillow the silky black of the Japanese. Both men are taken by surprise by the figure running towards them, all coltish legs and speed.

Edward recognises Eddy, and feels a sudden, sickening pulse above his right eye. The boy comes to a halt, barely out of breath, freckles standing out against his pale face. 'Pa, come quick. The doctor says to come straightaway.'

...

Edward steps into the tiny room at the back of the flat that they have made into Ruby's sickroom. It is late afternoon, but the curtains are partly drawn, and he squints as his eyes adjust to the gloom. There is the small bed in the corner with the patient in it. There is a table with a cup and jug. Eliza sits in a chair beside the bed, an empty chair beside her. He does not look at her face, which is turned away from him towards the bed. He is frightened of seeing her face. They have come to watch Ruby die.

It is very hard for him to believe this.

Only this morning Ruby had told him she would ride a horse as soon as she was better. Reaching her hand to tug at his beard and whispering, *Giddy-on-up*. Asking him for lemon drops, and to see her sisters, from whom she was quarantined. Saying she could feel their old cat, Tom, sitting soft and heavy on her chest. She was clearly unwell, unusually lethargic, but very much alive.

But the doctor did not like what he saw on his second visit. What her parents had thought was a restorative nap turned out to be a coma. 'She's shutting down,' the doctor told them. 'You might want to sit with her until the end.'

The end? What end? She is only eight years old.

Edward moves stiffly, sitting down in the empty chair. The shape of his wife hunched over the bed makes him queasy, bloated with dread. He can read the grief in her bowed head, a resignation that is utterly unlike her. Surely they can hope for a miracle yet? That broad, rounded back blocks his view of Ruby, and he shuffles his chair closer to the bed.

His heart races: she could be sleeping! Her eyes closed beneath the straight black fringe, the rise and fall of her chest. But leaning closer he hears the shallow, rasping breath, and sees the terrible pallor, like a line of chalk, around her mouth. He wants to stretch out on the bed beside her, but it is narrow, no more than a cot. Instead he reaches out to take her hand between his, and is disturbed by its rubbery coolness. He stares at the dimples, those doughy imprints just above the knuckles.

'Edward,' says Eliza, in a rough, low voice. 'Help me onto the bed.'

They manage to seat themselves, widthways, on the bed, with their backs against the wall and their feet hanging over the edge. Then they place Ruby across their own bodies: her head on a pillow in Eliza's lap, her feet resting on Edward. The bed creaks loudly with every move, but Ruby does not stir. She does not so much as blink. They cover her loosely with a white lambswool blanket.

Eliza cannot stop stroking and petting Ruby's face and hair, and Edward cannot stop watching it. The small face with its dull red rash, the desperate need in those hands. His shirt against the wall is cold and soaked with sweat. Her feet resting like sandbags on his lap. The room has filled up with a musty sweet smell, like damp and rotting hay. If they stay this way forever, thinks Edward, it would be alright with him. It is a closed, looping sadness; a form of joy, compared with death.

It is much later now, perhaps midnight, or closer to morning. He is chilled in his summer suit, numbed from sitting so long, and damp along his left leg where Ruby has wet the bed. A bitter taste lodges in his mouth and throat.

'She's gone,' says Eliza, her voice quiet and hollow.

Something gaping, abyss-like, opens within Edward. A dark and limitless gulf where he might fall, and never return. He swallows, and his mind seeks out a ledge from which to cling.

She is gone, but he has had the weight of her feet on his thighs for hours now, will feel them there, he is sure, for several more. In fact, there's no reason they cannot stay here till morning, or later if they wish. They can watch over her, and hold her, have her picture taken, cut a lock or two of her hair. They can tell their favourite Ruby stories, and then, and then—

And then?

Chapter Five

AUTUMN 1890

Edward takes the photographs out of the envelope. There is Beaver, shirtsleeves rolled to the elbow. Dark-haired, stocky, stiff and serious—as he never looked in real life—holding a wallaby. Its timid, pale face emerging from dark fur, its body limp, ready for skinning. Framed by a mess of trees. The dead wallaby and Beaver somehow equal, devoid of animation, life. But he was never like that. Never still. Beaver hunted, skinned and cooked animals, cleaned his gun, chewed twigs, whistled: he lived his life in motion.

You could never take a true photograph of Beaver. And for his part, Beaver never put much stock in their camera. Even as they travelled around the country-side trying to make a living from it. It was Edward who had to coax and charm their portrait subjects: fly-blown miners with dense, wayward beards; rich station owners in British clothing; glazed-eyed publicans. Edward who had to tickle babies beneath their chins, compliment plain and surly eldest daughters. Edward who lined up the pictures and squeezed the bulb. Beaver would busy himself with the horse—leading it to graze, brushing burs from its mane—or later on with the boat. When the picture was taken Beaver would disappear beneath the heavy cloth, apply the chemicals and emerge with the photograph. Mostly he did not look at the photographs; they were of no more interest to him than an out-of-date newspaper.

It was Edward who loved the camera—that souvenir from the future. For if the camera was possible, what else was possible? The camera was such a leap from the paintbrush, the pencil; one could not help but think the future would be unrecognisable, marvellous.

The next photograph shows their clumsy, flat-bottomed rowboat. Shaped more like a child's drawing of a boat than any actual boat. With chunky oars, knocked-together bunks and a filthy canvas awning. How did they live for four months in this ancient, leaky craft? For it was ancient in the summer of fifty-nine when they found it, beached on the banks of the Murray at Echuca, where Beaver promptly traded their horse and cart for it. Beaver dancing around it as though it was a rare discovery, making little whinnies of delight. 'We'll take the river to Adelaide,' he said. 'We'll be explorers. We'll see the fierce river tribes and live off the land, and it won't cost us anything.' He climbed into the boat, stretched himself out on the bench seat and propped his feet on the gunwale. 'Edward,' he said, '*this* is the life.'

It took them almost three days to find and plug all the leaks.

...

'Edward? Can I come in?'

Eliza. Her voice through the door enough to bring it home again: Ruby is dead. Every moment now one of forgetting or remembering. All his time divided in this way. Looking at photographs, forgetting. Eliza's voice, remembering. Bumping into the same slab of fact, over and over, pounding himself.

She had shown no fear, had trusted her father and mother would take care of her. Had submitted to their cold cloths and stroking hands like a minor deity used to such attentions. Believing she would be well in no time, that no harm would come to her in the home where she was loved. She trusted them, and they held her close, and watched her die. Watched as the coma settled on her like a black cloud, dulling everything that was once bright and alive in her. Inhaled the decay on her breath. Studied the rise and fall of her chest. Felt for the vague, distant beat of her pulse. Until finally they were sitting over her slack and lolling corpse, pressing their lips to her cheek that once bunched with her smiles but was now limp, rough as sacking.

Edward puts the photographs back in their envelope. 'Yes. Come in.'

Her whole face looks swollen, the eye sockets bruised. They stand in the small room among rose-patterned arm-chairs, wool rugs, Chinese vases and two lifelike ceramic kangaroos. A dull, stony light makes its way through a small window, landing dismally on everything. Eliza sighs.

'I came in here for a reason, but now I can't remember why.' She folds her hands and rests them on her stomach. Precise and gentle hands that held and rocked the corpse of their child. Holding the rag-doll body to her bosom as if to feel some last current of life.

'Oh, that was it. My paper.' She walks over to one of the low, lace-covered tables and picks up a thin newsletter. Edward already knows what it is: *The Harbinger of Light*, a spiritualist paper with accounts of recent séances, unexplained phenomena, communion with the dead. *Mrs Biggles of Brighton reports that during her Friday séance a mirror hanging on the wall cracked in two for no apparent reason . . .*

Eliza fans herself with the pages; the room is airless, too warm. Edward looks across at her, tries to smile. 'Where are Ivy and Pearl?'

'In their room. Playing with the tea set.'

A present from D'Ama, the miniature tea set was an instant favourite: tiny silver spoons, ceramic cupcakes, sugar cubes made of glass, and the teapot with matching cups, handpainted in mint-green and pale yellow stripes. While Eliza had objected over its expense, Edward had worried they might somehow feel bribed: be good, don't cry and you can have this lovely toy. But the girls had not only loved the tea set on sight, they seemed innately drawn to its ritualistic potential. They hosted an endless series of tea parties, pouring, stirring and serving with solemn intent. And at every party a place was set for Ruby. 'Two lumps for Ruby,' he heard Pearl say one day, stopping him in his tracks. The way she said it: so natural, so happy. And he thought then how perfect D'Ama's choice was, as if he'd somehow known that, despite the sadness in the house, the girls still needed permission to play and to dream.

Edward wonders if he should look in on them. The desire to see all his children comes over him like a fever, hot and consuming, at all hours of the day. But no sooner does he see them—clear, trusting eyes, fragile limbs—than he feels afraid, knowing there is no way to keep them safe.

'You'll be here for dinner?' asks Eliza. She has been on a mission to restore all household routines. Family dinners and sing-alongs, bedtime reading, trips to the park. Crying only at night; waking with a face as puffed as an Easter bun.

'Eliza.' Put your head on my shoulder. Cry if you want. Rest. 'Don't work too hard.'

She gives him a look—deeply blank, like a sleep-walker—and leaves the room.

...

Edward stands on the rooftop. The wind comes in short, fresh bursts, whipping his shirt into sails. The sun is setting, the world tinted pink and gold. Buildings look soft as sand. As though he could slide harmlessly over rooftops, down walls and onto the street, then dust himself off and walk away.

The book is heavy and he shifts it to his left hand. *Black Beauty*. How Ruby had worried over that horse. Her small face pinched and tense as he read aloud the whippings, neglect and overloading endured by the big-hearted beast. Edward knowing it would all come good in the end, but Ruby too young to know or even guess this. Then—her sudden illness. She had never heard the ending, where the horse finds a true and happy home. My God—why had he not read it? Skipped ahead, rushed through it. He was her father, he should have reassured her, given her comfort.

So he has come up here with some idea of reading the ending. Sending the words heavenwards.

But the sunset has thrown him. That rose-coloured light, the fiery wheel of sun sinking behind the church, the spire tipped golden. He cannot see its beauty without hurting, knowing Ruby will never see it. Sunsets, beaches, cherry blossoms, stained glass—the list is endless, and it drains him.

He looks around and sees an old packing crate. Grey with weathering and cobwebs. Sinks onto the rough wood and, still holding the book tight, lets the sobs tear through him.

...

Lying in bed beside Eliza. He feels her muscles tense on waking, steeling herself for the day ahead. The smallest breath between waking and rising, and she is out of bed. He hears the gentle pat-pat of water poured and scooped up by her hands. Faint rustle of towel. Footsteps, and the dry scrape of fabric meeting skin. Ordinary domestic sounds that reveal nothing of the sheer will it takes to make them.

'Shall I heat some water for you?' she asks.

'Don't trouble yourself. I'll get up now.'

'It's no trouble. I need some anyway.'

'If you're going anyway . . .'

Lying in bed, he feels the underwater feeling, like tons and tons of water bearing down on him, keeping him heavy and separate from everyone. And running through it, a dark thread, a buried line of guilt, and a sense that he has always known this was coming, that life has been too good for too long. He has felt the thread and ignored it, but this morning, cocooned in his warm bed, eyes closed against the day, he follows it slowly but steadily back to the source. He sees: a deep mineshaft, and at its bottom, a man lying face down in mud and water. One hand stretched out like a bright starfish against the purplish mud. Lucky Cho. Well. He is not surprised.

He hears her footsteps coming back towards the room. It is time to get up. Get up, he tells himself. And, at the third telling, he does.

...

Days pass. Below him, in the Arcade, people come and go. Edward stays mostly in the flat. He wants to be near his children. It is Linda who herds the younger ones in and out of his presence, ducking her head like a royal page. Pearl who climbs onto his lap, warm as a pup. With his eyes closed, it could be Ruby. Eddy talks about cricket, regardless of who is listening. Grabs the iron poker, drops his weight into his knees, and swings carefully, high into the air. A worn Persian carpet beneath his feet. Edward eats an apple, and the children eat apples, the harsh tearing of apple flesh suddenly loud in the room. Ivy wants a story read, but Edward has no heart for it and passes the book to Linda, Ivy darting puzzled looks between them. Or he does read, his voice echoing in his head, his mind jumping ahead to the next sentence. Nothing seems to separate one day from the next. Until the end of the month, when D'Ama comes, according to custom, and takes Edward to the baths.

...

It is a double nakedness. Edward is out of his house and out of his clothes. Each step along the corridor is hard on his bones. His flesh above and below the towel is soft and white as flour. He feels acutely his ageing, mortal body, and at the same time quite separate from it.

He opens the cedar door and walks into a dull, compact heat. D'Ama is already in the room. He seems to take no time changing, as though he dissolves the clothes from his body at will. He is leaning into one corner, his shoulder touching the gold outline of the Moorish castle, his collarbone sharp as a razor.

At the funeral, when they hugged, Edward had felt those bones, bird-thin, and smelled the old tobacco in his blood. And D'Ama had said, She was your favourite—the only words that gave him any comfort that day. And not because they were true, necessarily, but because they seemed to excuse his overwhelming, almost decadent grief.

But now it is D'Ama who looks grief-stricken, grey-skinned. 'He shot himself. Joy found him in the bedroom, after breakfast.'

And Edward realises D'Ama has been talking for some time. He cannot possibly ask him to repeat himself. He must concentrate. Who has shot himself? Who has Joy found?

'He was supposed to face court today. Over the land deals. Corruption.'

D'Ama rests his head against the wall. Silence.

James Endicott. Edward thinks of his big, barking laugh. The boyish smile that made people trust him. The gold-lust in all our hearts. On the goldfields, in the cities, it's all the same. Edward can still taste the excitement of coming out on the boat: a thick, sea-salt paste at the back of his throat, the thought of all that gold waiting in the ground.

'People trusted him,' says Edward, watching D'Ama's eyes snap open.

His look, when he replies, is severe. 'People are damn fools.'

Chapter Six

1891

Edward presses his palms to his hips and bends forward, trying to catch his breath. His heart shudders in his chest, pumping the blood to his face, and to his hands, which are red from dragging the heavy bag. He smells the muddy-clean scent of the soil through the hessian, and looks with satisfaction at the row of earthenware pots, round and crude as any ancient cauldron. He has always planned to make a rooftop garden. So when D'Ama had complained about the pots—imported for a Tuscan villa on Mount Macedon, the owner of which could no longer afford the villa, let alone pots—Edward spontaneously bought the lot. He bought soil, a watering can and seeds. It will all take longer with seeds. But there is a magic to it, watching the life spring up out of nothing. And he thinks the children might like it: early-morning watering while the city wakes below them, the thrill of being the first to see the green shoots emerge.

Edward watches as Pearl and Vally drag the second bag onto the rooftop, Vally's straining child muscles like apricots tucked beneath his shirt.

'That was *heavy*,' says Vally, as Pearl dusts her hands on her floral pinafore. They stand together, squinting into the sun. Two bright figures on the grey rooftop. Sunbeams glance off Vally's blond head. It is a beautiful day.

'We'll bring the rest up now,' says Edward. 'After we get it all going, the two of you can have first pick of the seeds.'

Edward pours soil into the first pot, stopping an inch below the rim. He tamps it down, surprised at just how good it feels: perfect warmth, a crumbling looseness. He sticks a finger into the dirt, then sinks his whole hand to the wrist. Plugs directly into a memory of helping his mother pull carrots: drone of bees, dirt jammed under his nails, his mother's dirt-hemmed skirt. Telling him: *Roll your sleeves up, Eddy. Use a bit of muscle.* Their laughter when he pulled out a carrot as long as his arm, and him, almost giddy at having his mother to himself, anxiously listening for the baby's cry.

'Which seeds grow the fastest?' asks Vally, squatting down beside him. His elbows resting on his knees, his hands cupping his face. He has spread all the seed envelopes on the hard stone around him. 'I want my seeds to come up first,' he says, rocking for emphasis. 'I want to grow spectacular flowers, and give them to Ma. What kind of flowers does Ma like?'

Pearl stands behind him, holding her elbows and looking doubtful. Edward glances down at the envelopes. He has mostly chosen kitchen plants: mint, thyme, parsley, sage. There's also lavender and rosemary: notoriously slow growing. Later on he will buy some ready-grown plants, such as orchids and jasmine. His children, it is only just dawning on him, are probably expecting the plants they see at their local park, the Royal Botanic Gardens.

'I want to grow something pink,' says Pearl. 'Otherwise I'm going downstairs.'

Edward stands up, brushing the dirt from his hands. 'What a pair of gardeners, keen as rabbits. But did you know the most important thing you can grow is food? If you can grow food, you can survive just about anywhere. You'll never starve.'

'Why would we starve?' asks Vally. 'What's happened to our money?'

'Nothing, nothing has happened to it. What I'm saying is, imagine if you were the only person on an island—the lighthouse keeper, for example. And every month the supply boat brings you your food, but one time it fails to arrive. A smart man would have his own vegetable plot—a few potatoes and beans—and he'd survive, he'd be fine. Now,' Edward makes a quick survey of the envelopes, 'Vally. You say you'd like to grow something for Mother. Did you know that her favourite vegetable dish is mint peas?'

Vally shakes his head.

'Well, she goes mad for mint peas, simply mad for them. And you can't make mint peas without mint.' Edward holds up an envelope and gently shakes it. 'And as for you, Pearly-buttons, you might like to start with lavender. Lovely pinky-purple flowers, and smells enough to make a bee swoon.'

Pearl giggles. 'Bees don't swoon.'

'You've never seen a bee swoon? Oh my, what a poor sheltered child!'

It was hard getting hold of even two of the children. Eddy, it would seem, has joined every sports team in town, and Linda, who has taken to drawing, spends long hours gazing at apples and pears stacked together in a bowl. As for the others, Eliza is constantly taking them to the beach, the park or out visiting, when all Edward wants is to gather them under one roof. It was almost unbearable having to break Ruby's death to them, and he cannot lose the feeling that he has ripped a hole right through their childhoods. For what is childhood without the belief that something—our parents, destiny, God—can stand between us and death?

And now it seems he wants to restore the illusion, to keep them close and, in doing so, keep them safe. While Eliza has taken to keeping them busy.

Edward can already picture the vivid green of the plants against the red-brown pots, the grey rooftop and the blue sky; a primary-coloured retreat, private and full of cheer. He can almost smell the grassy sweet mint crushed between his fingers, and see the look on their faces when those first, eager shoots push up through the soil.

'The first step is to prepare the soil by breaking up the largest clumps. You want a nice, loose soil so the roots can grow straight down without too much trouble.' Edward leans over one of the pots to demonstrate, and is pleased to find that Vally and Pearl soon follow, the three of them kneading and sifting the earth, with Pearl on her tiptoes, grunting as she works. Then she steps back and holds out her hands: stiff-fingered, caked with dirt.

'Just bring your hands together like this,' says Edward, banging the dirt from his palms. 'And don't worry too much about your hands getting dirty, that's all part of the fun. When we're finished, we'll give them a proper wash.'

Pearl wrinkles her nose and dabs daintily at the dirt. When she lowers her hands, she is careful to keep them away from her dress. Vally scoops a handful of soil and begins to flick it, grain by grain, towards her, until she gives an indignant squawk. Edward decides to ignore it.

He shows them how to level the soil, how to plant in rows, how to gauge the depth of the hole by the size of the seed. Amazed at how the knowledge comes back to him from dim boyhood, like a faithful pet. The gentle sun on his hands, and the children working so quietly he can hear them breathe.

He takes one of the envelopes and pours a dozen or so seeds—ant-sized and dun-coloured—into his palm. He lays them out in shallow trenches, light brown against dark brown, like stitches in a coat. He moves quietly, almost reverently, grateful for the task, the sun, the children; close to being content.

'Look at this,' laughs Vally. 'They forgot to put the seeds in.' Edward turns to see Vally upending the envelope over his hand, a thin line of seeds pouring from a corner and onto the ground.

'Why don't you pay attention?' cries Edward, as the last seeds bounce wildly onto the stone, rolling into every crack and crevice. 'Why don't you use your brain?'

Vally drops to his knees to salvage them, his face flaring red. 'S-sorry. I didn't see them. Honestly, I didn't.' He looks helplessly at the ground. 'They're awfully small.'

Edward is instantly ashamed. Losing his temper over a packet of seed—what on earth's the matter with him? The boy is clumsy, nothing more, not a scrap of meanness in him. It's Edward who has spoiled the morning, breaking the spell of its pastoral calm.

'I'm sorry, Vally, I should have mentioned it, how tiny some of them are.' He hands over another envelope, patting him on the shoulder. Letting his hand rest a moment on the thin, warm shirt. 'It's hard to believe something so small could grow into a plant.'

From the corner of his eye he can just see Pearl, crouched low to the ground, wiping her hands on the stone.

...

The children have gone downstairs, leaving Edward to pack up beneath the full midday sun. Waves of weariness breaking over him. He finds the half-empty envelopes, folds them and stuffs them into his pockets. Yawns deeply into his hands. He takes a broom and sweeps up the mess of dirt and seeds, lulled by the rhythmic ksh-ksh of straw on stone. Almost asleep on his feet.

Then he hears Ruby's voice, as clear as the day: '*I would have chosen strawberries.*'

That it's only in his head is also clear to him. But the cadence, the phrasing, are unmistakeably hers, and strawberries are her all-time favourite. So what, in the end, is the difference between hearing her speak, and this, whatever this is?

Feeling only a little foolish, he chooses to reply out loud. 'I know, Ruby-red, I'll get you some next time.'

And is hit with a bolt of pure happiness.

He wants nothing more than to get inside his office now, to close the door and sink into his chair and nurse in private this strange form of joy. A flight of stairs, a stretch of corridor: that's all he has to navigate without being seen or heard.

But the number of times he has been intercepted by Owens—the man must be part bloodhound.

Edward bends down and slips off his shoes, grinning to himself. Shoes in hand, he inches down the staircase without making a sound. Creeps along the corridor, burglar-style, on the balls of his feet. Why has he never thought of this before? He should start wearing slippers to work. He should build a trapdoor and lower himself from flat to office on a foldout ladder. His reverie is cut short by the sight of D'Ama, leaning against the office door. Cream leather boots, a black cravat, and hands in the pockets of his green checked suit. D'Ama nods hello and raises an eyebrow at the shoes in Edward's hand. 'Does your father know you've been out all night?'

As they step inside the office, Edward sees D'Ama's face stiffen with shock. Unopened boxes of books stacked several feet high cover most of the floor. A pile of cardboard rainbows leans against the window, partly blocking the light. A cuckoo clock in the corner prevents the door from fully opening. The impression, Edward realises, is more storeroom than office. And in the centre is Edward's desk, scattered with a handful of papers, the inlaid surface shining gently in the half-light.

'What the devil,' mutters D'Ama, picking his way through the boxes and stopping short at the visitor's chair. Perched on the seat is a blue and silver hen, staring back at him with beady eyes.

'That's Chicita,' says Edward, slipping into his seat. 'A novelty for the Arcade. She's mechanical—you put a penny in the slot there, and she cackles and lays an egg! A tin egg, that is, with a miniature toy inside it. But come,' Edward gestures vaguely, 'put her down, and take a seat.'

D'Ama wedges the hen into a gap between two boxes. Then he sits down and holds up his hands towards Edward, the fingertips blackened with dust. 'How long

has that been sitting here?' He reaches for his handkerchief and begins to wipe each finger clean.

Edward struggles to remember: a week, a month, or
is it more? 'Maybe a month,' he says, sounding less than
certain.

D'Ama folds his handkerchief and puts it away in his
pocket. 'Not too many pennies going into it, then.'

Edward joins his hands together and places them
on the desk. He resists the urge to stroke the mother-
of-pearl, to reach for its silky comfort. He knows he
has been lax about the business lately, he doesn't need
D'Ama to tell him that. But he will listen to his lecture
and then, when D'Ama leaves, he will be alone with his
thoughts of Ruby.

D'Ama taps his fingers on the desk. Then he sighs,
pressing his hand to his head. 'Remember when you still
had the market stall and I had that warehouse on Spen-
cer?' His voice is gentle, disarming. 'Remember when I
told you it was time to leave the market and set up a
shop of your own?'

Of course Edward remembers. For D'Ama had somehow got wind of a secret plan to close down Paddy's
Market. They were going to redevelop it, to make it
weatherproof and uniform and clean. They were going to
get rid of the carnival acts, the troubadours and con men,
the preachers on their splintered boxes, and the Chinese
with their animal medicines, their loud brass gongs. They
were going respectable. And when they tore the market
down, everyone would need to relocate. Edward knew
what that meant: the scramble as stallholders looked for
new spaces, with landlords rushing to put up the rents.
So he did what D'Ama advised him to: found a store-
front immediately, before the rush, and set up a shop. A

proper shop, with four walls and a roof. A shop he ran for almost a decade, before going on to build the Arcade.

'I knew you were headed for bigger things, Edward, knew it from the moment we met. And what better proof than the Arcade? It's really a tremendous achievement.'

Edward is under the eerie impression he is listening to a eulogy.

'But now I'm telling you once more that it's time for you to get out. The economy will soon be in a full-fledged depression. And you won't survive it, Edward. You haven't got the stomach for it. You haven't got the right mindset—not since you lost Ruby.'

Edward sucks in too much air and starts to cough. 'Hold on, D'Ama, hold on. What are you saying here? If the Arcade has a problem, I need to know so that I can fix it.'

D'Ama smiles grimly. '*If* there is a problem. Why don't you talk to your manager sometime, instead of devising new ways to hide from him? Owens will tell you how bad the figures have been these last twelve months.'

Edward had, in fact, seen Owens the day before, his round face hazy with sweat, the monthly figures in hand. And Edward had tried to make sense of them, he really had. He had run his fingers down those columns of numbers, and a curious thing had happened. For while he could remember how it used to feel to decipher the numbers—a sense of control, a beautiful order—he could no longer do it, nor care that this was so.

Edward realises that D'Ama isn't smoking, and something cold settles in his bones. 'I can't "get out" of the Arcade, D'Ama, it's not some corner shop that I happen to run. I can't just pack up and wipe my hands of it, move on to something else. The Arcade is no ordinary business, it's, it's . . .' Edward gropes for a way to say it. It's the best of him—his hopes and ideals, his higher purpose—willed into solid form.

'I know it's more than an income to you, Edward, I'm not an idiot. But I'm telling you, you're going to lose it all anyway. The city is going to be decimated—bankruptcies, shop closures, joblessness—before we see it get any better. It's happening quicker than any of us thought. At least if you fold the business now, you will still have your capital and some money in the bank. But if you run it into the ground—and, make no mistake, that's exactly where you're headed—you'll end up with nothing. And that means nothing for Eliza and the children.'

Edward grabs his throat, alarmed at its sudden tightness. 'But I could still save it, couldn't I? If I stayed, and really fought?'

D'Ama makes a low sound through his teeth, a dubious whistle. 'Look, I've given you my best advice: get out, and get out while you can. Otherwise you're risking your family's future.' He stands abruptly, knocking the hen with his knee and setting off its loud, maniacal cackle. He stands there, glowering at the hen with his arms crossed, before throwing Edward a last worried look and leaving the room.

Edward thinks: so this is how James Endicott felt, learning of his ruin. An expansive fear, a desert of fear, pure and arid and airless. Remembering with shame his lack of pity for the man. Those round blue eyes, the cleft chin like a careless slip of the knife. He wonders how Joy got the blood off the walls, if she had to paint over them.

And why are his hands so cold? He stares down at them, gripped into fists on the desk.

. . .

'Cocoa? I have made us some lovely hot cocoa.'

Eliza has found him, sitting in the half-dark drawing room, light slanting in through the tilted venetians. She rests the silver tray with its two cups on a low table, and sits in the chair facing him. A milky glaze already on her lips.

Edward gives her a weak smile. She doesn't yet know about D'Ama's visit, that their lives hang by a thread. And he wonders if he should tell her. She has a fine straight logic and does not scare easily. She is not some foolish girl. He sits up straighter in his chair, no small feat with its swollen headrest and deep curving back, and thinks of how to begin. *D'Ama believes we might be in a spot of bother . . .*

Eliza clears her throat and throws him an apologetic look. 'It's funny, what one misses most.' She picks up her cup, holds it just below her mouth. 'It's her voice I miss, her constant chatter.'

Edward is startled. He thinks about what happened on the roof and how to explain it. 'But don't you find that it's still there, in a way? That you can sort of play it in your head?'

Eliza sniffs, and a single clear droplet falls into her cup. 'They say at the séances you never hear their real voice anyway. But imagine being able to talk to her, Edward, even just the once!'

They are wrapped in the dense, blanketing smell of the cocoa. Edward slides towards her. He covers her hands, the warm cup still between them. 'Is that what you want? Do you want to go to a séance?'

Eliza drops her head, and for a moment their foreheads touch, like one rock rolling against another before coming to rest.

Chapter Seven

1892

Edward is humming. He nods to the polar bear and takes down his hat, feeling the weight of it. It pleases him, this weight. The solidity of the businessman preparing for work. A briefcase would be nice. Instead he touches the chain on his pocket watch, finds reassurance in the flex of the metal. His shoes polished to a black shine beneath him.

But the domestic is ever-present; the fried, kitchen smell of pancakes clings to him from breakfast. And he can hear the footsteps of his children moving around the flat. As he takes to the stairs the footsteps grow quicker, and he glances up at the third-floor balcony to see Pearl and Ivy staring down at him.

'Pa, look!'

'Look, it's snowing.'

They open their fists to drop white flecks of paper, and bob down to gather more. Doubled up with laughter, they lean on the railing as the snowflakes fall on Edward. Landing on the brim of his hat and on his jacket while he stands there, motionless, like a figure in a snow dome.

Then he wraps his arms around himself and pretends to shiver wildly. He stamps his feet and dances around, as though trying to get warm. And, spurred on by their manic laughter, he carefully mimes the making of a snowman, crowning the creature with his own top hat.

By the time he reaches the fernery, he has shaken off the paper and donned his hat once more. But he is no longer early for the meeting he has called, and arrives to find his workers have already gathered. Their skin showing dull in the grey morning light, twice-filtered through clouds and glass. The damp, earthy air over-hung with perfume. The women eyeing one another in their stiff, clean dresses, and the men looking at the ground. Nobody looks at Edward; bad luck can be cast with a glance.

He places himself beneath an overhanging frond, and sees the broad, ridged trunk scarred with the names of lovers. *Walter and Gertrude forever. I love Hilda Desmoines.* He wishes them well. He looks for Owens and finds him: round, shiny face and royal-blue bowtie, like the prize ribbon on a pumpkin.

He clears his throat and the sound stops the room dead. 'Ladies and gentlemen, I'd like to start by thanking you all for coming. I know some of you have had to come in early, and others on your day off.'

Thirty faces stare back at him and not a single smile. He rubs the back of his neck and pushes on.

'I know that many of you are concerned by recent events in our city. You've seen shops close down, fami-lies queuing for handouts, and even people begging in the street. We are certainly living in difficult times.

It's only natural that you might also wonder what lies ahead for the Arcade. That's why I've called you to this meeting.'

Edward feels his way through the unyielding gravity of the room. 'Of course, the city is our lifeblood, and it will come as no surprise to hear that the Arcade is suffering too. People simply do not have the money they had twelve months ago. If we don't find a way to adapt, if we don't make some critical changes, the sad fact is we won't survive.'

A twitch of anxiety passes through the crowd. Edward swallows and darts a look at Owens.

'Now, some of you may disagree with my approach, and that's fine, that's nothing new . . .' Finally a smirk creeps across some of the faces and Edward is almost glad. 'But in order for this to work—for the Arcade to survive, in fact—I am asking for your full and absolute cooperation.'

He clamps his jaw to keep himself from grinning. 'The Arcade is getting a band!'

The idea had come to him in the days after his talk with D'Ama. Moving around in a fog of fear, he had found himself repeating his own weak defence: *The Arcade is no ordinary business.* Like a child playing with an old cape, believing it makes him invisible. Haunted by this flimsy response to a very real threat. But as the words replayed themselves—at dinnertime, on the rooftop, in bed—it had struck him that they ran in two directions. If the Arcade was no ordinary business to him, the same was true for his customers. For them it was many things: a resource, meeting place, fun house, opportunity, retreat. It was expansive, big-hearted; it was whatever they needed it to be.

To cut it back, he believes, would be to kill it. His best hope is to keep growing, to anticipate the city's needs. It's radical and risky, but he feels in his bones it is right.

So he will hire the best band he can. And in the months ahead he will add a lending library, and fill a room with optical illusions. He will swish his cape and make the depression disappear—at least from within these walls.

But first he must sell them on the band.

'Every afternoon and evening, a band will come to the Arcade and give a free performance. With its help, we will provide the one product that everybody in this town really needs and nobody sells. Can anybody guess what it is?' Edward, who loves riddles, peers eagerly into the crowd. But the wary faces staring back at him don't seem in the mood for guessing.

'Good cheer! Plain, old-fashioned good cheer. It's in short supply everywhere, but we will soon have it in spades! It will set us apart and keep them coming through the door—whether they have money or not. Those with money will spend it here, and those without will remember us and come back when they *do* have a penny to spend. The band's role is to send a clear message: leave your cares and worries at the door.'

Edward throws his arms wide. 'And remember, *we* are the face of all this good cheer. Smile! Welcome them. Be friendly and kind. Let them read in the cane chairs, let them eat their sandwiches in the fernery. Let them touch the trinkets and the toys. No one is too poor or downtrodden to be welcomed into our midst. Every single person must feel it in their hearts: this is a place where I belong.'

Edward pauses for breath, and a wave of murmurings and throat-clearings breaks across the room. He tries to make it out, to gauge the effect of his words. 'Does anyone have any questions?' he asks, trying to look encouraging.

'I do. I have a question,' says the sunken-eyed, whippet-thin caretaker, Juniper Griggs. 'Would you mind telling us straight who's going to lose their job?'

'Lose their job?' repeats Edward, scratching his ear.

Griggs draws a breath. The crowd seems to stand behind him, its energy bulking out his angular frame. 'With due respect, Mr Cole, I think we all know what *critical changes* means.'

It hits him like a slap to the head: they are waiting to hear about their jobs. They have waited since their arrival this morning, since he called the meeting earlier in the week. And in their apprehension, he could have addressed them in Russian and received the same response.

'Thank you, Griggs, for bringing me to my next point.' It should have been his first point. He sees it all so clearly now: he should have set them at ease at once. 'I have made a careful study of the roster, and it seems to me that if we are all willing to cut our shifts by an hour or two a week, then no one will lose their job.'

Griggs draws back and lets out a puff of surprise. This seems to trigger a chain of sighs, exclamations, shoulder-rolling and head-nodding from the formerly still crowd. They gather into small groups, patting backs and shaking hands, just as if he has declared the meeting over.

Edward stands awkwardly, right foot forward, poised to deliver the rest of his talk.

Did they really think he would sack them? Sure, D'Ama had called for it, insisting he trim all the fat. And in a rare moment of dissent from her husband, Eliza had backed him up. But to cut a job now was to put a man on the street. It meant his family might starve.

And besides, he could hardly launch a policy of good cheer by sacking people.

'There is one more thing!' he calls out to the increasingly festive crowd, as one man pulls a mouth organ from his pocket and a woman hands around a bag of nuts. 'Don't forget to request your favourite songs from the band. There's nothing like a favourite tune to spread good cheer!'

...

Edward opens the door to his office and sees the letter on his desk. White, square: an ordinary letter. A shiver of alarm runs through him. It is too white, too crisp in this room full of dusty bookshelves and smeared windows. Even the peacock in the corner—once so proudly iridescent—now dresses in a modest veil of cobwebs. The letter, by contrast, seems demanding, brazen, ready to impose itself.

When Eliza comes, he is sitting at his desk reading the letter a second time. She is dressed in heavy black velvet, her plump figure lost within its folds. Edward wonders where she's heading.

'What is it, Edward?' she asks, in her usual calm way. But there is strain in her face, tension in her neck and jaw.

'Nothing to be too alarmed about.' He smiles gently up at her. 'But it seems that Benson—red-haired fellow from the print department—has borrowed a sum of money without troubling to ask first.'

He sees her lips press together, the flare of her nostrils. 'How much?'

'Hmm. Well, it sounds rather a lot—a thousand pounds. However . . .'

Eliza gasps. She utters something very like a curse. Edward decides he has probably heard wrong.

'However, he owns up to the fact in this letter here, and I've no doubt he'll pay it all back.'

Eliza has begun to pace, her hands clasped before her. She stops and looks at Edward. 'You'll fire him, of course.'

Edward leans back in his chair. 'I haven't decided about that yet. I've only just read the letter.'

'You say he works in printing?'

'Yes, he works the press.'

'Go ask him to print up a notice then—Cole's Book Arcade: we welcome thieves!'

Edward could not have been more shocked if she'd leaned over and punched him. He has never heard her talk in this bitter, mocking way. He drops his gaze from her face, and sees that her hands are shaking. It dawns on him then how frightened she is, how tightly fear has wound her. He lowers his head in shame. He has failed her, his own good wife. Exposed her to uncertainty, potential ruin.

He must get on top of things. He must restore some order. No more surprises, he vows, raising his head. No more revelations.

'Eliza,' he says, quietly but firmly, 'there's nothing for you to worry about. I have everything under control.'

But she has already turned her back and is walking towards the door. 'We mustn't be late for the séance,' she says.

...

A plump, dimpled woman leads them through the house, past dark-wood furniture smelling of beeswax and orange, paintings of sheep and rolling green hills, and a ceramic beagle, curled up on a sideboard. They enter a study where a man reads a newspaper, a red setter drooling at his feet. There they meet briefly with Abel Cornish, master of the house. A giant jelly of a man who could crush all three of them in a bear hug if he chose, but who instead wobbles a few words of greeting and returns to his papers. The dog opens one eye and lets it close again.

The domestic charm does not help Edward. He thought he'd have no qualms about coming to this séance, but his heart bangs inside him like a fist. It's not the sharp, clean fear of physical danger—a gun at the head, a bull with horns lowered—he could deal with that. It's the stealthy, smouldering fear of unknown things, of buried things. Things best left alone.

'I believe you already know Mrs Endicott,' says the plump woman, as they move into a room with curtains drawn. Edward runs his hands down his pants to take the sweat off them.

The room is lit by tall red candles in silver holders. A long mahogany table stands in the centre, and several people are milling around. He sees Joy Endicott, tall and thin, with blue veins snaking up her long white neck. She wears all black, and a mourning ring made of jet and human hair. She is taking a bowl of violets from the table, moving them out into another room. He sees an older woman, silver combs in her thinning hair and a stark, bird-like face; she is introduced to them as Miss Heaver, a spinster recently out from England. He sees a young woman in a headscarf, and a Chinese man in a smart striped suit.

'May I introduce Mr Quong Tart,' says their hostess, and Edward knows the name: he is an entrepreneur from Sydney, and rather well known. But for a second he sees another face: full lips, soulful eyes, the calm appraisal of Lucky Cho. The two men shake hands, but Edward barely notices. It has never occurred to him that Lucky Cho might one day speak again. The horror of it turns his bones to paste.

At this point, their medium, the dimpled Mrs Cornish, tells them all to take a seat. She is in her forties, but her voice is girlish with the hint of a lisp as she tells them she has a good feeling about today's séance. She describes how she will move into a trance, in order to contact her spirit guide, an Aztec king from the fifth century. She says his name is unpronounceable to modern tongues, but that they may call him Ip-hut-il. Iphutil will speak to them using her mouth. He will answer questions and pass on messages, but only regarding certain spirits; the spirit world is wide and he does not know everyone. She asks them all to please join hands and to clear their minds of interfering thoughts.

Edward's blood beats like a drum: Lucky Cho, Lucky Cho, Lucky Cho. Like a telegraph to the spirit world.

For pity's sake, he tells himself, clear your mind. Think of something else. He thinks of the mint growing on the rooftop, the pin-prick holes where something has eaten it. A leak in the kitchen roof. He thinks of Benson, working up the courage to write his letter. Then he takes a breath and clasps hold of the hands on either side of him, Eliza's cold, Joy's long and cool. He glances at Eliza, sitting straight as a schoolgirl, and lightly squeezes her hand.

There is some commotion to the right of him. The woman with the half-starved face is leaning over, whispering in Joy's ear. Edward senses the problem: she will not take the Chinaman's hand. His heart fills with wild hope; they will have to cancel the séance! But Quong Tart simply stands, casually, without fuss, and changes place with the woman in the headscarf, the medium's niece.

Mrs Cornish instructs them to relax and to not be afraid. They may experience some strange and inexplicable things, but they will not be harmed. Then the candles go out, though no one has touched them, and there is no smell of wick smoke in the air. The people around the table are dim shapes now, a pale flash of teeth or eye.

Edward shivers violently.

Mrs Cornish begins to hum, a high-pitched atonal sound. Her eyes are closed and her body sways, her head lolling with the movement. Edward tries to keep his hands steady and hopes he can keep them dry. The smell of burned sugar fills his nostrils.

Suddenly the medium's eyes open, the whites standing out in the gloom. 'I have a message,' she says in a deep, halting voice, completely unlike her own. 'The message is from someone who last saw this world on a very black night. Someone who died with the taste of liquor fresh on his tongue.'

Edward bows his head. The mineshaft, that starless night. Of course he cannot escape it. Let him be accused. Tears sting his eyes.

'Someone who breathed in water instead of air,' the medium intones.

Miss Heaver gives a small twittering cry. 'Why, that's Irvin, my darling brother!' Her eyes dart around the table, as though ready to be challenged. 'His ship was sunk in 1874. During a storm.'

And Lucky Cho died in a puddle of water at the bottom of a mineshaft. 1853. A two-ounce nugget in his trouser pocket.

Mrs Cornish moves her gaze around the table. Her face is angular, rigid; gone are the dimples, the cosy smile. 'He has a message for someone very close to him. A woman. He says to tell you the other side is peaceful and he wants for nothing. The spiritual world provides everything he needs.'

A woman. Saliva floods Edward's mouth, almost choking him with relief.

'Tell me more,' says Miss Heaver. She leans forward in her seat, clutching the hands on either side of her. 'Tell me,' she almost whispers.

The medium is perfectly still. 'He says to tell you it is like being in a garden. He says the souls are coloured like rainbows, they look and smell sweeter than any flower on earth. And a light falls upon them like sunshine, only softer and more beautiful, and they are always warm.'

Miss Heaver sighs and closes her eyes. Edward feels Eliza's hand grow warm in his. His breathing finally starts to slow. He can feel his shirt where it has stuck to him.

The medium continues. 'He says that he needs to warn you. That it is time to let go of your worldly possessions, to be generous and free, for they are only a burden and will mean nothing in the spirit life.'

Miss Heaver's eyes flash open, bright and alert. 'How do I even know it's Irvin?' Her lips are pinched and she crosses her arms over her chest. 'It doesn't sound like anything Irvin would say.'

Joy takes her hand from Edward's. She pats Miss Heaver on the arm. 'Why don't you ask for some proof? Ask for a sign.'

Miss Heaver nods slowly. Edward can now see quite well in the half-dark. He watches her as she snaps her order. 'Give me a sign that it's Irvin, then.'

Edward feels a strange tingling on his right thigh.

The medium opens her mouth and the words seem to pour out. 'He said he planned to marry once and that he didn't. He said you alone in the world know the reason why.'

Miss Heaver gasps and moans and then grips the table with her two hands, while the pressure on Edward's thigh grows stronger. 'It's Irvin, it's really him! Oh, my poor darling brother!'

Edward's thigh is growing warm, the sensation travelling up towards his groin. Then something sharp digs into his flesh, clearing his mind of Lucky Cho, filling it with another image: the hard outline of Joy's mourning ring. He grabs her hand, so hard he hears the bones crack, and pushes it away. At the same instant Miss Heaver's grip on the table loosens and she seems to swoon, slumping forward onto the table with a thud.

'Oh dear,' says Quong Tart.

Edward only just hears Joy whisper, *Think it over*, and then she is out of her seat, lifting her friend upright, fanning her face.

'Should we stop?' asks the girl in the headscarf.

'I'm fine, I tell you,' Miss Heaver protests, waving Joy aside.

'No one will mind if we stop,' says Quong Tart.

'By all means,' says Edward, his fury at Joy growing, encompassing the whole séance.

'Nonsense,' says Miss Heaver. 'I won't hear of it.'

Edward turns to Eliza, prepared to drag her out by the coat sleeves. But Eliza is staring at the medium with alarming intensity. 'Ip-hut-il? Ip-hut-il? Have you seen an eight-year-old girl by the name of Ruby Cole?' she says, rushing the words out, almost breathless.

Edward nearly groans. He bites his lip and waits. The whole table waits.

The medium sits in total stillness. 'No,' she replies.

Eliza swallows hard. Edward grips her hand, ready to pull her from the chair.

'I see—something,' says Joy Endicott. She is sitting back in her seat, gazing at the air above Eliza's head. Her white hands form a pyramid beneath her chin; her eyes are raised: she could be praying. 'I see a bird. A beautiful white bird, flying in circles above your head.'

They all stare at the empty air above her, Eliza tipping her head back to look.

Joy raises her hands to her mouth. 'Look at its eyes! The eyes are like two glowing rubies!'

'Ruby!' calls Eliza, now throwing her head from side to side. 'Ruby?'

'Oh, it's gone,' says Joy, lowering her eyes and resting her head in her hands, as if she is exhausted.

Edward feels as if his skin could blacken and curl. 'We're leaving,' he tells Eliza, half helping and half pulling her from her seat. He takes her by the arms and propels her towards the door, furious, and also a little frightened, for there is something sickeningly familiar in the image of a white bird, but he pushes it from his mind, guiding his dazed and subdued wife through the long hallway and out the front door.

...

Edward lies in bed, while Eliza undresses behind the wrought-iron screen; he sees the white flicker of skin through the metal. Thinking about the white bird of his dream, he decides it means nothing. Joy Endicott is no medium, though she is clearly other things. Licking at their grief like a rat on a battlefield, and for God knows what purpose. Heaven help her if she comes his way again.

The bedroom is icy tonight, the sheets stiff and cold. Edward absently rubs his feet against the mattress. What does she want from them? What should he tell Eliza?

No more surprises; that was his resolve only this morning. But to say nothing seems a kind of betrayal. And then there is Benson, who will not be sleeping well tonight, waiting on his fate. What does he do with a man who steals a fortune from him, then confesses of his own free will?

He hears the rustle of her nightclothes, the night-cracks of wood, the low sound of singing from the street. He has forgotten to close the window—no wonder he is freezing—and he rolls himself out of the bed. But the window is closed, the singing coming from their room. He turns to watch Eliza. Sitting before the bronze curlicued mirror, she is brushing her dark cropped hair. Singing softly in the candlelight. He climbs back into bed, hugging himself for warmth. Knowing he will not touch that peace. Not tonight.

...

Dawn brings a bluestone light to the city. The lamps are burning in Edward's office, and he stares out the window at the city's dark bulk. A cleaning rag dangles from his hand. A man who steals a thousand pounds is a man of some intelligence. It takes planning, and patience, and nerve. But a man who then comes clean about it, without being caught? Edward shakes his head. He pours vinegar onto the rag and makes a swipe at the pane, erasing the city in a milky smear. Did someone catch him in the act? Did Owens? He rubs and rubs until the glass starts to squeak. No, it wasn't Owens. Owens would have come to him first. He pours more vinegar. It's going to take some time. He has all morning.

When it finally comes—the knock at the door—his gut tightens. Clear morning light hits the brass doorknob, the clean-swept floor. The peacock waits, de-webbed and jaunty.

Benson comes through the doorway, his hair gleaming metallic, and Edward motions him to sit. Benson shakes his head and stands squarely in the centre of the room, so Edward stands, too, facing him across the desk.

'Mr Benson. Is it true you have stolen roughly one thousand pounds from the Arcade in the last two years?'

'Yes, sir, it's true.' The man's lips barely move.

Edward lifts a page from the desk. 'And is this your own confession? You wrote this and left it here?'

Benson's eyes flick downward. 'Yes.'

Edward crosses his arms and holds them at the elbows. 'It seems to me you got away with it—why own up now?'

Benson pulls a face, a wince of reluctance. He stares at the ground. 'With all respect, Mr Cole, why does it matter? I'm guilty, isn't that enough?'

'Perhaps it doesn't matter—it might not matter in the least. But I think you might humour me all the same.'

They face one another, the cuckoo clock chipping away the seconds. High on his cheeks, Benson begins to colour. 'I was gambling, Mr Cole, and I owed a lot of money, and the men who came after it were—not gentlemen, if you get my meaning. They were pretty rough.

I have a son, as you know, and a wife.' He swallows and holds out his large freckled hands. 'So I took the money, thinking to keep my family safe. And now they're safe.' He shrugs. 'And I must pay for what I did.'

Edward's skin begins to tingle, right at the base of his skull. 'I agree, Benson, you must pay. You absolutely have to pay.'

Intelligence, thinks Edward. Conscience, and heart. Exactly the kind of man he wants for the Arcade.

'So how about ten per cent of your wage every week? Until you pay it all back?'

Benson looks confused. He glances at the peacock, as if it might speak and make sense of things. 'You're not sending me to jail?' he asks, a note of uncertainty in his voice.

'Jail? How do you expect to pay me back from jail?' Edward drums his fingers on the desk. 'If you go to jail, I'll never see my thousand pounds again.' He moves around the desk, closer to Benson. 'You're to pay it back, do you hear? Every penny. A thousand pounds is a lot of money. By the way, you don't still gamble, do you?'

'No, sir, I don't. I swear on my mother's grave.'

'Very well,' says Edward, turning to stare out the window. 'Weekly payments will have to do.'

Within seconds of Benson leaving, Eliza comes bustling through the door. It's too much to hope that she hasn't seen him, all that freckled mass moving through the corridor. She will ask about his decision, and she will not like it, but he must be firm. It is his Arcade; he knows best how to run it.

'Good morning, Edward. Why, it's sparkling in here!'

She beams at him and drops a basket on the desk. A warm, yeasty smell fills the room.

'Oh, I tidied a little. Spot of cleaning here and there.'

'Is that why you left so early?' She gazes around the office. 'Without breakfast? This bread has come straight from the oven.'

Edward's stomach growls, and she lets out a laugh. Then she folds her hands on her stomach, looking serious. 'If you're not too busy, may I ask you something?'

Edward nods and waves for her to sit. Be firm, he tells himself. You have a plan. You're the boss.

'Do you think we might have someone to dinner this week?'

Edward, who dislikes entertaining, brings his hands together. 'What a wonderful idea! By all means, let's have someone over.'

Eliza looks taken aback. They haven't thrown a dinner since Ruby died.

'As long as it's not Crank,' he adds, wagging his finger. Crank, a phrenologist who works out of the Arcade, had once come to dinner and read the bumps and dips of the children's skulls, causing an uproar when he declared Vally had the makings of a genius.

'Oh no, not Crank,' laughs Eliza, for she was the one who had to console Vally when he failed to read Ancient Greek, or play Mozart by ear. 'Rather, I was thinking about Joy Endicott, and how lonely she must feel since her husband died. Don't you think she might like the company?'

Edward tries to speak; his tongue feels swollen, enormous. 'I really couldn't say,' he says.

Chapter Eight

1893

Edward steps out of the Arcade and walks down Bourke Street. Past Hosie's, with its green-tiled doorway and soupy, cabbage smell, past the empty barbershop with its wall mirrors and tilt-back chairs. Edward's shadow, leaning towards the road, dipping into the gutter. A single carriage rolls down the street. He waits for it before crossing, grit blowing against his face.

The footpath is dotted here and there with people, like the main street of a country town. Not like a city of half a million people.

Is it some kind of holiday? Even the GPO—that three-tiered sandstone palace—has an air of desertion, autumn leaves gathering on its steps. Edward looks down at the old sugar bag in his hand, full of the week's takings. He knows it's no holiday.

It feels, strangely, almost like it did when he arrived in fifty-two. At first, the streets were full of people—hundreds of people who had disembarked from ships—but few planned to stay in the city more than a day or two. Just long enough to pick up supplies and ascertain the best way to get to the goldfields. Edward, who had been chronically seasick on the voyage over, gave himself a few days to find his feet again, and was amazed to see how the city emptied out in that time. How it went from lively port town to ghost town overnight. And all the while there was a feeling in the air that the action—the real centre of things—was elsewhere. As today it seems elsewhere.

Edward rounds the corner. He sees the tobacconist's and, peering past the gold lettering on the window, he makes out the dim interior. The tobacconist, his thumbs hooked behind his braces, a glass case full of pipes, the glint of tobacco tins. Four men propped against the countertop. If the world is ending, thinks Edward, they don't seem to know it. He smiles into his beard.

As he passes by, the door swings open, sending a gust of dizzy-sweet tobacco smoke into the street. A small man stands blinking on the footpath. 'Well, what do you know,' he says, shaking his head at Edward. 'They've gone and closed all the banks!'

Edward has to see it for himself. It is only a couple of blocks to the London Bank, his bank, and he walks briskly through the quiet streets as grim-faced men begin to pass him, coming from the other direction. He grows conscious of the bag bumping against his thigh. A man in a crumpled suit stops to ask him for money, and Edward hands him coins from his pocket. Receives his thanks steeped in sour wine.

Outside the bank a small crowd has gathered. Men in sombre-looking suits, butchers in soiled aprons and bakers laced with flour like half-hearted mimes. The air rumbles with their anger and shakes with their outbursts.

'Where's our money?'

'You can't hide forever!'

'You lily-livered, money-grubbing fiends!'

Behind them stands the bank's expressionless stone façade, with its oak and copper reinforced doors. Closed but not barred. Closed from within.

...

Edward sits in the worn antechamber outside Deakin's office, the chair beneath him hard and cold, the room smelling of damp and wood smoke. Deciding whether or not to knock on the door with the frosted-glass panel stencilled with Deakin's name. He has passed by other offices—an accountant, a dentist—in the same small corridor, and a coat-rack with bare wooden limbs. He wonders if it might embarrass Deakin, to visit him here.

It was Eliza who insisted that he come. He has not seen Deakin since Ruby's death. Deakin had sent flowers then, and a note in his flawless hand. It was Edward's private belief that Deakin, the father of three girls, could imagine only too well the hollowing grief of losing a child. That he has stayed away not through indifference but through a fear of his own deep empathy. It's the only explanation that holds with his character as Edward knows it.

Edward stands and knocks on the door, and after a few seconds Deakin opens it, some dark emotion in his eyes.

'Ah, Edward. How in God's name are you?'

The office is small, its one narrow window overlooking a drab laneway. Beneath the window is a low Turkish couch, and a potted palm bent towards the light. The damp smell is stronger here, musty and close.

'I should have come to see you, Edward. How are you? Are you alright?' Deakin sits at his desk, with Edward sitting opposite. A thin light comes through the window, and the steady clatter of hooves drifts up from the street.

'Fine, fine. The family's fine. How are all the Deakins?'

'Oh good, you know, good.'

Deakin licks his lower lip. Behind him, on the cream wallpaper, is a framed photograph of his wife, Pattie, her strong young face looking downward, a bunch of wild-flowers in her hand. Something unyielding in her sweet look.

Deakin makes a sudden grimace at the small, cluttered desk between them and throws up his hands. 'To tell you the truth, Edward, I've sunk myself a little, with this market downturn. And not just with my own money.' He makes a noise of disgust. 'My father's too.' He nods at the shelves of books which line three walls of the room. 'That's why I've returned to practising law. It's not changing the world, I'm afraid, but it is paying my debts.'

Edward nods, and as he shifts in his chair his foot nudges the sugar bag, heavy at his feet. 'If there's anything I can do to help . . .'

'Oh, no!' Deakin jumps up from his chair. 'I mean, thank you, no. It's not as grim as it sounds. I shouldn't complain. I suppose I just miss being at the centre of things.' He smiles. 'Well, the centre of the antipodes, anyway.'

Edward watches some of the old animation return to his friend's face: the hint of wry humour, a spark in the depths of his eyes. He suddenly misses their long, impassioned talks, that wild longing for the future. How different it would be to share his hopes and plans with this man, instead of Owens and his doomsday scowl, or the cool pragmatism of D'Ama.

'Why don't you come for dinner tonight?' suggests Edward, surprising himself. 'Eliza has started having people around on Friday evenings, and she complains I never invite anyone.' He pictures them after dinner, himself and Deakin, a pot of tea, and talk of every kind: the nature of greed, the potential of the north, the dangers of isolation.

'I'd love to, Edward, though I'd better check with Pattie first. But tell me, what brings you to these humble quarters?'

'You've heard about the banks?' says Edward, leaning forward slightly.

'I heard that people panicked and tried to withdraw all their money at once.' Deakin shrugs. 'Naturally, the banks ran out of coin. But they'll get more from overseas, and it will all settle down.'

'But in the meantime,' says Edward, spreading his hands on the desk. 'I have the small problem of where to keep the Arcade's takings.'

Both men turn to look at the cast-iron box on legs in the corner of the room.

'You wish to use my safe?' says Deakin.

'Eliza would rather I didn't keep the money at the Arcade, not with the family living upstairs. It would be great to have somewhere close by that I could trust.'

Deakin covers his mouth with his hand and begins to laugh. 'I told myself I'd see that safe full of money someday.' He shakes his head. 'It's good to be right about something.'

...

Edward looks down at the small, darkly roasted bird on his plate. It is not chicken but a fine-boned quail, sitting in a jellied pool of onion and quince. Its slippery bones demand some attention from the diner, and its spiced gamey smell demands a certain respect. A snuffling sound falls over the table.

Edward looks around at his family and friends. On his right sits Eliza, cheerful and attentive, hands expertly ripping apart her bird. Beside her sits Joy Endicott. Gone are the dark mourning clothes that never suited her, the high lace collars. She wears a low-cut green dress, hovering on the bounds of decency. Bird fat glistens on her lips. She sits beside the children, Eddy, Vally and Linda, serious and poker-faced in their parody of adulthood. Vally, a perfect shadow of Eddy, laughing when he laughs and eating when he eats. At thirteen, it's his first adult dinner, and he fears being sent to bed with the younger children. Eddy swings his restless legs beneath the table. Linda slouches over to hide her rampantly developing breasts.

D'Ama sits next to Linda in his plum velvet suit, cufflinks flashing like sovereigns. Beside him sits his guest, Quong Tart, compact, shaven and smelling of anise. Speaking, to their surprise, with a mild Scottish accent. Edward has not seen him since that dreadful séance. And on his left is Deakin, who seems lively tonight, following every conversation with mild hilarity.

For Edward, it's a struggle to be among so many people. Mobbed by sensation. The clash of silverware, a mouthful of onion, Eliza's laugh, Joy's white skin. Not knowing where to look. What to do with the clamour of emotion: his curiosity towards Quong Tart, a nervousness he blames on Joy, the tangle of affection, yearning, gratitude, boredom, love. What does he do with it?

Mostly he stays quiet. A headache begins to snake its way from shoulder to skull.

'What have you done with the wine?' asks D'Ama, eyes darting everywhere.

'Why, it's here in front of you,' says Eliza, pointing out a bottle.

'Not that turnip juice, my dear, I want the Bordeaux, the bottle I came with.'

Eliza looks at the sideboard, and D'Ama stands to retrieve it. Back in his chair, he opens the bottle and pours a glass for Quong Tart. 'It's dreadful, Edward's wine, and you mustn't ever drink it out of politeness.'

'My husband never drinks, you see.' Eliza smiles broadly and leans towards their guest. 'But we have no objection to others enjoying a drop with their meal.'

'You might think otherwise,' says D'Ama, 'if you happen to be the one drinking it.'

Quong Tart looks from D'Ama to Eliza. Then he grins and raises his glass. 'No wine could possibly offend when the company is so agreeable.'

'Well put,' says D'Ama, also lifting his glass. 'Though I see you're still drinking my Château Margaux.'

'I admire a man who doesn't drink,' says Joy, rotating the knife in her hand, a strip of light playing across her throat and face.

'A sign of character,' agrees Quong Tart. 'I usually stick to tea myself.' And he goes on to describe the string of tea salons he runs in Sydney: the Elite Dining Hall, where gold carp swim beneath a shimmering waterfall, and the Moore Park Zoo, where an elephant once stole the scones from a customer's plate.

'I would feed it *all* my scones, and swing off its trunk like a rope,' declares Vally, in a sudden excess of spirit.

'And it would snap *you* like a tree branch,' counters Eddy, shaking his head.

'Tell me, Mr Quong Tart,' says Linda, blushing vividly, 'does your work take you, ah, overseas, to Scotland?'

'To Scotland! I'm not selling oats, you know. It's tea, it comes from China . . . but now that you mention Scotland, I do have a wee bagpipe collection . . .'

'The bagpipes!' yells Vally, leaping from his seat. 'Did you bring them? Can I play?'

'Ah, no. Sadly I did not. But I did bring some China tea for you all to sample. I hear you poor folk only get the Indian stuff, am I right?'

As soon as the plates are cleared they gather down the end of the table to watch Quong Tart unpack his tea set. Out comes a smooth bamboo box, long and rectangular, with slats in the lid. Out of that comes a column of small, bowl-shaped cups, each one nestled inside another like a beggar's palms. The cups are sun-set colours: saffron bleeding to orange, orange to red. He places each cup on the bamboo slats, his fingers fluid and exact.

'Have you ever tasted China tea?' Eliza asks, speaking to Joy in low tones.

'No. I always believed it inferior.'

'It certainly looks very impressive . . . all this ceremony. I feel rather grand!' Eliza laughs and turns her smile upon those around her.

Quong Tart disappears into the kitchen, returning with a kettle and Louma, the sour-faced cook. He holds up an unglazed brown ceramic teapot, and pours boiling water into it from the kettle. He swirls it around and tips it out into a waiting bowl. 'To warm and season the teapot,' he explains.

He then takes out a white ceramic canister, a green dragon curling its way around it. He scoops tea from the canister into the pot. He pours in boiling water and immediately tips it out again.

Louma shakes her head. 'Again he tips it out!' She crosses her arms and pouts her disapproval.

'That's to wash away the dust and give the leaves a bit of a tickle. Here, smell this.' He waves the teapot at Edward, who is startled by its complex and elusive scent. Floral yet earthy, like a single jasmine trodden into soil on the far side of a garden. And just as startling is the feeling that comes over him, a sweeping tenderness for the furthest reaches of the globe.

'Do you still have your headache?' asks D'Ama, passing Edward a small amber bottle. He holds it in his palm, the pain throbbing steadily behind his eyes. And something else, in the off-beat, a thought pulsing, trying to take shape. He unscrews the cap and shakes a few drops into his mouth, wincing at its bitterness.

'Perhaps the young lady would like first taste?' Quong Tart holds out a cup to Linda, orange in colour, with a fine crimson rim.

'Go on and try it,' says Joy, and Linda comes forward, smiling, almost forgetting her shyness, plump-cheeked and buxom in her rose-coloured pin-tucked dress. She takes the cup, as everyone watches, without turning red. She closes her eyes and raises the cup to her lips.

'Why, it's the loveliest tea in all the world!' she says, blinking in surprise, still holding the cup aloft. And Edward sees, through his pulsing vision, the colours of the dress and the cup blurring, re-forming, settling into a kind of rainbow. Tea and rainbows; it makes perfect sense.

...

'I've just started importing this,' says D'Ama, pouring a clear green liquid into three small glasses, holding the label to the lamplight. 'Tell me what you think.'

The men are sitting back on the couches, except for Edward, who sits perched at the couch's edge. Even so, he feels himself tipping backward, sinking into the dip. He plants both feet firmly on the rug.

'Is this what they call green fairy?' Deakin licks his lower lip. 'Tastes like licorice, only hotter. I rather like it.' He takes another sip. 'It won't give me visions, will it?'

'It depends,' says D'Ama. 'Sometimes it just knocks you out.'

'That isn't what you gave me for my headache?' asks Edward, but D'Ama shakes his head.

'That was laudanum. It's what I always take for my head.'

Quong Tart thrusts his glass towards the centre of the room. 'Here's to great imports!' he calls, lifting the glass high.

'That reminds me,' says Deakin. 'Where did you get your accent from?'

'From the goldfields,' laughs Quong Tart, swallowing his drink. 'Where else?' He tells them the story of his parents, dying on the goldfields within days of each other, leaving him destitute, an orphan at the age of five. How a Scottish miner took pity on him and raised him as a son. Even teaching him to play bagpipes.

'Edward was a goldminer,' says D'Ama. He sits with his legs crossed, exposing the perfect white sole of his shoe. 'You'll never hear it from him, though; he never talks about the goldfields. Not the right background for an intellectual bookseller.'

'That's not true,' says Edward. He feels intensely strange. He feels the conversation move in waves, as though the words are in liquid form, nudging and swaying him. 'There's not all that much to say about it.' He sees the rug at his feet is divided into squares, and each square contains a tiny maze: blue on yellow, brown on orange, red on pink. Each maze identical at first, until one looks closely at the tiny variations . . .

'Did you strike it rich?' Deakin's voice seems to come out of nowhere, booming in Edward's ear.

'Oh, hardly, no. I made more money when I gave the whole thing up, started selling lemonade to the diggers.' The conversation recedes, like sand pulled by the tide— like being drunk, he thinks, with a stab of shock. Placing the sensation after forty years of abstinence. But he can't be drunk; can a man get drunk by association?

'Did you hear that? The man sold lemonade! The whole place teeming with thugs and thieves, and there's Edward: *Forget about the moonshine and malt liquor, chaps, I've got something really refreshing!*' The men laugh, and D'Ama leans over to top up their glasses. 'Quite a chequered past.'

'Oh, do be *quiet*, D'Ama.' Edward's face burns; thankfully the room is dim. When will the conversation end, why can't he steer it elsewhere? Inside his head, his thoughts are luminous and clear as stars, but they cannot cross the fuzz, like a band of wool around his skull. At least his headache is gone; he can be grateful for that.

'I think it shows great initiative,' says Deakin, turning suddenly to face Quong Tart. 'I mean, have you seen the Arcade yet?'

Quong Tart shakes his head, his skin hazy in the lamplight. 'No, but I want to go first thing tomorrow.'

'No you don't,' says D'Ama, setting down his glass on the low lacquered table. 'By then it will be overrun with vulgar hordes. You want to see it tonight.'

...

Edward holds the lamp out in front of him as the men make their way down the stairs. Their shadows like a mountain range, their footsteps drumming the wood.

At the ground floor, Edward swings the light in a circle, and everywhere it shines there are books. Books in the tall shelves lining the walls, and in the shorter shelves dividing the room into a series of alcoves and aisles. Books curving snake-like on tables, or piled into pyramids. Books on trolleys and countertops. The men wander the aisles. They seem almost shy, carefully rounding the ghostly white wicker chairs. Turning away if they happen to catch their reflections in the brass columns.

Quong Tart stands beside Edward. 'I've never seen so many books.'

Edward guides him to one of the taller shelves against the wall. Below waist level, the shelves give way to deep drawers with neat white labels and handholds recessed into the wood. 'Open it,' says Edward.

Quong Tart slides out the drawer and lets out a low whistle. There are books on Chinese history, Chinese languages and culture, and several large, luxurious volumes on Chinese art.

Edward slides open the drawers on either side. 'Folk-tales from around the world. And over here, animal husbandry.'

He stops, the lamp still swinging from his hand. 'But you've all seen a book before. Why don't I show you something different?'

Edward leads them, feeling warm, buoyed, the four of them tucked within the fuzzy circle of light. They pass the music room, its trumpets and violins snug in their cases, the printing room stinking of grease. Thoughts of a tea salon kick at his psyche, like a baby desperate to be born. The Arcade needs a tea salon, nothing could be clearer. He thinks of all the people with their flasks and sandwiches, gathering in the fernery for lunch. The people want a place to drink without getting drunk. They want to be refreshed and to be nourished when they visit. And a tea salon—a Chinese tea salon—will have culture, it will have ceremony. They can even read books on China while they wait for their tea. He loves Quong Tart for making him see this; he is burning with brotherly love.

'Don't talk to me about protectionism.' D'Ama's voice is thin in the high-ceilinged room. 'That's simply lazy colonial rot. It's wrapping industry in cottonwool. And you know what you'll get for it? Inefficiency—and that's if you're lucky; corruption if you're not.'

'Not to mention those import tariffs.' Deakin's voice is deeper, with hints of vibrato. 'That could make life rather tricky for an import baron.'

For a moment, their footfalls are the only sound.

'So what about pensions then, D'Ama? Do you support the idea of pensions, or do they just make the orphans and widows lazy and uncompetitive?'

D'Ama snorts. 'Let them have their pensions. And spare us the sight of widows like Joy Endicott parading themselves like cows at market.'

Deakin lets out a gasping sort of laugh.

'Here we are,' calls Edward, standing inside a grand arching doorway and holding up the lamp. Above him, in gilded gothic script, gleams the word *Wonderland*.

Edward flicks a switch and the walls light up. The room is one long corridor, the walls inset with glass display cabinets, like those in a museum. But as they begin to walk its carpeted length, it seems there are to be no stuffed pythons or Egyptian mummies. Instead, each glass panel frames a view into the impossible. The first shows a polar landscape: blue water and icebergs—achingly white—that seems to stretch without end. Defying the logic of the small square frame. The more one looks, the further it stretches: no boundary, no horizon, just limitless distance.

Deakin taps lightly on the glass. 'I can't see how it's done. Is it mirrors?' He moves closer, his nose almost touching. 'Those lunatic explorers, just imagine.'

The next frame shows a volcano, a rocky brown cone with a lake of flaming liquid at its centre. From this lake, shooting skyward, is a spout of red-gold lava, electric against the black night. The single jet of lava soaring higher than the ceiling, higher, it seems, than the Arcade's own roof.

Deakin rests his palms against the glass and shakes his head. 'How's it done, Edward? You have to tell me.'

Edward smiles. He takes him by the arm and draws him to the next frame, where Deakin suddenly shouts, 'An Architeuthis! Surely not—this has got to be a hoax.' He stares open-mouthed at the huge rubbery mass: small malignant eyes, a sharp, pointed beak, and bright purple suckers on its tendrils. It's a squid, but of massive proportions, as big as a whale: a giant squid.

'But Edward, I always thought they were mythical, something dreamed up by whalers on their long voyages. How did you get it, is it real?' Deakin tugs gently at Edward's sleeve. 'You can't keep me in the dark, not on this.'

Edward swells with unshed laughter, with a deep, companionable joy. He loves these men, their decency, their singular souls.

At the far end of the room they find D'Ama, in partial darkness, lighting his pipe. As they approach he steps to the side, revealing three full-length mirrors mounted onto the wall. The three men—Edward, Deakin and Quong Tart—are confronted by three grotesque alter egos. Deakin's head is enormous, his lips like two pink eels mating on his face. Quong Tart has shrivelled up into a wasted figure, a deflated balloon of a man. And Edward, holding the lamp before his body, is a brilliant circle of light, his tiny bearded head sitting at its apex.

Deakin and Quong Tart burst into laughter.

'I could get arrested, with lips like this.'

'I've heard of wasting your life, but I always imagined it took longer.'

Smoke drifts from the corner, where D'Ama chews his pipe, and appears in the mirrors, eerie and broken.

'What is that—ectoplasm?'

'No, I think it's the misty moors of Scotland.'

'Edward, this is sensational.'

Edward has seen the warped mirrors dozen of times; in fact, he had them specially commissioned. They never fail to tickle him, but tonight—tonight he is transfixed. He sees something soulful in their faces, something totemic in their ruined bodies. They are absurd yet truthful, like the Minotaur or Ganesh.

He swings his lamp to the right and the circle of light disappears from view, leaving a ghoulish, thin torso. He swings the lamp back and the light engulfs everything, like a star exploding.

'Edward seems to have found a new love,' says D'Ama, one hand on his elbow, the other on his pipe, as he and the others walk back towards the exit.

...

The bedroom smells of musk, of sleeping animal; it smells of lavender and powder. Edward undresses in the dark. He feels his way into the bed, beside the warm mound of his wife. He listens to the gentle ocean of her breathing, tries to match it with his own. But the night still buzzes in his blood. Tea salons and widows' pensions, orphan boys, the Minotaur. And that feeling, that high, relaxed feeling, like opportunity and friendship rolled into one. Like being drunk. And he lets himself remember: the intense camaraderie, the exotic tang, of drinking around the campfire with Lucky Cho. The bottle so smooth in his split and calloused hands. Rubbing his thumb across the rounded lip of the rim. Listening to Lucky Cho tell stories of China. Of a monastery, high on a mountain and so remote it could only be reached on one week of the year. In perfect weather. That if pilgrims did not make the trip in this time, bringing supplies for the coming year, all the monks would die. The monks would know the beauty and brutality of life, their vulnerability essential to their learning.

Edward had loved that story, the way it rippled outward in his thoughts. How many stories were there, how many cultures, wisdoms? He could dwell in such a story—imagining the high snow-capped peaks, the monks shivering in their crimson robes. Watching those black dots in the snow, the distant pilgrims. In dwelling there, he could tune out the sickening crack of gunshots, the snarling dogs. While the fire and the whiskey formed a blazing balm for the loneliness of being twenty and so utterly far from home.

'Eliza.' His voice neither soft nor loud in the room. She mutters something and it sounds like 'sleeping'. If only he could tell her about the tea salon. Another way of opening the world to people. Of hinting at its stories and its richness. Suddenly, a baby's wail comes tearing through his thoughts, making him jump and throw back the covers. But it is only the alley cats, yowling in the street, their desperate cries falling just short of human. Making him think, for some reason, of Joy's hand on his thigh at that séance. A tight, quivering feeling in his belly and groin brought on by the memory, the sound of the cats. He will have to go downstairs and chase them off; he could never fall asleep with their crying in his head.

Chapter Nine

1894

The girls run downstairs, their white dresses like birds giving chase. Pearl holds her dress at the knee and turns back to Ivy, dark hair wrapping her neck and face. Their hands hover over the bronze rail, and descend, here and there, for balance. Ivy is laughing and breathless. The sun, pouring through the glass ceiling, gilding arms, faces, hair. Edward watches them, stunned with love. Stricken when they round the corner, out of his sight. Running to their adult selves. In no time they will be grown, as the others have grown; all except Ruby. Loss wells in his throat.

He goes in search of Eliza, to steady himself. He tries the kitchen first and finds pots on the stove, heavy steam, the smell of stewing bones. Then he sees her, backing out of the pantry, a large ham clasped in her hands.

'Oh, hello there. Are you hungry? Shall I make you a snack?'

'No, I was just thinking: why don't we take the children to the beach today?'

She rests the ham on the bench, which is crowded with jars of sauce and pickles. Dried herbs hang on the wall behind her.

'The boys have gone rowing. And Linda will be at Jane's all weekend. But Louma will be back from the market soon. We could leave then, and take the babies.'

Edward could kiss those downy cheeks. He could kiss her tender, practical hands.

'Marvellous. A cosy company of Coles. A frolicking family foursome.'

'Hmm,' says Eliza. She steps back inside the pantry, her next words muffled and faint. 'You'd better make it a frolicking fivesome. Did I not mention that Joy is coming?'

...

With an hour to go until their train leaves, he has time to stop at the print department. He has begun to see the advantage of owning a press. Not the commercial advantage of publishing books and compendiums to sell in the Arcade—he has long recognised that—but the personal advantage of publishing whatever he likes. He has begun writing pamphlets. Modest tracts on topics that take his fancy: the dangers of smoking, the foolishness of fashion, the importance of hobbies, the history of the apple. He leaves the pamphlets on the Arcade's counters, beside the registers, for people to take as they please. It's a pastime of his, a minor indulgence.

He stands now in the doorway of the printing room, watching Benson work. The machine is heavy, cast iron and black with grease, but elegant, too, with scrollwork and enamelling. Despite his large frame, Benson moves easily, precisely, the power of his body held in check. Like the hops farmer Edward lived next door to growing up.

His barrel torso barely contained by his Sunday-best shirt when he came to hear Edward's father preach, his hands dwarfing the hymnal. It was to this man, John Shearer, that Edward had first confessed his hopes of striking out on his own and seeing the world. John Shearer had given no advice, neither for nor against this plan. But he had taught him the names of constellations. He had asked for Edward's help come harvest time and, when the work was done, let Edward hang about dreaming in the bare, coarse fields. Giving him a break from his nine younger brothers and sisters. The man was trustworthy—that's the word that comes to mind now—and Edward senses the same quality in Benson, in spite of everything.

Benson looks up and sees Edward in the doorway. 'Good morning, I didn't notice you standing there.'

'I know, you were deep in concentration. You seem to have a real way with that machine.'

'Oh, I don't know.' Benson rolls his shoulders and glances down at the press. 'I like it, though. I like figuring out her kinks. See this part here? If it gets jammed I've learned to run a knife into the gap, to help it release.'

Edward looks. It looks like a machine. He cannot make out the part in question. 'I'm pleased to hear it. A man should like his work. It's not all about putting bread on the table.'

Benson reddens. He rubs the back of his neck and stares at the ground. 'Well, I consider myself lucky to be doing that much.'

Edward clicks his tongue. 'The past is the past, Benson. I never go there myself, burned the passport, if you like. The present and the future, that's where we work our influence, where we should direct our energies. Speaking of which.' Edward takes a piece of paper from his pocket, covered in his fly-away scrawl. 'If you wouldn't mind printing this up?'

'*The Real Cause of Colour in Mankind*,' reads Benson in his mild voice. He reads in silence for a few minutes before looking up. 'You're saying that racial differences are superficial and don't determine a person's essential character.'

'In a nutshell, Benson. With a little science thrown in for good measure.'

'And you think this will change the way people think?'

Edward has been asking himself this very question. For all his love of words, rhetoric, books, it seems to him lately that some beliefs are so ingrained they require something extraordinary in order to shift them. But the thought is young; he doesn't yet know what to do with it. 'Oh, even if it plants a seed,' he replies. 'If it plants a seed, that's something.'

...

He waits in his office for the women to come and collect him. The air is warm after days of hot weather, and when he opens the window street sounds rush in: bells and hooves and the jangle of a cable tram. He sits on the edge of his desk. On the back of the door he has pinned several maps, of Japan, India and the South Pacific. Pink mountains and yellow deserts, coloured by hand. He is staring at the red egg of Easter Island when the door is thrown open and Ivy rushes in, a bucket swinging wildly from her hand. Her eight-year-old body is round with baby fat, her eyes the colour of honeycomb. Pearl is trailing her, the same height but thinner, hair and eyes gypsy dark. 'We're going to be late,' she says, pointing to the cuckoo clock. 'The train leaves in twenty minutes.'

'Guess where we're going?' calls Ivy, skipping circles around them.

'I've no idea,' says Edward, shrugging his shoulders. He glances at the bucket in her hand. 'Are we going to Ballarat, to look for gold then?'

'No-o-o.' She giggles.

'Now *that* I would like,' says Pearl. It's no secret that she hates the sand and will, on their return, remove every last grain from her clothes and shoes. 'If I found a lot of gold I could buy Mrs Endicott a mansion. Like the one she used to have.'

'Me too!' calls Ivy. 'A mansion. Or a poodle!' Her eyes are bright, her cheeks apple-red. A little too red, thinks Edward, looking closer. He turns to study Pearl.

'Come here,' he says, cupping her chin with a shaking hand. Her cheeks, usually pale, are also very red: two spots, high on her cheekbones. Pain shoots through his collarbones, his chest. He can still recall the exact feel of Ruby's sandpaper skin. 'Do you feel hot? Is your throat sore? Your face is all red.'

'Oh *that*,' she says, squirming free. 'That's from playing dress-ups with Mrs Endicott.' She tugs at his sleeve. 'Come on, Pa, we'll miss the train.'

Edward stands too quickly, unsteady on his feet; black dots swim before his eyes. Powder, he thinks. Face paint! Whatever it is they call that muck. He takes a breath, tries to calm himself, waiting for the room to stop its spinning. The word, he believes, is rouge. His very own babies, painted like harlots.

...

'Can we, Pa, can we?' The girls dance on the spot. The donkeys are a hundred yards down the beach. Children

114

are already queuing for rides, wide-brimmed hats shielding them from the sun. Behind them stretches the sea, flat and blue and glinting like broken mirrors. Edward nods and hands them some coins. The girls take off, sand clouds rising in their wake, Pearl dusting sand off her dress even as she runs. The air is thick and still. Edward leans his back against a tree trunk.

Joy takes a wooden fan from her bag. She swipes the air, half-hearted as a cat. 'This heat is roasting me alive.'

'Hmm,' says Eliza, taking a book from her bag and laying it on the blue wool rug. She pats at the damp spots beneath her eyes and chin.

Edward gazes at the water. He sees a single white sail in the distance. Closer to the shore, he sees the sprawling wooden buildings of the sea baths. 'I might take a dip later. Cool the system.'

Joy wrinkles her nose. Her skin is still white, though no longer translucent. 'I loathe the sea baths. All that damp wood closing one off from the world . . . like a great watery coffin.' She turns her head to the water. She seems sadder in profile. 'I think I would like to swim in the open sea. To dive like a bird, without thought or worry.'

Edward happens to agree with her. He does not support the law against public bathing, finds nothing immodest in the act of swimming. But coming from Joy, the words seem wanton, unladylike. The opinion of a woman who bedizens children. She has wormed her way into the bosom of his family, but that doesn't mean he has to like it. He keeps his agreement to himself.

'You couldn't make a law that would get me into the water,' says Eliza, frowning at the baths. 'I'll keep my feet on dry land, thank you very much.'

Edward rubs his hands together. 'I wouldn't need a law. I'd simply scoop you up and throw you in.'

He is startled by Joy's husky laugh; she does not laugh often. She turns her green eyes towards him. 'I can imagine what the papers would say: *Crazed bookseller tries to drown wife in sea.*'

Edward shakes his head. 'And here I've been making the mistake of paying for my advertisements.'

'Oh, they'd be lining up at the door, alright. Blood-thirsty, that's what they are.' Eliza nods in emphasis.

Edward raises his eyebrows at the book on the rug. 'Enjoying your murder-mystery, dear?' he asks. Eliza purses her lips, before breaking into a grin which shows every one of her small front teeth.

A vendor rings his bell nearby. In the distance, Ivy and Pearl have almost reached the head of the queue. The donkeys pace their small strip of beach, led by men with red ropes. Eliza opens her book and fans herself before beginning to read.

Edward picks up a handful of sand and lets it sift through his fingers. Feeling its gritty softness, its radiant heat. The heat of the day seeps into his flesh, muscles softening like butter. He breathes in salt air, hints of roasted nuts. He closes his eyes against the glare of the sand, just for a moment.

Dreams unfold instantly. He is carrying a heavy tapestry, gold and brown, almost buckling beneath its weight. But he must hang it like a curtain, and soon, before the tea salon opens. He stands on a chair and tries to thread it through a row of hooks. But no matter how he lines it up, the tapestry hangs crooked and bunched. And his arms ache, his muscles are beginning to tremble. He unhooks it and starts again. Then he notices the room is filling up with people, and he realises it's the opening of the tea salon. He has to get the curtain up! And what about the tea, has he even ordered it yet? What will they use for tables and chairs? He better not drop this priceless tapestry, he thinks, as it slips from his hand and crashes to the floor.

He starts awake. Eliza is reading. Joy is watching a couple of children run past, trailing a long piece of sea-weed. He looks over to see the girls riding their donkeys, Ivy wriggling with excitement; he has only slept a matter of minutes.

'Ivy's waving,' he says, raising his hand. Eliza looks up from her book and waves as well. Pearl sits straight in the saddle, both hands gripping the pommel.

'Ivy's fearless, but she's still very young,' says Joy, watching and shading the sun from her eyes. 'Pearl reminds me of myself, trusting neither man nor beast.'

Edward bristles: his daughter is *nothing* like Joy. 'Pearl is prudent, that's her nature. She doesn't trust strangers. But she does trust her parents. She trusts the people she ought to trust.'

'Ah,' says Joy. 'Children should trust their parents. Wives should trust their husbands. And all will be well with the world.'

Edward frowns, unsure of her point. 'Well, naturally wives and husbands must trust one another. You can't possibly object to that, can you?'

'No. But perhaps one can trust too much, and think too little. I trusted James completely, you know. It never occurred to me that he might commit fraud.' She swallows and lowers her head. 'Or take his life.'

Edward is shocked to hear her say such a thing aloud. What does she expect: absolution, pity? But Eliza looks up quickly, the pages of her book falling shut.

'You mustn't blame yourself, my dear.'

'Oh, I know it doesn't change anything. But tell me, who would you blame, if your husband did those things?'

Eliza opens her mouth; the girls dismount from their donkeys and start running back towards them.

'Your husband would never do those things. You can say it, it's the truth,' says Joy, lying back and covering her face with the fan.

...

Edward enters the men's bathing pavilion: a long rectangle of sea water fenced in by wooden pylons. He stands on a platform at the water's edge, bare skin tingling. He understands the theory behind these enclosures: protect the bathers from sharks, and the public's modesty from naked and near-naked bathers. But in the moments before he wades in—while the limbs of men and boys churn up the water and their voices crash off the wood—it suddenly strikes him as madness. The whole calm, glittering bay spread before them, and here they gather in one small pen, like sheep in an abattoir. He feels the cold shock of water on his thighs, pelvis, ribs, and then he's swimming, the silky sea like a second skin. Quick bursts of breaststroke, lengthening out into smoother strokes, weaving around the other bodies, like some great benign shark.

Of course they'd swum in the Murray, him and Beaver. Whenever they got to a part of the river that was deep and wide, Beaver would shuck off his dilapidated moleskins, his filthy shirt. He would swim a careful circuit, checking for submerged branches and rocks. Then he would swim for the joy of it. His arms would slice through the water, his body would part it, clean as a fish. Nobody swam like Beaver. There was no excess movement, no splash. Just his streamlined body and his wide-split smile. He would coax Edward into the water, at a time when Edward could barely keep afloat, and teach him basic strokes. Edward, who on the boat over from England had lived in mortal fear of drowning, who viewed all bodies of water as a liquid grave. And he'd come to like it. The freedom of it, after sitting cramped up in the boat. And the way his skin felt stripped clean for hours. Once, absorbed by their lesson, they had been surprised by natives: varnished bodies rising out of the water just a few feet away. Edward and Beaver had frozen, unsure if they were in danger, their single rifle stowed inside the boat. But the natives had, through pantomime and gesture, expressed their curiosity over the white men's skin: they had only seen it clothed before, was it white *everywhere*, they wanted to know?

Edward collides with a dense, slippery object: a swimmer, coming from the other direction. He raises his hands in apology. 'Do forgive me. I wasn't looking where I was going.'

'No, no,' says the stranger. 'My fault entirely. I'm a landlubber, through and through.'

Edward swims more carefully now, head above the waterline. That incident with the natives had come as a relief, for they'd heard tales of whites being speared along the river. Of course, they were not actually any safer for their encounter, but he'd found himself relaxing all the same. That was the thing—a pamphlet might appeal to your reason, but it wouldn't make you relax your guard once it was up. Experience: that was the key. Coming face to face with what you fear.

Edward approaches a man floating on his back, his great hairy torso like an island, partly forested.

Swimming around him, he almost collides with another man, who is animated, deep in conversation.

'It sent him broke, you know. Along with his visits to a certain widow we know . . .' He addresses the island, who rises from the water now, showering Edward with the run-off. He looks familiar to Edward, his round face, the jowls like sandbags.

'Was he offering consolation, or merely seeking it?' asks the island, eyebrows shooting upward. He is a massive man; surely Edward would remember meeting him?

'Ah, who knows?' says the friend.

The island runs a meaty hand through his thin wet hair, then leans over and winks at his friend. At that moment, Edward places him: he's Abel Cornish, husband of the medium.

'One could say it didn't bring him much *joy* in the end,' says Abel. His friend laughs so hard he swallows water and begins to choke.

...

The moment they set foot in the house, the girls scatter: Ivy to find her brothers, Pearl to change and shake out her clothes. As Edward and Eliza carry the picnic hamper and rugs into the hallway, Edward almost trips over a large striped cat, the same marmalade colour as their carpet.

Eliza sniffs at the rugs. 'Would you take these to the rooftop for airing?'

Edward nods and gathers them, smelling of skin and salt, into his arms. He is thinking about Joy, her hand on his thigh at that séance. That slender white hand with its indigo veins. Thinking, too, about the words he overheard at the baths. Back home, in this corridor filled with cricket bats and umbrellas, it's hard to be sure what, if anything, he really heard. Remembering, too, the water in his ears and the noise of the place. But he cannot shake the feeling they were talking about Joy. Or the feeling it gives him—a churning deep in his gut—whenever he thinks of her hand.

'How does Joy Endicott support herself?' he asks. 'Being the widow of a bankrupt?'

Eliza frowns. She is flushed, tired-looking. She runs a hand across her face. 'Well, I don't know exactly. Perhaps her friends help out. I believe she receives some donations from the séances she helps to run at the Cornishes'.'

'I see.' Edward nods and stands there holding the rugs. The cat wanders past, brushing his leg with perfect indifference. His thoughts have left him confused, restless, slightly combative. 'You don't find it distasteful that she makes money out of the grief of others?'

'Well, no, Edward, I don't.' She unties her bonnet, lets it hang in her hand a moment, the hair beneath flattened. 'That money is earned by relieving people of some of that grief. By making them happy.' She shakes the bonnet briefly and hangs it on the polar bear.

'But how do you know it's true, all this talk of spirits?' says Edward, treading on more dangerous ground. For Eliza continues to attend the odd séance, though never with Edward, who always makes some excuse.

'Well, I don't,' she says, shocking Edward to the core. 'But I know it makes people feel better.'

But he thought she believed! He thought that, rendered vulnerable by her loss, she naively, sincerely, believed every word. He stares at her, the hard lines of grief from nose to mouth that formed after Ruby died.

'But if it's untrue . . .' he stumbles, not knowing how far he can take it.

'I never said it was untrue. I just feel that one shouldn't dismiss happiness, in whatever form it takes.' She picks up the hamper, throwing him a look both defiant and kind, and disappears into the kitchen.

...

He hangs the rugs out in the lemon twilight. The evening has a dusty taste. He feels dry—his skin, his mouth, his thoughts—a desiccation of body and soul. Drained by the hours in the sun. Drained by the odd exchange with his wife. He doesn't quite know what to do with himself. He will go downstairs, he thinks, to his office, and collect the pamphlets that Benson must have printed by now and left there for him.

But inside his office he finds more than just the pamphlets. He finds Benson, a balding stranger and the peacock standing neatly in a row like bachelors at a ball.

'I hope you don't mind us waiting here like this,' says Benson, hunching his shoulders. 'But I thought you might want to hear this.'

Edward motions them to sit, but with only two chairs in the room they all remain standing.

Benson steps forward. 'May I introduce Mr Gabriel? Simon Gabriel, this is Mr Cole.'

Edward shakes hands with the short, pale stranger. He has a high, bald forehead, mutton-chops and a mild expression. Edward glances at the desk for something to offer them: paper, inkwells, a few old apple cores.

'I asked Mr Benson if he might introduce us,' says the man, his eyes as soft and brown as pudding, 'after he showed me your pamphlet, *The Real Cause of Colour in*

Mankind.' He speaks with the hint of an accent, something more lilting and rhythmic than English. 'You write that skin colour is a superficial trait and that it does not determine a person's character. I not only agree with you, Mr Cole, but I can prove it.'

Edward wonders if the man is a scientist. He exudes a calm authority, an unruffled air. 'Please continue, Mr Gabriel, you have my utmost attention.'

'Consider this for a moment. If a man was born black and lived as a black man for thirty years, and then—indulge this, if you please—his skin changed to white, would he still be the same person? According to your pamphlet, he would. Well, I'm here to tell you, I *am* that man. I stand before you as a white man, but this is not how I was born. I was born in Mauritius some forty years ago, and I can tell you now, I was born black. As black as an Indian.'

Edward stares at the man, who begins to roll up his sleeves to the elbows.

'My parents are black. We moved to Portugal when I was young and I grew up there, an ordinary black man. Please, take a look at me.' He rotates his pallid forearms for Edward to see. 'Now, take a look at this.' He removes a photograph from his pocket and hands it to Edward.

There, staring at the camera with his soft eyes and mutton-chops, is Simon Gabriel. A little thinner, a little younger, and with skin the colour of dark brewed tea. Edward feels his own skin become charged from the back of his knees to his ears, every hair standing.

'But how . . . how did this happen?'

Simon Gabriel pulls a wad of paper from the same pocket. 'It started changing about ten years ago, small patches at first. I was living in Mildura by then and I consulted several doctors, both there and in South Australia, but none of them could explain it. By the time I turned completely white—after a year or more—they were thoroughly baffled. But I have kept their reports as proof of my situation, and will gladly leave them here for your perusal.' He places the wad, bound with red ribbon, on the edge of the desk.

Edward's mind has begun to race ahead. Is this it? Is this the extraordinary *something* to shake people out of their prejudice? This pleasant, articulate, cultured, black and white man? And if so, how? What does he *do* with him?

'Thank you so much for coming to see me, Mr Gabriel. Your story is very powerful, truly remarkable.' He reaches over once more to shake the man's hand, clasping it firmly with his own.

'This might well be a first,' laughs Simon Gabriel. 'While people happily shake my hand believing me to be white, I can't say that anyone has ever tried to shake it a second time on discovering that I'm really black. No, I believe this is the first.'

Edward laughs too. He smiles his gratitude at Benson, standing quietly off to the side. Then he turns back to Simon Gabriel. 'May it be the first of many,' he says.

He takes to the stairs, needing to share this with Eliza, and rushes into the flat. He finds her drinking cocoa in the sitting room.

'Let me fetch you a cup,' she says, but he shakes his head. He already feels slightly feverish and the room is dense with heat. He removes his jacket, his one concession to the weather, and his shirt is patched with sweat. He sits in his armchair, careful to keep his dampness off the fabric. He tells her about Simon Gabriel. Simply, calmly, not wanting to influence her reaction. When he's finished, he watches her lick the milk from her upper lip.

'He sounds like a very interesting man,' she says, placing her cup on the table. She sinks back into her chair, her feet lifting from the floor.

'Intelligent, too,' Edward can't help adding. 'Did I mention he speaks four languages?'

Eliza nods and half closes her eyes, giving her a sleepy look. But Edward knows she is thinking deeply.

'It's like the pamphlet you wrote.'

Edward leans forward. He tries to keep his voice neutral. 'Yes, how do you mean?'

'Well, you wrote your pamphlet arguing there was no difference between black and white. And then this man, Simon Gabriel, comes along, and it turns out he's been black and white both. But surely, all the while, *he's still the same man.*'

Edward springs forward and pats her lightly on the knee. 'Exactly, my dear! My own thoughts exactly. But tell me,' he drops both his hand and his voice, 'now that I've found him, what do I *do* with him?'

Eliza waves her hand in a sweeping, regal gesture. 'Why, Edward, must I think of everything?'

...

By the time they are ready for sleep, the bedroom is baking. A breeze flaps the lace curtain, but it is warm, a northerly. Bringing voices, footsteps and hints of rotting vegetables into the room. The sky is navy, nursing a swollen moon.

Eliza sits on the bed, removing her small beaded slippers. Edward yawns and moves to the basin. He splashes water onto his face, letting it run into his beard and down his shirt.

'I might go with Joy tomorrow, to buy some velvet for a dress for Ivy.' She kicks her slippers beneath the bed. 'Joy says she saw a turquoise that would suit her just so.'

'Ah, Joy. Is it really such a good idea, having her spend so much time with the girls?' His pulse quickens—what has he said? Eliza may be placid and good-tempered, but she is fierce as a lioness in defence of those she loves.

'In what way? A good idea, in what way?'

'In the way she puts that, that . . . vulgar face paint on the girls!' He feels himself firing up, and knows his only option is to run with it. 'Ivy is eight years old, for crying out loud, and Joy had her painted like a lady of the night!'

'Oh, Edward.' Eliza swipes the air, batting away his words. 'They were playing dress-ups, that's all. Remember the time Vally went African with the charcoal?'

He begins to pace, momentum his only ally now; he knows that if he stops he will fold. 'You said yourself, Eliza, just this afternoon, that she even accepts money from men.'

'Edward!' She rises from the bed, her hands clenched into fists. 'She was left penniless, as well you know. If she accepts money, on loan or even as gifts, who are we to judge her?'

'It's not about judgement. It's about the kind of example she sets for our girls.' He feels he's made a solid point, one that will be hard to dispute. And Eliza does seem to falter. Her face looks pinched as she runs a hand through her cropped grey hair. Then she takes a breath and seems to draw herself taller.

'Remind me, Edward, what kind of example is Benson setting?' She drops her hand and smooths the folds of her flannel nightdress. 'Tell me, please, how Benson is deserving of our compassion, our kindness—and let's not forget, our forgiveness—when Joy is not?'

Edward feels himself felled, side-swiped; he didn't see it coming. And she knows it, her eyes gleaming metallic in the moonlight. For a moment, she seems to see right through him, through to his weakness, his lust. Edward flinches beneath her gaze, which is surely heavy with disappointment. They were only thoughts, he wants to tell her, he would never act on them! In fact, they barely seem to belong to him, coming as they do of their own accord. But then her face seems to soften, and she offers him a half-smile.

'Besides, I like having Joy around,' she says, moving to turn down the sheet, and climbing into bed. 'She makes life interesting.'

Chapter Ten

1895

Edward sits on the rooftop, leaning back into the carved teak bench. Potted lime and frangipani surround him, and a breeze brings city smells: smoke and coal and dung. From here he can see other rooftops, birds, a tarnished sky: grey as old silver. His scarf keeps the cold out.

'Get ready for some changes, Ruby-red.'

'What kind of changes?' says Ruby. 'You won't take away Wonderland, will you?'

Edward shakes his head. 'No, my gem. Not after I searched the oceans for a giant squid, and all those pretty shells. All so I could bring home the beach for you.'

Ruby beams, her dimples on perfect show. The wind picks up, whistling through nearby chimneys; chimney smoke melds with the sky. 'It's going to rain,' she says.

Edward scans the clouds. A bird takes off from a neighbouring rooftop, cuts effortlessly through sky. Ruby is his eternal baby. She will always love animals, the sea and her family; it is written in the heavens, immutable. The other children will grow up, of course, shedding their childhoods like old skins. Already there is Linda, nineteen and brimming with romance. Her days spent sketching flowers, reading novels, trying out new ways with her hair. Eddy, at seventeen, has a man's body, an athlete's body, lithe as a deer. They will choose their own paths; it's what he's always wanted for them. So what devil of human nature whispers the thought: what if one of them were a little more like him? Only a little! He pictures an autocrat, someone fiercely independent, a successor with a vision both original and bold. But devoted to Edward's vision too. A thought that hangs around the corners of his mind, sly as a pimp.

He will not indulge such a thought; they must follow their own dreams.

He suddenly remembers his mother—standing before their ivy-covered cottage, flanked by his young brothers and sisters—on the day he left home. Her rough-skinned fingers touching his face as she handed him a small sack, telling him to open it later. Letters, he had thought, from his brothers and sisters. After three days he had looked inside and found not only the letters but money. Money she had saved for him from the time he was a child, some of it as old as himself. His sweet, blue-eyed, worn-out mother.

Misty at the memory, and his mother dead thirty years.

He is still blinking when he hears footsteps on the stairwell, and D'Ama appears, a small glass in hand. He sits down next to Edward and takes a bottle from his red striped jacket. A couple of raindrops land like stains on his cream pants. He pours himself a drink. 'How's life, Edward?'

Edward runs his hand along the bench, feels the splintering of weathered wood. 'Splendid, thanks, D'Ama,' he replies.

'Mmm,' says D'Ama, tasting his drink, his mouth pursed with pleasure.

The brandy smells of soft fruit and heat. A smell Edward loathes on anyone but D'Ama. That acid-sweet stench, betraying preacher, banker and felon alike. On D'Ama, it seems to mix thoroughly with its host, like dressing on a salad.

'This visit from Quong Tart: is it business, or a social visit?'

'He's going to help me find staff,' says Edward, as a gust of wind rips the words from his mouth. 'For the tea salon.' The wind doubles back, slaps their faces, fills their eyes with grit.

D'Ama blinks rapidly. 'You mean Chinese staff?'

Edward rubs his eyes and nods.

D'Ama lowers his head, shutting his eyes to the wind. 'You won't make a lot of friends in this town, giving jobs to the Chinese, and during a depression.'

A passing train blows its whistle, long and low. Edward can smell the bay. Raw and sulphurous, smell of voyages, risks. The blind excitement of arrival. Stepping from boat to pier, like a hero in a myth, the moment already destined. His whole life leading him to this city at the bottom of the world, brimming with gold. Or so he had felt.

'I might make some Chinese friends,' he says.

D'Ama grins and raises his glass in salute. His skin is grey in the dirty daylight, his eyebrows very black. The bones of his wrist protruding and thin, his Adam's apple bobbing sharply.

'You know, I am waiting,' says Edward, tapping the bench, 'for the lecture, the warning, the judicious advice.'

D'Ama tucks the bottle away and straightens his cuffs. He is careful not to let his suit brush the damp leaves of plants. 'There's only one thing I *can* say.' He leans in close, grabs Edward by the shoulder and looks him in the eye. 'You'd better brush up on your mahjong.'

...

'A freak show. You are turning this Arcade into a freak show,' says Owens, sweat beading on his forehead, droplets forming before Edward's eyes. He imagines Owens' body dotted with saltwater reservoirs just below the skin. An entire wetland, populated with tiny fish and birds, thriving in his agitation. A species of dwarf crocodile lazing beside an artery.

Owens puffs out his lips. 'Are you listening, Mr Cole?'

The men stand in the book department, twenty minutes before opening. Other staff members are beginning to arrive, throwing them curious glances. Edward thinks: perhaps it would have been better to have started this elsewhere.

'Yes, I'm listening, Owens. It will not be a freak show. It will be educational. Lessons for mankind.'

Owens looks to some of the other staff and seems to draw support from them. 'I fail to see, Mr Cole, how putting this—man—on display could possibly teach anything to anybody. He is, quite simply, a freak of nature. Put him in a carnival if you must. But do not involve the Arcade in such cheap showmanship!'

The whole room is listening now, Edward can feel it, their attention like magnets charging the space. The light patter of voices has stopped. The only sound is the scuffing of Juniper Griggs, sweeping his broom ever closer. Edward declines to give them a performance. He motions to Owens and they begin to walk. They pass the open door of the print department, Benson leaning over the press with a rag in his hand. They walk until they reach Wonderland, and stop before its golden letters.

'Mr Gabriel will stand here, in this doorway, greeting people as they pass through. Discoursing with people, if they choose. People will then be invited to make a guess as to his nationality, and to write their guesses in a book. Nothing shall occur that is cheap or undignified, I can assure you of that.'

Edward smiles at Owens, who stands beneath a cardboard rainbow. Orthodox Owens, who has never once sided with innovation, has never welcomed change, but has worked for Edward, loyally, competently, for twenty years now.

Owens squints up at his boss. 'And then what happens?'

Edward rocks on his heels, energy like lightning wanting out through the soles of his feet. 'In a week or two I will reveal his background and whether anyone has guessed it correctly. People may then judge for themselves whether there is any difference between a black man and a white one.'

Owens moves his jaw from side to side. 'That's all? That's all that will happen?'

Edward cannot help but notice it: the rainbow ends precisely on Owens' bald spot.

'Yes, that's all. No bearded lady wrestlers, no two-headed goats, I'm afraid. Just the charming Mr Gabriel, passing the time of day.'

It is almost impossible to work after this exchange. His delight at silencing Owens, his anticipation of Simon

Gabriel in his starring role as himself. It had taken him months to see it: let the man be himself. He will impress and charm them and, when they discover he is black, they will have to concede he is inferior to no one.

If this is not excitement enough, tonight they are hosting a party for the opening of the tea salon. So rather than going to his office to attend to paperwork, Edward finds himself roaming the Arcade, trying to walk off his agitation. He marches back through the book department, thinking to check on a new display there, and is glad, when he arrives, that his earlier audience has dispersed and the Arcade has opened for the day.

The display is right by the entrance: a red wooden cut-out of a hot-air balloon attached to a genuine woven-wicker ballooning basket. Across the balloon in black letters are the words *Tom Sawyer Abroad*, and the basket is filled with copies of this latest adventure book. At least, it's supposed to be. For even though there is a table stacked with copies of the red leather-bound novel, customers seem to prefer reaching into the basket and taking a copy from within. So Edward spends a few minutes moving copies from the table into the basket until it appears full once more. Nobody knows, not even his staff, that the basket has a false bottom and is not nearly so deep as it seems.

He is standing back to admire his handiwork when a man strolls through the Arcade's entrance swishing his bullfighter's cape, black with red lining and frayed at the hem. He is followed closely by another man, dressed like a Turk, his white baggy pantaloons tucked into ankle boots. The third member of this party wears a rabbit-skin jacket and Roman sandals. They walk single file, their long hair falling almost to their shoulders. Edward guesses they are nineteen, twenty at the most.

Bringing up the rear, his gold hair shining, his fifteen-year-old's face flushed with importance, is Vally.

'Oh, hello there, Pa,' he says, as though this were the most normal of scenes, as if he has come by with the chaps from the cricket club.

'Hello, Vally. And hello to your fellow friends.'

Vally makes a small bow, blushing deeply. 'I'd like you to meet Golding Ford, Axel Jones and Robes Robison. They write smashing plays, Pa, and act in them, too.'

'Ah,' says Edward, offering his hand. 'Men of the theatre.' On Golding's wrist, he notices, a bracelet made of shells.

'Great place you have,' offers Axel, with a flick of his cape.

'Could do with a little more Wilde,' adds Golding. He stands with one knee bent, one sandalled foot resting on the other. Robes has wandered off. He finds a cane chair and collapses into it, his pantaloons spread about him like a giant nappy.

'Wilde, yes, I see. Thank you, gentlemen. I'm always open to suggestions, just so you know.' Edward takes his leave, grinning to himself. Not only amused but thrilled by his youngest son. Such a show of independence, such wilful branching out! He had better stay out of the way, let the boy get on with it.

...

The band plays 'Golden Slippers' and everything speeds up. More people arrive. Talk is louder. The piano player bites his lip, a lock of hair bobbing wildly. The violinist turns scarlet. Louma, festooned in frilly cap and apron, brings out yet another tray of food: a goose-shaped dish of pâté and a whole smoked cod. Edward picks up a crusted rabbit pie and takes a bite. Juice spurts onto his beard and a drop lands on the freshly painted floor. He takes a napkin and bends to mop it up. The party is in full swing, his family and friends all around him. Edward stays on his hands and knees a moment. Staring at those gleaming egg-white boards. Breathing in the sour paint fumes. *Oh, dem golden slippers!* He's finally done it. The tea salon: real at last.

And he presses his palm against the hard, blank floor.

A baby—eyeing him from across the room—makes a sudden beeline, crawling with speed on sugar-brown limbs. Curls bouncing, lips glazed with spit, it halts right in front of him. Holds up a puffy finger. And gives him a look, so pure, so unmediated, it seems to impart some vital wisdom. *Oh, dem golden slippers, oh, dem golden slippers!* Drool overflows its lips, sploshes onto the wood.

Edward gets to his feet, and Ivy and Pearl swoop on the baby, Ivy lifting it high into the air. Vally makes a noise of disgust. 'Why do girls turn primitive when babies are around?' he asks, causing Joy to laugh out loud. 'They make those clucking, cooing sounds.'

'Well, *I* don't,' she assures him.

'No, you *don't*,' he says, with firm approval. Strutting in a suit with corduroy trim. Behind him, the walls are bright with new murals: Mandarin palaces with curled-moustache roofs, geese floating on ornamental lakes. An entire wall is lined with real bamboo, pole-thin and vibrant green, growing in pots, with a black and white panda showing through the gaps. Red cut-glass lanterns hang from the ceiling.

'Oh, dem golden kippers,' sings Vally, helping himself to the cod. Joy laughs again, her jade earrings swaying.

Across the room, Deakin arrives, and is instantly greeted by the hawk-eyed Miss Heaver. Her silly bird-face angled upward, her hands twisting in a girlish gesture. Her body rustling drily inside a brown lace dress. But every time Deakin tries to step around her, he is foiled; her footwork is pure pugilism. In moments she has worked him into the far corner of the room, ducking beneath a bower of silk blossom. Deakin fingers his tie. He peers over her head, eyes large and dark and wild.

'Excuse me,' says Joy, picking up a drinks tray. Moving to the rescue.

'She looks smashing,' says Vally, through a mouthful of cod. And she does. A lilac watered-silk dress skimming her body. Wheatfields hair piled high on her head. A relaxed way of moving and a ready laugh. Freckles trek across her nose.

Deakin, spotting her approach, almost buckles with relief.

Edward is startled by the roar of laughter from the opposite corner, where Quong Tart holds court. Eliza and Linda with heads thrown back and chipmunk cheeks, carved by the same hand. Quong Tart and Simon Gabriel, arms linked across the shoulders, kicking their legs in a highland jig.

Owens, in his yellow bow tie, gulping lemonade. Eddy rolling up a piece of ham and cramming it into his mouth. D'Ama waving around a glassful of wine, mid-story with Benson, and not spilling a drop.

And for a moment Edward is struck by a sudden affection for all these people, a tender clarity, as if seeing each of them as they truly are, and loving them regardless. Remarkable, fallible, human.

'Are you, um, deliberately guarding those pies?' asks Eddy, as he reaches a long arm around him. Edward shakes his head. Eddy holds up a small pie and halves it with his teeth.

'Oh, glory, am I going to marry that Louma,' he says, drifting off. He wanders over to the corner where Quong Tart has begun handing out some small item, and as he gets to the edge of the group he holds out his hand and is given something too. So fluid in the way he holds his palm out, and is not left to wait, hovering awkwardly, even for a second. How easily he walks through life, thinks Edward.

'Look,' says Pearl, tapping him on the arm; she has come up soundlessly beside him. In her outstretched palm lies a brown curled shell. 'Quong Tart gave it to me.' Her eyes are dark and luminous as oil.

'What's it for?' he asks.

She rocks it gently in her palm. 'You can eat it. And inside is a piece of paper, with your fortune on it.' She closes her hand into a fist. 'But I'm saving it,' she says, slipping it into her pocket.

And just like that, he's reminded of Lucky Cho. The thin slant of his shoulders, his pockmarked skin. The way he saw signs everywhere: a crow call before dawn, a red bandana tied to a tree, the numbers on his miner's licence. And the signs were always for luck; he never did forecast misfortune. Sharing with Edward his whiskey, salt pork, rice, for more was coming, he had read the signs. I'm blessed, he would tell Edward, as they dug into hard-packed earth, born on a lucky day. Even when it poured rain for a week and the mud sucked at their boots like newborn devils, Lucky Cho remained cheerful. The bad is always balanced by good, he told

Edward, just wait and see. Two days later they found a two-ounce nugget: grey and gnarled and glittering in the drying mud.

'Are you coming upstairs? We're starting the séance,' says Joy.

Edward blinks. The band has stopped playing and is packing away their instruments. 'No. I might join in later.'

She moves away, leaving behind the scent of jasmine. Edward can see that she's beautiful, and that others see it, too: Miss Heaver and Deakin, who follow her with their eyes; Quong Tart, who raises his glass to her as she passes. More people are leaving the tea salon now, moving through the red-curtained doorway.

Deakin waves and makes his way across the wide, near-empty room. 'Sorry I was late. I just got back today from the Bathurst convention.' He runs a hand across his eyes and up through his thick dark hair.

'No, no, glad you could come. How was the convention? Are we headed for federation yet?'

Deakin offers a tired smile, his skin the colour of whey. In need of air, and apples and sunshine, thinks Edward.

'Anyone would think we're suggesting something radical. Like executing the Queen. Not just bringing some hodgepodge laws under a federal banner.'

Edward nods and gestures at the table behind him. 'Would you like something to eat? Or to drink?'

'No, thank you.' Deakin attempts another smile, glancing at the floor. 'But there is something I do need to ask of you. Now that the banks are back to normal . . .'

'Oh—you need your safe back! Of course, of course.' The banks have, in fact, been sound for some years. But Edward has enjoyed the twice-weekly ritual of walking to

Deakin's office. Standing for a few minutes in the dark, masculine privacy of that book-lined room. The exchange of a story, joke or complaint. Edward sometimes saving up his offering for days: *I spotted Rolf Boldrewood in the fernery the other day . . . reading one of his own books!* Small everyday threads, the binding of their friendship.

Deakin spreads his hands, palms upward. 'I only ask because of a new client I have . . . rather sensitive, needs his privacy.' He clears his throat. 'If he were to see a prominent citizen, such as yourself, waiting in the corridor, or leaving my office . . . well, it's a nuisance, I know . . .'

'It's quite alright.' Edward feels the slight dip of disappointment in his gut. But today is the opening of the tea salon, a grand day, a celebration. He will let nothing dampen it.

'Why don't we meet here for a cup of tea now and then instead?' he offers, and is gratified to see a deep-creasing smile spread across Deakin's face.

'Let's do that,' he says, putting his hand into his pants pocket. 'And before I forget . . .' He hands Edward a thin slip of paper. 'I picked this up from Quong Tart— my fortune, apparently. But I think it belongs to you.'

The paper so fine that Edward's skin shows through. And printed across it in smudged black ink: *When it is dark the sun no longer shines, but who shall forget the colours of the rainbow?*

His love for Deakin, for Quong Tart, for humanity, makes it hard for him to speak. Such goodness in this world. A fine omen, too, for the tea salon.

'Thank you, Deakin. This means a lot to me.'

And then the sudden sound of feet on floorboards, a herd on the move. And pushing through the red curtains: Miss Heaver, followed by Linda, Pearl and Joy.

'I'll tell him myself,' declares Miss Heaver, and Edward notes the shrill satisfaction in her voice as she hurries across the room, pitching herself like an emu, her bird's head jerking on her thin neck. She stops before him, nostrils flaring. The others form a semicircle just behind her, Linda's hands twisting in a semaphore of anxiety, Joy resting a hand on Pearl's shoulder.

'*Mr Cole*,' says Miss Heaver, with heavy emphasis. 'I cannot imagine what you hope to achieve by all of this. As you stand here admiring your new salon of *foreign inspiration*, your baby daughter is sitting on a China-man's knee as if he were Santa Claus. And your *wife* is holding hands with a black man, *apparently* in an effort to contact the spirit of his dead uncle—as if live black men are not sufficient we must have some deceased ones as well! And what I want to know is, when will you act like the head of your household and put a stop to all this?'

Edward watches the pulse flickering in her temple. He glances back at the curtain, expecting to see Eliza, hoping she will deal with this. But the curtain remains still. It seems unlikely to move again, like the curtain on a stage where the show is long over.

Edward scratches his head. 'I hope Mr Gabriel and Mr Quong Tart have done nothing that might offend you?'

Miss Heaver snorts and waves away the words with rings glinting. 'I'm talking about the principle of the matter, and you know it. I never know what I might find when I come here—there could be a whole *room* full of Chinamen or a tribe of blacks. Well, that won't happen because I refuse to set foot in this house again. There, I've said my piece, and no one can say that I don't speak my mind. Goodnight to you all!'

'Goodnight,' says Edward, his spirits rising. The night is not ruined. This bothersome woman will leave and, with luck, he will never see her again.

Miss Heaver makes a stiff curtsy to Deakin. She nods briefly to Linda, and looks at Pearl with a sad smile, shaking her head and reaching out a hand as if to brush her cheek. Then she glances at Joy. 'Let's go,' she says. 'And do not forget the coats.'

Joy's eyes are as bright and hard as glass. She looks over at Deakin and their eyes meet briefly before Deakin looks away.

Miss Heaver walks towards the curtain and does not look around when she speaks. 'You will get nothing from me if you stay here. You might as well come now and fetch my coat.'

Joy drops her head and walks to the coat stand. She takes down a white ermine coat and holds it out for Miss Heaver to thread her arms through. Joy ties it closed at the throat. She takes down another coat, a white fox, and puts it on.

'Please don't go,' says Pearl, suddenly, tearfully. 'Stay here with us.'

The women do not look back. They cross the floor-boards, silently, like arctic creatures crossing snow.

...

Edward has stayed away from Wonderland all week, not wanting to give away by word or gesture the smallest hint of Simon Gabriel's blackness. But on this, the final day of Simon Gabriel's hidden identity, he cannot resist the urge to see it for himself. He positions himself just over the threshold of Wonderland and waits there, top hat in hand.

In less than a minute he sees a man approaching with large, jolly features and a chequered waistcoat. He bows to Simon Gabriel, who politely returns the bow. They begin to speak in French. In French! Simon Gabriel can speak French and German and Portuguese, and he offers the customers a choice of languages, including English, in which to converse. Edward is totally absorbed, even though the rapid, lilting poem of a language is beyond him. He would like to know languages. But what he does hear is Gabriel's confidence and his easy, untroubled manner. A man undamaged by years of hostility and prejudice. They laugh together at something Gabriel has said, and at the same time someone laughs inside Wonderland; Edward is caught in a warm eddy of mirth and goodwill.

By the time he steps forward, out of Wonderland, the two men are shaking hands. The man in the waistcoat looks across at Edward, and begins to bow and dance on the spot. 'Hello there! Mr Cole himself, if I'm not terribly mistaken?'

Edward smiles and accepts the man's hand, his big pink fingers like the teats on a cow.

'My name is Xavier Fields, and I was just talking to Mr Gabriel here—a fine fellow, a man of the world, one might call him. But he certainly doesn't make it easy to guess his provenance!' Fields shakes his head and wags a bovine finger. 'He can talk about Russian politics, Her Majesty the Queen and the American War with equal and perfect ease.' He presses his fingers to his lips, his smile leaking out on either side. 'But I think I have managed to figure him out, nonetheless.'

'Really?' says Edward, stroking his beard, sure to keep his own smile hidden. 'Then you must go and write your guess in the book, with all the other guesses. Today is the last day, if you didn't know.'

Fields chuckles and shakes his head again. 'That French did throw me at first, I'll admit it. Not native French, no, but no book French either.'

Gabriel raises an eyebrow. He is dressed in a neat brown suit, his thinning hair brushed back from his forehead, his pale face smooth and unperturbed.

'But then I remembered a man I met once, at the races, in seventy-nine, I think, or was it eighty? Canadian, he was, but from the French part, Quebec. Spoke a bit like our Mr Gabriel here.' He looks at Edward and gives him a deep wink. 'But Canadians are not so unusual, I believe, so I asked myself, why run a competition over a Canadian?' He leans over suddenly and claps Edward on the back, hard, and almost topples him. Then he lowers his voice to a piercing whisper. 'If I write it in the book, it will give the game away—that man's from Alaska, or I'm a monkey's uncle!'

They can't help it; Edward and Simon Gabriel laugh loudly, helplessly, tears even streaking Edward's cheeks.

'Am I right? Is that why it's funny?' Xavier Fields smiles uncertainly. 'Can you tell me what the prize is?'

...

Edward sits at his desk and takes out a new page. It makes a clean, white space on the massive carved desk, like the desert on a map. No matter how cluttered his office becomes—towers of books leaning up against the shelves, piles of newspaper and magazine cuttings, a telephone perched on a tea-chest—a new page is all he needs to calm and focus his mind. The outside world dims. He no longer hears the deep, constant rumble of Arcade sounds: voices, footsteps, instruments, registers, cackling hens. He is in the white zone of thought.

He takes a pen with black ink and writes: *65 guessed he was an Englishman, 39 a German, 27 a Frenchman, 16 a Scotsman, 14 an Italian, 8 a Jew, 6 a Dutchman, 6 an Irishman, and 17 other nationalities were guessed, but none guessed that he was a coloured man.*

Edward is so excited his hand shakes. How could they have guessed? There is no quality, no essence exclusive to black or white. It was a perfect demonstration. The simple truth for all to see. A wave of exhilaration leaves his skin vibrating. For once, he wishes he could put down the pen and shout the words, sing them.

And, as always in his excitement, he feels the shadow of past excitement. The coiled joy of setting off in the boat with Beaver to see the country for themselves. Edward gripped by the explorer's zeal, certain he would discover plants and animals, meet the natives, take samples, fill notebooks. Encounter the very spirit of the country. Singing, *Row, row, row your boat, gently down the stream* to himself for days on end. Wanting to sing it aloud, to startle birds from the trees, to rip through the dense, hot afternoons, but held back by his natural shyness. *Life is but a dream.* And in those first glorious weeks—the boat drifting easily with little need to row, and Beaver so full of stories and good cheer—it was.

Edward takes up his pen again, keen to finish his paper, to get it into the Arcade. Almost laughing at the astonishment it will cause. When suddenly he pictures Miss Heaver, eyes shining with hostility, her face animated with self-importance. And a sliver of doubt settles over his good spirits. He thinks of Joy. They will not see much of her now, he is sure. And he should be glad; it is what he has wanted all along. He remembers Pearl's face, her look of panic, the sudden tears, the one child of his who never cries. No. There is no relief in Joy's absence, only a complex knot of pity, sadness and disappointment. He had wanted Joy to laugh at Miss Heaver, to tell her to take her furs and go home alone. He had wanted her to shine.

Edward begins to write, fanning the last spark of his excitement.

Chapter Eleven

1896

The brass is dull brown and cool to the touch. Edward pours polish onto a cloth. He works in a spiral, rubbing the column, turning it golden. He tastes metal in his mouth. The cloth grows warm beneath his hand. For each column he takes a new cloth, for every second column a new bottle of polish. He has the rhythm of years. He wears an old suit without a mark on it.

He woke early this morning. Into a dawn with birds still sleeping. Drinking cocoa by five; he sleeps so little now.

He must remember: to order more tea, choose Vally's present, phone the zoo.

He rests, his palms flat against the metal.

He has been reading Darwin, late at night, sunk low in an armchair. It is worse than cheese, or a huge meal, for his sleep. He dreams: constellations of coloured ants on the Arcade glass. Wild horses running down a slope, ridden by apes.

The tarnish leaves a grey film on his hands and he keeps his sleeves rolled. Now and then as he rubs, he thinks he feels a pulse. A hidden heartbeat. As if he is a farmer rubbing down a beast of the fields. Whispering sweet praises.

His knees press into the floor, hard as hammers. He must kneel to reach the awkward spot where the column meets the floor. He has lifted his jacket out from under him. The bright metal shows him his own straight nose, the thick wool of his beard, a group of men behind him.

He glances up at the large wall mirror to see a man fly through the air.

At first he is puzzled: why does Juniper Griggs lie flat on the ground? It takes a second for his brain to mark the punch, to see the violence in the pure, swift movement of Benson's fist. Men are rushing over to the prone figure, and another man holds Benson by the arm. He does not need restraining. He stands so still and pale he is like a tree drained from the roots; standing only out of habit.

...

He has asked Benson to wait for him in the tea salon. But when Edward arrives he finds the big man—hunched over a small table, his hands clasped and pressed to his mouth—is not alone. Beside him sits a subdued Simon Gabriel. Edward is surprised, for he should be upstairs by now, at work in the lending library. The man has a genius for library work, a talent for suggesting the right book, or finding misplaced volumes, which seem to leap from the shelves at his approach.

The girl brings their tea. She is smiling and pearl-toothed, tiny in a gold cheongsam. Red cut-glass lanterns give her skin a dark glow. She bows and turns away, her small figure framed by bright background murals. Steam rises from the pot, and Edward breathes in pastures and pine trees.

'You must both try this tea,' says Edward. 'I don't sell this; it's kept on hand for special guests, and myself. An oolong, picked by monkeys.' He pours out three small cups. 'It's what I served to Mark Twain when he stopped by. And do you know what he said?' Edward basks in his memory of meeting the great man. 'He said, I had a monkey once, but all it ever picked was its nose.'

Simon Gabriel nods and spoons three sugars into his cup. Benson plays with a crumb on the tablecloth. The cloth is a dusty pink, its red fringe parted by the knees of the three men. Simon Gabriel holds out the sugar to Edward, who shakes his head. Queensland sugar; Edward has been reading about it. Tropical heat and rain-soaked soils, armies of snakes hidden within the twelve-foot canes. All the cutting done by Chinese, Italians and Kanakas. The breadth of this land in the north hard to imagine, cattle stations the size of Wales. If Edward were a young man now, making his way in the world, that is where he would go.

'I think it should be me who goes,' says Simon Gabriel. To Queensland? Did Edward say all that aloud? Sweat springs to his brow and he rubs it, willing his mind to the table. He stares at Benson's hand, balancing the cup in its broad palm. A boxer's hands, or at least they were once. He wonders how it feels to hit a man for money, to will the tearing of flesh and the snapping of bone. To shed empathy like some old coat and move in the ring without compassion or pity. And what is lost in this exchange? How does a man put the coat back on and live the rest of his life?

'I will not tolerate violence in my Arcade,' he says.

'I should go, not Gabriel. I'm the one who lost my temper and hit that ignorant sack of bones.'

'But you were standing up for me,' says Gabriel.

'I should not have hit him.'

Edward is overcome by tiredness and a sense of estrangement. Who are these men, sitting at the table? Like all men, they show their faces to the world, but what lies beneath, in their hearts? After all, he can list what he knows about Benson on one hand: a former boxer and gambler, married with one son, a solid worker. He thinks he has gleaned other qualities—a deep conscience, a calm inner strength—but what if he's wrong? What if, instead of these, there lies a deep anger, a compressed and hidden violence?

The truth is, the punch has sickened him. Griggs' nose cracked like an egg, the heavy blood flow staining his teeth. Dragging himself across the floor, away from Benson, with animal whimpers. Like something from the goldfields, where the most shocking aspect of the violence was its casualness, its everyday nature. Lucky Cho thrown into the dirt for laughs. One man standing on his fine-boned hand while another shouted, *Get up, you lazy dog, you miserable piece of filth.* They had seen a man with his foot shot off, and another with a broken jaw, using a chisel to grind his meat to paste. But the Arcade is not the goldfields. The Arcade, thinks Edward, is the opposite of violence, the opposite of fear, of all the forces that close us off from the world and ourselves. The Arcade is the opening up.

How could Benson commit such an act, in this place? His punch did violence not just to Griggs but to the Arcade itself.

'You've let us all down,' says Edward.

Benson drops his head and stares at the tablecloth.

'Tell him,' says Gabriel. Benson tightens his jaw. Around them, the din of cups and saucers and voices fills the silence. The tea salon is almost full, the waiters and waitresses pouring and bowing and clearing with speed.

Simon Gabriel turns to Edward. 'Griggs called me dog shit. He said that only dog shit turns from black to white.'

Edward flushes, but Gabriel waves the words away. 'I've heard it all before, it means nothing to me, nothing. If a man dislikes me for being born black, I can't help that. But if I leave the Arcade, it makes things simpler. No more tensions.'

'But you didn't do anything! I'm the one who hit him, remember? For God's sake, Simon, you didn't *do* anything.'

Edward is still reeling from Griggs' words, their nastiness, their crude and demeaning intent. Why would he say such a thing? Hasn't he worked side by side with Simon Gabriel, seen what kind of man he is? He feels himself descend into a numbing bewilderment. How to rid the world of bigotry if he can't even rid the Arcade of it?

Benson struggles to meet Edward's eye. 'I can pack my things now. Or see out the week, if you prefer.'

'We need to do what's best for the Arcade,' Gabriel insists.

Edward slaps the table with the flat of his hand. Cups clatter in saucers and Benson's tea spills over. Edward feels his neck and face burn. 'What is best for the Arcade,' he begins, while both men stare at him with open mouths, 'is that no one should presume to tell me how to run it.' Edward takes a breath and lets it out slowly, looking down at his stinging hand. 'Benson, what you did to Griggs was appalling, indefensible, and must never happen again. I expect you to step in as care-taker—sweeping, mopping, and so on—until Griggs has recovered. But I have no wish to lose you, and by that I mean either of you.'

The people at the neighbouring tables have turned in their seats to stare. One old woman looks at Edward through a lorgnette. As though he has come to sing for them.

Edward smiles into his beard and looks across at the woman. 'Those rotten flies,' he says.

...

Edward hurries towards the Little Men. He thinks it might be best to go out for a bit, to leave the punch, its queasy aftertaste, behind. He steps into Bourke Street to find the sky filled with enormous sugar-whipped clouds. Spring warmth peppering the air. He stands for a moment, breathing the smell of horses and humus. Then he turns into Swanston Street and heads for the station: he will treat himself a trip to the zoo.

The footpath is crowded with schoolboys, all elbows and knees and outgrown blazers. Edward weaves his way through them, only to find the path ahead half blocked by a makeshift stall. Two Indian hawkers banging their copper pots together. They wave at Edward, as if he is an old friend, red silk scarves around their necks. Edward waves back, and decides to detour down Little Collins.

He will go for the monkeys. He has always loved the monkeys, and reading Darwin has renewed his fondness for these comical cousins. He used to visit them at the

Botanic Gardens, back before the zoo was built, back when he still worked the pie stall. Working nights, so that his days stretched vast and free. Weather that was very hot or cold would see him stationed at the library, but on the days when the sun showed demure through a veil of cloud, he would often go to the gardens. One time, he saw a monkey steal an earring from a woman who was leaning through the bars for a closer look. A well-dressed woman, she had hooted her disbelief—a string of vowels so formless it was hard to tell her sounds from the monkey's own.

He has been thinking lately that the Arcade could use some monkeys. He pictures a room on the second floor—bright and spacious and filled with the creatures. His customers in quiet contemplation, reflecting, perhaps, on their own animal natures. Observing those tribal instincts, so often the cause of man's own troubles.

Besides, it would be awfully fun.

Without thinking, he has cut through a series of laneways, taking his old route to Deakin's office. Moving through the disused bluestone alleys, cool with puddles and shadows, and further from the station with every step. He smiles at his error, exiting the alley opposite Deakin's building. At the same moment, a woman steps out of that very building and they stand facing one another. The small empty road between them. Joy, frozen, with one hand raised to her head. He sees the pale fur, her red-rimmed eyes and the damp handkerchief in her hand. And—in the second before she turns away—a sort of grim triumph in her face.

The image stays with him, like the after-effects of staring at the sun. Green eyes, exposed white flesh of the throat. He goes straight home. He will not speculate on what he's seen. Sweating now inside his buttoned frock-coat. Squinting, the midday glare magnified by every glass and sandstone plane. He waves half-heartedly to the Indians. Almost dizzy as he approaches the bright rainbow, the blinding white façade. Then stepping into the cool entrance, enveloped in the soft gauze of filtered light. Resting beside the Little Men as they turn their metal signs with a melodic *dink*, *dink*. The sound as welcoming as a dog's lick of the hand.

Edward undoes the buttons of his coat. He walks through the book department, sees the rich gleam of the brass columns, the clean silver mirrors. Golding Ford and Vally, slouched in cane chairs, reading: Golding frowning intently, his rabbit-skin jacket thrown across the back of his chair, and Vally fingering his shoulder-length hair and the string of beads around his neck.

'Golding, Vally. You might as well be the first to hear the news,' says Edward, swept up in a sudden rush of impulse and resolve. 'The Arcade is getting monkeys.' He feels better already. Blood coursing through every vein. Revitalised. Vally and Golding stare up at him in astonishment, Vally looking more boy than man at this moment, his blue eyes blinking rapidly, his tongue darting in and out of his mouth. While Golding remembers to close his mouth, to pull his features back into a look of mild amusement. Well, look at that, thinks Edward. I even managed to shock the bohemians.

...

It is much harder to shock Eliza. It is the end of the day and he takes the stairs quickly, buoyed by his new project. His body is good for its age, responds well to the upward push of each stair. The secret is fruit, cartloads of fruit, and no alcohol, no tobacco. He has brought his family up on fruit, and they're a red-cheeked mob. Only Eliza has a tendency to crave chocolates at odd hours. He finds their silver wrappers buried in armchairs, flattened in the pages of a book.

He finds her in the dining room, arranging flowers in a vase, happy gerberas taken from the rooftop.

'My dear. I have just purchased four very fine pairs of monkeys,' he says, resting his hands on a chair back.

Eliza turns to look at him, hands still busy with the stems. 'Of course. Should I prepare the guest bedroom, or put them in with the children?'

Edward moves towards her. He touches one of the petals, feels its silky flesh. 'I'm going to convert the second-floor storeroom. And ask the man who did the tea salon murals to paint it up like a jungle.' He pats her lightly on the arm. 'But you *could* make them a banana cake.'

...

The sunlight through the windows is sharp as razors. It is Melbourne light, not the smudged light of the tropics. Do they miss the tropics, he wonders? Do they miss the rustling of leaves, waiting for predator or prey, the surprise of it? He sits by the cage, stroking a monkey through the bars, his sleeve bunched at the wrist. He loves the southern light. People call it a harsh light, but that is ignorance. It is a pure light. You see every hair, every whisker. He feels the monkey twitch and relax, twitch and relax.

He has been dreaming monkeys. He follows them into underground sewers, rank and dripping, or old mining tunnels. When they are far enough away from other eyes, they reveal to him their secret: they can really talk.

He wakes to tell Eliza his discovery, only to be told, 'You were talking in your sleep again, Edward.'

Edward stretches his right leg, then his left. He has been sitting too long. The monkey moves away, glancing back at Edward. He watches them for hours, measuring time by the changes in light and the stiffness in his knees. He is compelled by them as by some ancient shadow play. He sees himself in their faces, their curiosity. A monkey will study a new object until it fits somewhere into its picture of the universe. We are their descendants, and we are more alike than different, we are branches of the same tree.

Why are the churches so scared of this connection?

It has been so long since Edward believed all the churches had to say. As the child of a minister he had, of course, prayed long and hard and studied his bible until every inch of his child's soul pulsed with belief. He had seen hell in his vivid young mind: devils with horsewhips, men and women roasting on spits with blackened skin and mouths split in agony. He had seen the ark built, slow plank by slow plank. Then, at age twelve, he had discovered stargazing. Lying back in the tall grass behind their cottage, watching stars break through the dark fabric of night. And his neighbour, John Shearer, had taught him a little about the constellations. Clusters of stars with stories full of passion, anger, revenge. He would lie there, hemmed by marigolds and lavender, his back itchy-damp, murmur of voices from the house, and think about great winged horses and giant scorpions. Until it dawned on him one night that the bible was stories, too. Two sets of ancient myths, two ways of showing us the world. And his belief slipped away. Not in God, but in a church that insisted that it alone knew and spoke the truth. He saw no need to tell his parents. All he wanted was to hold and examine his discovery at quiet moments.

It wasn't until he met Lucky Cho that he began to think about religion again. The stories he could tell! Edward looked forward to the end of each day, when they would finally lay their gear down, scrape the dirt from their hands and build a fire for the evening meal. All day they worked in near silence, speaking only when a task demanded it. Because the work was hard, and bent their backs, and made the muscles in their legs shake with fatigue. And because it was dispiriting, pawing through the brown slops, trying to find that wink of gold. But in the early evening, when they made the fire and cooked their meal, Lucky Cho would come to life again. Telling stories in his gentle voice, invoking a cast of honourable warriors, vain emperors, cursed villagers and foolish wives. The air full of the sweet-bland smell of cooking rice and wood smoke. All this set against the goldfields, its daily fights, robberies, accusations of robberies, murder. There was a sense a man could kill out there and get away with it.

But in Lucky Cho's stories there was always some final accountability to man or god. It took Edward some time to unravel the various religions Lucky Cho spoke of: Confucianism, Taoism, Buddhism. 'But which one do you believe in?' Edward had asked him.

And Lucky Cho had smiled with whiskey-glazed lips and replied, 'All of them, a little.'

He had seemed so serene, telling stories as the fire burned down to its amber heart. The drink never seemed to agitate him, just made him pause a long time between sentences, and fall asleep in his clothes. But the drink burned for hours inside Edward. Burned through his doubts, worries, fears, and left him feeling destined and invincible. He could recapture the sense that he was on a grand adventure. Or he could lie back and look at southern stars, feeling as safe and sound as his twelve-year-old self.

'Do you mind if I come in? I need to speak to you alone.'

He turns towards the voice, and green eyes meet with his, just as they do, over and over, in his memory of her outside Deakin's office. She stands in the doorway in an ivory dress, her bare arms hanging by her sides.

Edward waves her into the room. Three of its walls are newly painted, with thick, snaking branches and heart-shaped leaves. A fourth wall is lined with windows letting in big rectangular blocks of sun. Joy shades her eyes with one hand while the other touches a diamond at her throat.

He remembers the way Pearl and Ivy used to run to the window, checking for her carriage, their noses pressed slug-like against the glass. And he feels a sudden hot pity for the woman. Who will ever love her the way his girls do?

'You should visit the girls while you're here. Or, if you prefer it, they could visit you.'

Joy shakes her head. 'No, I don't think so.'

Edward watches the diamond rise and fall at her throat. It looks strange for a moment, a hole in her skin through which light is escaping. He blinks, and it's a stone once more.

'It's not that I wouldn't like to.' Joy's hand moves from hair to throat, then falls to her side. Wild simian hooting erupts from the cage, and she jumps back, hands to her mouth. 'I didn't see them there . . . sun in my eyes . . .'

A chase has begun. Blurred brown bodies, flying through space, and high, excited chatter. Joy watches it for a moment, then turns back to Edward, her face grim.

'My latest hobby,' he says with a smile.

Joy rubs her arms as if to warm them. She has always felt the cold, he remembers, and the heat. As if her skin wasn't made for this world.

'The police are investigating the affairs of Mr and Mrs Cornish. Deakin found it out somehow. He has advised me to have nothing further to do with them.'

Edward almost slumps with relief. Of course: a lawyer advising a client. The most natural reason for Joy to have been at that office.

'He's a fine man to have as your lawyer.'

When Joy laughs it is a brief, bitter sound. 'He didn't tell me for my sake but for his own. He also told me he couldn't continue our . . . association. In case some connection was made, between them, and me, and him.'

Connection? What connection could be made between Deakin and Joy? But Edward knows the answer, has known it all along. Disgust and envy wrestle in his gut. How many people, people that he knows and respects, indulge themselves in such passions of the flesh? Is it happening everywhere, like some rampant, insuppressable disease? It is alarming and oddly exciting. Dizzying as the drop off a cliff.

'Why are you telling me this?' His voice is gruff and low. 'I don't think you should be speaking of such things.'

'I want you to know what kind of man he is,' she says, opening her hands to show her soft white palms. 'You think you can count on him, but you can't. He's driven—politics is everything to him. He told me he couldn't live without me, but it turns out we're all dispensable, in the end.' She begins to pace and to rub her arms once more. 'You and Eliza were good to me. You're the only ones who never wanted something from me.'

She looks suddenly boneless. She takes a hold of the cage, as though to keep herself upright. Edward also feels a weakening, a lethargy. As if they could stand here forever. Looking at one another. Breathing in the musky, animal air.

An image comes to him: two monkeys joined in a slow, rhythmic mating. A sight he has seen dozens of times. But the thought—vivid and unbidden—fills him with panic. He begins to cough. And as he does, a monkey's electric scream rips the air, so that the sound seems to come from some deep place within him.

The monkey has seen Joy's hand within the cage. It has sprung forward, shrieking and expecting treats. But Joy has leapt back, a look of horror on her face, as though the devil himself were in that cage. 'They're just like evil little men,' she says. 'How awful they are!'

...

It is several months before he sees the small article in *The Herald*. At the other end of the breakfast table, Eliza is cracking walnuts with bone-snapping force. *Mr and Mrs Abel Cornish, of Brighton, appeared in court yesterday charged with extortion.* Edward rapidly scans the four lines: they will plead not guilty, they will appear again in August. No mention of Joy's name. He reads the article aloud to Eliza, who stops chewing on her walnut, her eyes growing wide. He watches her face darken; she has a natural hatred of dishonesty. She finishes her nut and swallows.

'Well. I don't believe Joy would have had anything to do with *that*,' she declares. Loyal to the last.

Chapter Twelve

1898

Leaves fly on the wind and brush against his ankles. She puts her arm through his. They pass by half-nude trees and the curve of the river, and a tram rattles past them. The sky is the colour of a newborn's eyes.

'Is it too windy? Should we go back?' she says.

She has the same eyes as her mother, yellow-brown, the colour of a lion.

He shakes his head. The gardens are often empty in autumn. He will stop and read the labels; the boast of Latin names in all that earth. Birds will drift on the lake, made lazy without children to chase them. The lawns will be smooth and green. A planet abandoned. He remembers von Mueller (before they broke him), spitting with excitement, saying, 'There could be a hundred new cures in this land if we knew where to look.' Casually wiping his mouth with his hand.

'Did I tell you I gave seeds to Baron von Mueller once?'

Linda smiles, brushes hair from her eyes. 'Yes, from your Murray trip.'

That river. Lying soft and brown as a kitten. The two of them setting off in their patched-up boat like a couple on a cruise ship; Beaver waving his hanky at the small, receding township, Edward making diary entries in his head. They had travelled easily at first. There was a current, and little need to row, and Beaver was a good shot for fowl and the little piebald bandicoots they came to favour. Then quiet and time to think turned to boredom, and the flies set in, and the heat. Mallee heat. It simmered them, reduced them to their elements. Edward grew silent and full of schemes. He would scour the banks at daybreak, foraging for native seeds that might one day be used for a garden, or for science. Glossing his days with purpose in that pale-green dawn. An explorer: proud of the rashes that trailed his skin.

Beaver, always a talker, took to rambling. Long tales of life on the station, of riding horses that would sooner jam your head into a branch than carry you, and others that would nuzzle you and steam up your shirt with their hot, earthy breath. Horses with names like Free Nancy and Bag of Bones. How the blacks had a special way with them, even the mean ones, how they whispered to them and always knew when they were sick. There were a lot of blacks, some living on the station and some nearby. Beaver had seen their secret ceremonies as a child, followed the flickering firelight and sat in the dark watching them dance and chant and smear their bodies with paste. And he had never told this to anyone, but he thought his mother might have been a black woman. She was dead, died in childbirth, they told him. They never told him more, and he never asked.

'But doesn't it bother you, not knowing where you come from?' Edward had asked him.

Beaver had shrugged and offered his gap-toothed smile. 'Well, in the end, I figure, I'll still just be me.'

And Edward had loved him for it. For being his essential Beaver self. No one else he knew lived so completely in his own skin. Every night, Beaver would fall asleep within half an hour of the sun setting. As if no thought in the world could trouble him enough to stay awake. Lying hard on his bunk the way fish lie dead on a pier. The goldfields had ruined sleep for Edward. It could take him hours to drift off, only to wake suddenly as a branch groaned in the wind. Then he would reach over and prod Beaver on the arm, just to marvel at how little it disturbed him.

How on earth had he lost touch with Beaver?

He can see the distant sheet-metal sheen of the lake. They have left the path and she does not complain, the hem of her dress translucent with damp.

There was never another man like Beaver. What would he be like now? Like Edward, he must be in his sixties. But would he still hunt, swim and ride with perfect ease? Would his body ache with age? Would he live in a city, catch the train, keep his money in a bank? Edward shakes his head. He will always think of Beaver in that moment in the river. Surrounded by blacks who rubbed their own skin, and gestured for the two of them to rise from the water and show themselves. Edward had stalled with fear. But Beaver had got up calmly and made his way to where the water was knee deep. Stood there with perfect dignity. While the blacks had screamed with laughter to discover that a white man's penis was indeed truly white.

In the herbarium the light of a high window falls on their hands and on the flattened plants. Sheer and weightless, not plants at all but their trapped spirits. He shows her the ones he collected himself, his name written in von Mueller's looping hand. Edward had been broke then, shabby looking, but von Mueller had not cared, had fed him cake and listened to the account of his trip as though Edward had returned from a voyage with Cook himself. They were all pioneers then. The next time Edward saw him, von Mueller had lost his position at the gardens. A botanist, he had been replaced by a landscape gardener.

'I think I'll sketch this one. I like the way it curves under itself, like a chicken's foot,' says Linda, her head tipped to the right.

Edward barely hears her. He is seeing von Mueller, stooped and frail, ordering books in the years before he died. A bachelor and childless, he had said to Edward, 'I'll donate them to the library when I go. I have no one, you see, my plans die with me.' And smiled to show he didn't really mind.

A chill touches him, rests on his shoulders like a stole.

...

He is cheered by the arrival of D'Ama and Deakin, dropping by for an afternoon drink. He ushers them into the drawing room, offering them tea, and brandy. The room is sun-warmed, though rain has started falling from a darkening sky. The walls are lost in wallpaper and shadow. The last of the daylight hovers in the centre of the room, pooling in D'Ama's glass. Steam rises from Edward's cup and vanishes.

'The judge was sneaking food into court, eating pigeon or quail or whatever it was. Sucking on the bones.' D'Ama lifts a milk-white hand, mimes eating from a bone. 'He's a glutton, that man, always has been. But the defendant, whose name was Quayle, thought the judge had it in for him.'

When Deakin speaks, his mouth is sunk into his glass, his body sunk deep into his chair. 'Ruffled his feathers, did it?'

'He thought his goose was cooked!' Edward slaps his hands against his knees. D'Ama finishes his drink and licks his lips.

'So what did he do, this Quayle fellow? Why was he in court?' Edward looks at D'Ama, who leans back, and crosses his arms.

'Oh, you know, I think he stole something small. It's what you'd call a *poultry* crime.'

Edward and Deakin groan in chorus.

Perhaps they will stay to dinner, thinks Edward. Remembering the long and lively Friday nights they used to share. What has happened to those nights? Deakin is often away. And Quong Tart rarely leaves Sydney. He says he feels safer there, where everybody knows him. Where he is not just a faceless Chinaman.

'I must say, I do feel for the man. Sitting in that court, sweating on his fate,' says Deakin.

And Edward wonders, is that how Deakin felt with Joy? Did he greet his wife, kiss his daughters on the cheek, eat his dinner, all the while waiting for his world to fall apart? How could he bear to lead a double life? But Edward thinks he knows. For the past, too, can be another life, a parallel life, not finished at all.

'Don't waste your pity on him. He was guilty, and stupid enough to get caught,' says D'Ama, reaching for his tobacco. The rain grows louder, a steady drumming on the roof.

Edward is suddenly irritated. 'Why should we only feel for the innocent and not the guilty? The innocent don't need our pity,' he says.

D'Ama cocks his eyebrow and shrugs. He sticks his unlit pipe in his mouth. 'Feel sorry for the guilty if you like. It's the stupid I've no time for.'

Deakin looks from one to the other, then throws back his head and laughs.

...

Neither of them could stay for dinner and, though Edward is disappointed, he is also a little relieved. He feels hollowed out, weary. He puts it down to the long walk through the gardens.

He makes his way to the kitchen, glad that it's feeding time. He loves the commotion made by the monkeys. The mad scramble when he arrives with the food, the way they settle afterwards. The uncomplicated affection. When he reaches the doorway, he sees his sons at the bench. Lean and golden-haired, they perch lazily on elbows. Vally dips his finger into a mixing bowl and licks it. The gesture is pure present, thinks Edward. The past is nothing to them, the future distant.

'Are you looking for the monkey food? I think I've found it,' says Vally, pulling a face, as Edward enters.

'No, I'm afraid that's for us,' says Edward, lifting two metal pails from the corner shelf. As the pails swing gently from his hand, the tender stench of cabbage fills the air. Vally groans and pretends to pass out, theatrically, like an opera heroine. Above all, Edward wants to talk to them, to keep them close, to know them.

'Who wants to help me feed these monkeys?' he says.

It is Eddy who takes the second pail and carries it to

the monkey enclosure. Vally has a rehearsal; he always has a rehearsal. Eddy greets the monkeys by name and they turn circles, simultaneously, like a dance troupe.

Edward unlocks the double-gated entrance and they step inside. The air is hot and tinged with dung. The food is gone in minutes, in a riot of screeching and bared teeth. Then Edward takes a paper bag from his pocket and hands around the nuts. A delicacy, they are eaten quietly in measured, dainty bites.

'What a lot of old ladies!' says Edward, looking at their shrivelled faces and hunched-up shoulders. When Eddy laughs, it sends a flush of happiness straight through him. How to get him talking, to keep him just a little longer?

The monkeys finish their treats. They twitter and angle their bodies for stroking. Edward pats their heads, their hairy backs. Eddy takes a monkey's face gently between his hands, and turns it from side to side.

'How are you, Business? Keeping out of trouble?' When he lets go, the monkey climbs straight into his lap. Business. First name Monkey. He had let the children name them and this had been Ivy's contribution. Eddy cradles the animal in his arms, smiling serenely, eyelids half closed. Like a holy painting, thinks Edward: Madonna with hairy child. A sunbeam plays on his hair like the touch of God.

'Down you get, spoiled creature,' says Eddy, scooping the animal from his lap and dusting the hair from his clothes. In three long strides he will be out the door.

'Tell me,' says Edward, casting with his favourite lure, 'if you were in charge of the Arcade, what changes would you make?'

Eddy stretches his arms, his back arching, and shrugs. 'Nothing. The Arcade's great, I wouldn't change it.'

'Why don't you take a minute to think about it? Don't worry about the money, or the practical side. Imagine,' Edward rubs his palms together, 'you could do anything you liked!'

Eddy scratches his ear and, like his mother, chews his lip in thought. Edward watches those blue eyes, clear as lakes. It seems impossible that they hold an inner, hidden life. Eddy frowns and shifts his weight from foot to foot. The monkeys chatter impatiently.

Eddy smiles, and his features sharpen with excitement. 'I know,' he says, suddenly, miming the swinging of a bat. 'Cricket bats! We could sell cricket bats. How great would that be?'

...

Vally is late for dinner that night. They have kept him some cold cuts and salad, and Edward and Eliza sit with him while he eats. He apologises through a mouthful of beef; the rehearsal went overtime, they are opening the play in less than a week. Eliza claps her hands together—they will finally see him perform! But Vally is reluctant. He claims the venue is small and cramped, the material often confronting.

'Do you think your parents are dull provincials?' she retorts. 'Have you never heard of a place called Cole's Book Arcade?'

...

They walk down the basement steps in single file. D'Ama and Edward remove their hats while Eliza takes hold of the handrail. The room is cool, encased in stone and dark as a cave. A young man approaches, bearing a candle in a jar, and offers to show them to their seats. They follow

167

LISA LANG

the fuzzy orb of his light past rows of packing crates and mismatched chairs. He stops and points out three chairs placed together in the fourth row. 'You should take these—the chairs fill quickly. The crates are brutal after an hour.'

A faint meat smell hangs in the air. Edward clutches the thin program the usher has given him. There is no light to read it by, but Edward has seen it already: *The Levitating Woman*, written and directed by Golding Ford. Starring Valentine Cole in the role of Blessington. It was Edward's idea to have Benson print them up.

'I simply love the atmosphere,' says Eliza, wiggling her shoulders.

'It's charming,' says D'Ama, unbuttoning his coat. 'There's nothing quite so arousing as a good dungeon.'

The room fills all at once, with young men and women and a certain loose energy. Greetings are called across the room and seats exchanged. Cigarettes and extra candles are lit. A woman enters the room wearing a navy-issue peaked cap. Another woman wears pants. Edward stares at her as she takes her seat on the crate in front of him, retying a scarf she has wound around her neck. Pants, thinks Edward, what a practical idea.

Eliza touches D'Ama on the arm. 'Do you think they're all thespians?'

'Oh, I don't know,' says D'Ama, nodding at the woman in the cap. 'Could be a bunch of sailors with an interest in the arts.'

As Edward's eyes grow used to their dim surroundings, he peers ahead to the stage. Sees the small platform made of raw wood and hessian. The lamps nailed at head height, and their thick spill of honeyed light. Something in this set-up, its makeshift nature, takes him back to the goldfields. The sweat and dirt taste of it, and a muscle memory of being young. The unwavering belief in greatness. The uncertainty, the urge to judge harshly, especially his own efforts. And suddenly he is nervous for Vally, his stomach in knots.

The actors walk silently through the centre aisle, past the audience, and step onto the stage.

'So avant-garde!' cries Eliza, but Edward suspects it's just a lack of curtains.

The audience grows quiet as the actors move into position. Vally stands to the right of the stage. At eighteen, he is a clear-skinned and happy boy, but Edward, seeing him on the platform, thinks he looks vulnerable and exposed. His Adam's apple jutting from the thin skin of his throat. Will he remember his lines, will he stumble? Will he be everything he hopes to be?

The play begins with a prologue read by Axel Jones, but Edward cannot follow a word. His eyes are on Vally, and all he can hear is the thud-thudding of his own heart.

Vally takes a firm step forward.

And from the moment he opens his mouth there can be no doubt: Vally is in his element. He inhabits the stage like a man in his own house, easy with himself. His childish features take on a new gravity, a serious kind of beauty, and Edward is transfixed.

The story unfolds. A man named Strider, played with manic energy by Axel Jones, decides to create a perfect community. He gathers a group of family, friends and strangers, and persuades them to follow him into the bush. They select and clear a parcel of land, where they build their own houses, grow their own food and make their own clothes. They sing folk songs and dance with one another around the fire. They abolish religion and money and governments, and everybody is content.

Then one night a man named Blessington dreams of a lady levitating above the lake. She is very calm and fills him with a sense of peace. For the next five nights he has exactly the same dream. Convinced that the community's safety and prosperity is somehow due to this lady, he declares the lake a sacred place. The children are banned from swimming in it and the men from fishing. Vally plays the part with great subtlety: is Blessington a visionary, a charlatan or simply deluded?

The community is suddenly divided. One group of people follows Blessington out to the lake and helps him to build a shrine there. They make a long wooden plank extending over the water, and cover it with flowers and candles. Another group goes to see Strider and complains: a shrine is a religious structure and forbidden by the rules of their community. Strider agrees to talk to Blessington. He pleads for the removal of the shrine, but Blessington refuses.

The group who made the complaint decide to start fishing again. They catch a great quantity of fish, and that night they make a large fire and hold a feast. But the people who eat at the feast get sick and one of them dies.

As soon as they recover, the group who held the feast go to see Blessington. See what you have done, they say, we have always eaten the fish from this lake!

But I told you *not* to fish, he replies. How can I be to blame? A great resentment brews between the fishermen and the people at the shrine.

Strider, fearing the community will disintegrate, calls a meeting with those who attended the feast. I, too, have had a dream, he tells them. And I know how to make the lake safe again. They follow him, silent and serious, back to the shrine. They take hold of Blessington and force him to lie back on the wooden platform that serves as the shrine. They tie him with rope. The plank is the exact length of Blessington's body; only his head hangs over the edge, his hair almost touching the water. From the shoreline the plank can no longer be seen. The entire community has gathered to watch. To them, it seems that Blessington hovers just above the water. His long blond hair, hanging down, looks just like a woman's.

This is the lady of the lake, cries Strider. Return to where you came from and bother us no more.

And he brings down the axe with all his might.

No one claps harder than Eliza. She jumps to her feet and claps until she's red in the face. The actors stand, unsmiling, and take their bows. Edward rises, dazed and elated, a single, clear impression in his mind. Vally was not just at home on that stage; he was more at home, more alive, than Edward has ever seen him.

...

Lying in bed, unable to sleep, Edward composes a letter to Quong Tart. Do you ever see sleep, he begins, as a lone flag flapping on a distant hill? The whole night spent walking towards it, through a landscape made from pieces of the day. Let me tell you how proud I am of my son Vally. I saw him come alive tonight, the way I do with my Arcade, and I knew that he had found his own dream. Edward rests a hand on Eliza's back, feels her twitching, mad-dog style, in sleep. Do you ever think of the future, the real future, after both of us are gone? Tell me what we do then. My other son is happiest in movement, like an animal, savannah-born. Perhaps that's why he loves the monkeys so. I miss that tea of yours, the one that tastes of wood smoke and fever. Come and see us soon, you should really meet the monkeys. With greatest affection, Edward.

Chapter Thirteen

1901

Edward stares at the wallpaper, realising that the white shapes on the black flocked background are swans. The room so full of people he had thought they were just pattern. He glances up at the white pressed-tin ceiling and the crystal chandelier. Taps his shoe against the white marble floor. A small room, but he has not seen this kind of casual affluence since the eighties.

'Tell me something, Mr Cole, if I may be so bold as to ask you a question.' The woman who leans towards him is extremely aged, her thin hair topped with pale, spindly feathers. 'What is *your* opinion of the dresses?'

The dresses? There *were* two mannequins, Edward recalls, over by the entrance, obscured now by all the bodies in the room. But he has barely looked at them. All his memory can summon is the hazy outline of two floor-length gowns, looking—with their tiny pinched waists—like two women caught by lasso.

'I must plead ignorance, madam, when it comes

to matters of fashion.' Edward bows slightly and the woman smiles. 'Until today I had no idea that the use of the lungs was optional.'

The woman nods. 'I found them a little *ornate* myself. Lovely, if only one had the kind of society one could wear them in.'

The noise of the room makes conversation difficult. Voices rebound off the floor and disappear into the high ceiling, so that everything is simultaneously loud and muffled. Edward takes refuge in the noise. He points to his ears and shrugs apologetically, feigning a little deafness.

The woman inhales. 'DID YOU SEE MRS ENDICOTT'S FEDERATION DRESS? MADE OF SIX DIFFERENT MATERIALS, ONE FOR EACH STATE?'

Nothing wrong with *her* lungs, thinks Edward.

Yes, he nods, he has seen the dress. He has seen Joy in her dress looking poised and radiant, as though born owning this Collins Street boutique. And he had felt proud of her.

'. . . AND VICTORIA IS REPRESENTED BY HER GOLD SASH—AND THAT'S REAL GOLD WOVEN THROUGH THE FABRIC . . .'

It was Eliza, of course, who insisted that they come. Eliza who had seen the heavy embossed card while sorting through the family mail, working swiftly with her letter opener. Look, she had said, holding it in the air, Joy is opening her very own boutique, and she wishes us to be there! Adding: we must go, of course, to show our goodwill, to show we bear her no grudge. The card was proof that there was decency in Joy: she had, in her success, remembered them.

Edward knew the kind of affair it would be: loud, excessive and dull. But he lacked the heart to object;

Eliza did not ask much of him. He had nothing but tenderness towards his wife of late, this woman and her steady love. Love in the way she laid out his newspaper and cocoa. Love in the way she wore her rainbow brooch. He saw love in the way she felled a fly that was heading for his dinner, and wondered if he was growing sentimental with age.

'MY HUSBAND IS ALSO A LITTLE HARD OF HEARING,' the woman offers, and Edward thinks it may have something to do with all her shouting. He peers over her feathers in the hope of spotting Eliza, and is rewarded by the sight of her—stout, majestically upright—moving towards him through the crowd.

'Edward, you'll never guess what Joy has just told me!' She nods hello to Edward's companion, then shakes her close, silvery hair in wonder at her news. 'She wants Pearl to come and work for her!'

'What did you say?' demands Edward, alarm in his voice.

The woman throws Eliza a concerned look before turning back to Edward.

'SHE SAYS SHE LOST HER PEARL CHOKER!'

...

Later that night, Edward sits in the clubroom with Deakin. They share a leather booth, surrounded by dark wood panelling. The air is grey with smoke. The clink of cutlery sounds a high note over the rumble of men's voices. The waiter approaches. He sets down a brown bottle with a handwritten label and turns silently away.

Deakin pours the drinks. 'To federation.' He raises his glass. 'And to those who believed.'

Federation. The word still sends something ballooning through Edward. A giddy optimism, like a child's love of Christmas. He grins back at his friend and lifts his glass.

'To those who made it happen,' he says. He takes a long swallow, feels the old familiar burn in his throat and chest. The stuff is finer than any he has tasted. Smoky and mellow and clean as new grass. Deakin holds out the bottle, and Edward accepts a refill.

Deakin then tells him of the final battles. The behind-the-scenes brokering and endless deals. The back-scratching and petty rivalries. Edward tries to listen. But he finds his gaze returning to the bottle. Another taste would be nice. He glances down at his empty glass, and at Deakin's hand, bobbing in the air. Until finally, after some minutes, the hand comes to rest on the bottle.

'What do you say, Edward, should we fix ourselves another?'

Edward watches him pour, and then takes the glass in his hand. He feels the heat in him rise to meet the heat in the drink. In seconds, he drains the glass.

He wakes with the deepest sense of something wrong. A mouth so dry he can't swallow. He groans into his pillow.

He dresses in the dark, by feel. Stumbling, reeling as though the floor is caving in. As though he is drunk. But knowing, finally, that he has been dreaming. He hasn't had a drink in nearly fifty years.

Once he reaches the rooftop, he sucks the cold air into his lungs. The sky is satin blackness, broken by stars. He leans back into the teak bench, and marvels at the intensity of his dream. How real it felt. Just like this wood beneath his hand. He used to dream of drinking, and of being drunk, when he first gave it up. Waking full of nausea and guilt. He would go and light the cauldron to boil the water to make the lemonade, and breathe in the steam to try to clear his head.

He feels the quiet presence of his plants, those dim, shaggy shapes that surround him. Enjoys the bright indifference of the stars. Shining for their own sake.

The stars don't care, but he has built a life. Made something of himself. When it might have gone so differently, after Lucky Cho died.

I'm sorry, he tells Lucky Cho. I'm sorry. But I have lived a good life. At least I've done that.

The cold has seeped inside his jacket. As he stands to leave, he moves on impulse to the roof's edge. He sniffs dampness and mildew in the air. He sees the foggy outline of the streetlights below, and a shadow moving between them. The figure stands a moment, directly beneath one of the lights, before slipping through the Arcade's side entrance. It's Vally, coming home.

But it's almost dawn! Edward had no idea he was staying out so late and it sends a light shock through him. He should really have a word. He turns from the edge and makes his way past the plants, careful not to brush too close and damage them. What could be keeping Vally out so late—drinking, gambling, girls? The boy doesn't even work. All he does is smoke and hang around that basement with his friends, writing plays. But Edward's dream is still fresh in his mind. Edward was twenty-one when he quit drinking, the same age that Vally is now. Maybe he should leave the boy be, let him make his mistakes. Let him figure life out for himself.

...

177

'Tell me you're dying and I'll consider it.' D'Ama crosses his arms and leans back in the chair. The office is tidy, bright with morning sun.

'I'm not dying. But the lawyers keep on at me. I turn seventy in a few months, and it seems to have roused them.' Edward shrugs. 'I told them I would nominate three people: you, Eliza and Quong Tart.'

D'Ama looks a little pale, his eyes bloodshot in the corners. As he glances at the clock, the bird emerges from its hidey-hole, cuckooing the hour with demented good cheer. D'Ama frowns and shakes his head.

'But we could never run the Arcade, Edward. You haven't thought it through. Quong Tart would never leave Sydney. This White Australia stuff has really hurt him, he feels the country has turned against him. As for Eliza—I do love the woman, but what does she know about business? Yes, yes . . .' D'Ama raises his hands to stem any interruption, 'that's why you've chosen me, because I know so much about business. But the truth is, Edward,' and he leans forward now, his voice low and confidential, 'my only real interest these days is pleasure. I plan on devoting myself to it.'

Edward scratches his head. An ant wanders across the desk, its body stark against the mother-of-pearl. 'Yes, well, that's fine, D'Ama. But I need to do something to satisfy these lawyers. If you could just sign the papers?' He smiles, pushing forward some pages on his desk.

D'Ama looks both pained and indignant. He throws his lower lip out and reaches for his tobacco. 'I don't think you quite understand the degree of my commitment. The pursuit of pleasure is a dangerous undertaking, especially at my age. I don't expect to see the year out.'

He strikes a match, begins sucking on his pipe. Those sweet, musty puffs hit Edward in an instant, but he only smiles, and tugs at his beard. He expected resistance; he does not expect D'Ama to ever run the Arcade. All he wants is to buy some time with the lawyers. Time in which to figure out his children: what they want from life, and what he wants from them. With Ivy only sixteen, and Pearl barely eighteen, how can he make decisions about the future? How can he leave the Arcade to one or all of them when their adult characters are only just beginning to show? It's true, the boys have little interest in the Arcade. But Linda has surprised him. Taking on the role, at twenty-four, of Owens' personal assistant, she has been filing and organising with missionary zeal. The boys, too, may discover their interest later; at their age, Edward had no idea what he would do with his life.

'Well, if you're planning on being dead,' says Edward, choosing a pen from a marble holder, 'I can't see how signing could bother you in the least. I'll consider it a parting gift.'

D'Ama snatches the pen from Edward and points it at the clock. 'So long as you do not bequeath me *that*.'

...

The bad night's sleep is beginning to weigh on him. He enters the tea salon with senses dulled, passing the bright blur of murals, the women sipping tea in their best town clothes. He picks a corner table, lets the gentle midmorning hum wash over him. Smiles vaguely at the waiters. When his tea arrives, he drinks it quickly, scalding his mouth. He takes a letter from his pocket. Smooth yellow page, a blue duck flying in the corner, and Quong Tart's exuberant script:

A man stopped me in the street the other day and asked me why I did not go back to China. I said to him: Because it's full of Chinese, and you know how filthy they are! Oh Edward, I am always laughing. You have no idea how much fun I have. At the Customs House they now keep me waiting so long to collect my tea that yesterday I took my bagpipes along to help pass the time. Well, they must really love the bagpipes, and they showed their appreciation by putting me to the head of the queue . . .

Edward smiles at his friend, but his mood is heavy. His joy at federation now tainted by this push for White Australia, this backward move towards some tribal unity. Rubbish printed in the papers daily. His Chinese staff unable to leave the country, to visit dying parents, for fear of not being allowed back. One of his waiters pushed down in the street for wearing a pointed hat. And Deakin making his speeches in parliament: common heritage equals common purpose, walking the thin line between populism and prejudice, not saying the Chinese are bad, but denying their rights all the same. Does he even believe all he says? The Deakin he knew embraced a wider world than that. Edward wonders just how many compromises, how many deals he has allowed himself to make.

And again he sees Joy—white with shock—outside Deakin's office.

'Salutations, Mr Cole.' A fur-clad figure stands before his table. Edward jumps in his chair.

'Oh, Golding. I didn't recognise you there. Is it really so cold today?'

Golding shrugs and pulls the moth-eaten jacket more tightly around him. 'We rehearse in the basement and it's *always* cold. Have you seen Vally? He didn't show up for our rehearsal last night and I was worried.'

Edward nods. 'I saw him early this morning. Go on up to the flat and see if he's there.'

Golding takes off with his low, loping walk, past the thin forest of bamboo, and the women trying hard not to stare.

...

Eliza stands at the curtain, gazing down at the street. The flat is quiet except for street sounds: carriages, trams, the odd whistle and shout. 'Such a lovely evening. People look so cheerful on their way home from work.'

Happy to be leaving work—the concept is foreign to Edward. He lives and he works; the two are not easily separated. But he likes that today, feeling tired, he has come upstairs early to sit, book in hand, in the company of his wife. Pink light falling on her skin, still smooth, and her dark silver hair. She places one hand on the rose-patterned curtain, brings the other to the brooch at her throat. A coloured rainbow, enamel on silver. In a moment of extravagance, he had paid a jeweller to make it. Wanting to give her something beautiful with no practical purpose. But wanting it to say clearly: this is for our life together.

'And to think Pearl will soon be among them.' Eliza smiles down at the street.

Edward shuts his book. Going to the opening and bearing Joy no grudge is one thing. But handing over his reserved and serious-minded daughter is quite another. 'Pearl will be well provided for, she doesn't have to work,' he says quietly.

Eliza nods without turning from the window. 'Of course. But it's a good opportunity for her to experience something of the world. I wish the boys would do as much—you know they spend half their time sleeping? How can they be so tired when they hardly do anything?'

Edward's mind drifts. He pictures a low Turkish couch beneath a narrow window. Joy's white flesh against the purple fabric. Her hair turned loose. Did they really use that office, he wonders, that couch?

'If she never marries, she'll be glad to have an occupation, glad of the diversion.' Eliza presses a finger to the glass.

Pearl not marry? Plain and sallow as a child, she has grown into a rare and remarkable beauty. Her dark hair thick and glossy, her thinness turned to slender elegance. As children, it was Ruby who had seemed destined for such beauty. Perhaps, with no more need for it, she had simply passed it on.

'But if she marries, having worked won't hurt her any either,' continues Eliza.

He could bring up the Cornishes! Joy's undesirable connections, her bad judgement in the past. Then he remembers: they were found not guilty at their trial. And enjoyed a triumphant return to society. Their séances now so popular, he has heard, they are booked out for months in advance.

And it occurs to him that he has no idea how Joy financed her boutique. There are thousands of pounds in those fittings alone. She is like a plant, he thinks, in his rooftop garden. Looking fragile, exposed, beneath all that sky. Taking from the sun and the rain. Drawing birds and bees, as well as weeds and mosquitoes. Before you know it, thriving.

Eliza leaves the window to come and stand beside him, placing her hand on his shoulder. 'I rather thought you might say something against it,' she laughs, tucking a strand of hair behind his ear.

Chapter Fourteen

1903

He watches the water—blue, white-tipped, ruched—watching for land. He sees the water is only surface-blue, that just beneath lies darkness, shadows, hints of awesome depth. Some days he has stood at the railings and seen grey dolphins threading the ocean, or flame-coloured fish leaping from the water, reflecting the sunset. He has seen a floating mass of dead jellyfish, clear, like body organs drained of blood. Today he is not looking for these or other wonders. He is waiting for a thin green line to show against the ocean's edge. His body, pressed to the rail, as though to drive the ship faster. Taste of metal on his tongue. His impatience growing the closer they get.

Five months he has been away from his family and the Arcade. Five fascinating, long and arduous months. The offer: a trip to Japan, expenses paid, to experience its culture and beauty, and to bring this knowledge back to the Australian people. He had learned of it through

D'Ama; some of D'Ama's Japanese business contacts were putting up the money. Hoping to fund, in their words, an ambassador of goodwill. It had been irresistible to Edward. A chance to see the world, to promote friendship and understanding between nations. To be the solitary adventurer once more.

And so it had been, at first. That brilliant, destined feeling of boyhood solitude had possessed him, so that even the stones, even a pebble, seemed alive, fresh with possibility. His first taste of seaweed: a revelation. Silky, mild and clean. The concept of food, of what was edible, broader than he ever thought. Raw fish and soybeans, and bizarre forms of mushrooms. The ritual of removing his shoes on entering houses left him vulnerable, but also liberated. He could feel this new world, literally, beneath his feet. The gentle snag of wool socks on tatami.

He had been taken to see the cherry blossoms, to a large park famous for its display. Dark limbs smothered in white. The blossom so unbelievably delicate and dense, like troupes of angels come to rest on branches. The air so sweet, as though filled with angels' breath. Edward was giddy with joy. He wished for only one thing: to share it with Eliza. But the act of wishing seemed to dissipate all his joy. He could think of nothing but her hands cupping those blossoms, her cheeks pink with pleasure. Of a treat they might share—young, salted soybeans—beneath a snowy bower. He missed her, and it took the shine off things. It came as a shock. But worse was the knowledge that his isolation-loving boy-self was no longer there. He had believed that the boy lived on perpetually inside the adult Edward. That all he needed was the right conditions and he would show. But the more time passed, the more Edward missed his wife and children. He wanted to see Vally, sprawled in a cane chair, reading Voltaire. Ivy Diamond grinning broadly, an orange segment where her teeth should be. He would walk the Arcade in his mind's eye, lingering in the tea salon and Wonderland. He would write long letters to Eliza every night. He felt lonely. He felt his boy-self, the one who revelled in solitude, was gone. As dead as his long-dead parents.

'Land. I can see land!' shouts someone on the deck. But Edward has already turned from the railing, the salt air stinging his eyes.

...

'Welcome home, Mr Cole!'

The voices roar in unison as he steps into the tea salon. Family, staff and their families, all gathered. Smiling and waving small Australian flags on sticks. Streamers hung from wall to wall, and the band ready to play. Familiar faces, and the tables offering sandwiches and lemonade. Tears cloud his eyes. And in his mouth a certain taste, muddy and sour, like the taste of his own lemonade, made fifty years before. So no detail is lost, he thinks, the mind keeps it all.

Owens comes towards him, shiny and pink-lipped. 'Mr Cole. I trust you'll find everything in order.'

Smugness rounding his vowels. Smugness in the letters he wrote to Edward every week. Letters so dry and devoid of sentiment that only their smugness revealed their human origins. Edward takes the small, damp hand in his own.

'Thank you, Owens. You've done exceptionally well, I'm very grateful.'

And he means it. Edward could not have undertaken such a long trip without Owens to keep his eye on things.

What he lacks in imagination he makes up for in thoroughness and care.

Owens clears his throat, his eyes rolling back in happiness. 'You should try the lemonade, sir, it's really rather good.'

The band begins, an upbeat tune full of trumpet, leaving Edward and Owens to nod at one another, the noise preventing further talk. Edward looks to where his family stand. Eliza is beaming, jubilant—this is all her doing—and Eddy stands companionably by her side. Linda, Pearl and Ivy look like sisters in a fairytale, with beaded dresses and flowers in their hair. He looks in vain for Vally, his absence a small shadow on the day. He sees Simon Gabriel, who is turning black again. Small patches on his neck and face like the markings on a banana. The greyhound profile of Juniper Griggs. Crank's bald head, polished to a marble shine. Only now, in the glow of his homecoming, can Edward fully embrace all he's seen. Only now is Japan completely alive to him.

After half an hour of mingling, handshakes and smiles, he goes in search of Benson. He finds him in his shirtsleeves, on the floor, a gang of young boys crouched around him. Marbles roll and chink together.

'Alright, Danny, hand it over,' says Benson. 'Fair's fair.'

The boy slowly takes a cat's eye from the floor. His jaw is clenched and trembling. He hands the marble to Benson without meeting his eye. Benson looks up at Edward and winks. 'Want to play?'

Edward looks from Benson to the boys and back. 'How soon can we get something printed?'

Benson shrugs his shoulders. 'We can go now, if you like.' He gets to his feet, dropping the marble back into the lap of the sulking boy. 'I already have one the same, otherwise I'd keep it. Don't go betting what you can't afford to lose,' he says.

Benson's movements are swift and precise, and Edward sits back to watch him work. The room reeks of turpentine and ink, and as Edward breathes it in he thinks of the alphabet sweating. He loves this room, its sense of industry and purpose. Now he feels it mesh with his own sense of purpose. He feels his time in Japan inhabiting him like a second person.

He thinks about the night they took him to see a dance ceremony. Those dancers with their faces painted white, blanking out all expression. How they inched across the stage with excruciating slowness. Nothing seemed to happen. Unable to follow the story, unsure if there even was one, Edward grew restless and bored. His knees ached and the wooden bench dug into his spine. He longed to return to the hotel, with its hushed library and deep chairs, but kept still for fear of offending his interpreter. His jaw shook with stifled yawns. Then the drumming began and, to his surprise, a shiver of anticipation ran through him. He sat forward and began to pay attention. The dancing and the drumming, brought together, seemed to express a sense of yearning not unlike his yearning for family and home. It was bittersweet, and welcome, a confirmation that our human existence is shared. When the drumming grew rapid and loud, and the dancers, kneeling, rose suddenly to their feet, hope surged through Edward. And he realised then that he was following the story, emotion by emotion. A communication so old and pure it raised the hair on his neck.

Now that he is home he has no words to describe this. Why, when he can recount every detail of a scenic train ride or a dinner with diplomats? He thought he might be able to talk to Benson about it. But sitting here, somewhat stiff in the ladder-back chair, he feels almost mute with confusion. It's as though he needs a new vocabulary to express himself. A whole other language.

'Is that word *then* or *them*? And over here, is it *effect* or *effort*?' Benson leans over, page in hand, and Edward smells the mustard on his breath.

He could tell Benson about Tokyo, the crowding and neatness and order. How the newspaper men fought one another to interview him. Calling him a writer, a philosopher. Printing his image from a woodcut.

He could describe the stranger who helped him to find the silk flowers he had promised to bring home for Pearl. Leading Edward through twisted lanes and narrow doorways into tiny, hidden shops. Speaking to storekeepers, who in turn pointed out other shops until they finally found the kind she had asked for. How the man bowed deeply before departing, seeking nothing for his time. He could tell Benson: dignity is everywhere.

Benson holds the page in the air and shakes it dry before he hands it to Edward. 'It's not your catchiest heading,' he says.

...

That night, Edward lines up fifty copies of *What 40 Eminent Japanese Say of the White Australia Act* on his bedside table and climbs into bed. Eliza asks if he thinks they might be stolen, if he wouldn't rather put them in the safe.

He will send them out to the papers and to parliament. He will stand in the Arcade and personally place them in people's hands. In Japan, they welcomed him the way no Japanese would be welcomed in Australia. It had made him feel ashamed.

The bedsheets are crisp and smell of pine trees, England. Reminding him of his childhood home. The bed shared with his brothers, and waking to the touch of hair, or fabric, on his face, and not knowing who it belonged to, them or him.

He looks at Eliza breathing softly in the bed beside him. Putting on his welcome-home party has clearly worn her out. He tried telling her stories to make her laugh and keep her awake, as he watched her eyelids droop and fall. But it's good simply to feel her warmth in the bed, to breathe the same air.

Earlier, she had been full of news and stories of the children. How Eddy had brought a girl home to dinner, only to spend the whole night silent and blushing. That it was Linda who entertained the poor girl, finally leading her from the table to see the monkeys. How much confidence Linda has gained from working at the Arcade. And did he hear that Pearl had sold a dress to the singer Nellie Melba? Sharing tea together afterwards in the boutique's tiny back room. Ivy had been green with envy, before promptly forgetting all about it.

Edward had listened from the comfort of his armchair, slippers on his outstretched feet. Gazing at the ceramic kangaroos, forever alert, their ears turned towards him. Drinking his evening milk, a habit he had missed in Japan. Watching the points of colour high on her cheeks.

And Vally, he had asked, what has he been doing? But Eliza shook her head, exclaiming, We never see him! Promising there would be a proper scolding for his having missed the party that afternoon. She had then launched into a long and detailed story of Louma finding a rat's nest in the guest room, behind the kitchen, and D'Ama bringing them a kitten in a pink bassinet.

Edward had relished every one of the homecoming rituals: unlocking the door to his office, the children unwrapping their gifts, Eliza throwing back the clean covers on the bed. They had absorbed him fully. So it is only now, with the household dark and sleeping, that he can examine the piece of news he received on disembarking at the pier. A porter, manoeuvring his bags onto a trolley, had asked him if he knew that Mr Barton had resigned. And before the name of his replacement was uttered, Edward knew, like a prophecy fulfilled, who the new prime minister would be.

...

In the morning, Edward eats and washes and dresses as if it's the first time he has done these things. Never has a grapefruit felt so sharp and clean in his mouth. Never before has he held the soap to his nose, inhaling its floral scent.

At the top of the stairs, Eliza stops him and brushes the dust from his coat with hard strokes from her palm. As if it were armour.

It is a plain, grey morning. He hears the crashing sound of Owens opening the shutters. Beneath his feet, the drying floorboards smell of vinegar. Edward grips the pamphlets in his hand, surprised to find himself nervous. He didn't sleep at all well. He could still feel the motion of the boat beneath him, and would wake now and then with the sensation of the ship sliding down a large wave, his feet braced against the mattress.

As he walks towards the entrance he is cheered by the sight of the Little Men, and decides to position himself just to their right. They churn their crank and display their signs with the usual neat efficiency, unfazed by the Gulliver in their midst.

The first customers through the door are immediately drawn to Edward. Recognising him, perhaps, or at least expecting some new gimmick or joke. They reach for the pamphlets with the eagerness of children seizing on sweets. Edward grins as the pile grows thin in his hands. He turns to the Little Men, tells them to look sharp, they have a rival.

Then the customers begin to return the pamphlets.

The first man approaches Edward silently, and hands back his pamphlet without meeting Edward's eye. The next customer is more direct. A striking woman with dark red hair, she tells Edward that if there is a joke, she seems to have missed the punchline. Edward replies that no, the work is meant to be serious, and she gives him a look of clear and unmistakeable disgust. A florid man in a paisley waistcoat begins to insist that Edward can say what he likes, but how would he feel if his own daughter was to marry one? Laughing loudly, aggressively, when Edward suggests he would hope to judge each man on his own merits. The man is still laughing when a young tough approaches them. Hands in pockets and a bit of fluff for a beard, he throws the pamphlet on the ground at Edward's feet and spits on it. Not a token spit. A quivering grey mass with something yellow at its heart.

When Edward walks back upstairs and feels his knees shaking, he blames it on the boat.

...

Two weeks later, he is smiling at the date on the newspaper, while his chest aches in every hollow. It is Ruby's twenty-first birthday. He has already been to the rooftop, placed a glass bowl full of strawberries beneath a flowering rosebush. It was an exceptional morning. The sun bathed the rooftops in gold and a bird hung high, like a slash drawn on the sky. He said to her, you will never be an adult, but that is not a bad thing. Felt the cool flap of her wings.

Now he is at the breakfast table with the morning paper. Eliza's knife chimes a note against the butter dish, a higher note against the saucer of jam. Edward turns the page and lets out a surprised *oh*.

'They have reviewed my pamphlet,' he says.

Eliza lays the knife on her plate and sits up straighter.

He throws her a glance before beginning. 'The heading is, *No Piebald Australia*.'

He stops to clear his throat, a toast crumb stuck in his gullet.

Mr Cole prophesies that 'the humanity of Australia will in turn revolt at the selfish and inhuman law (as he terms it), will probably relax it, and finally abolish it altogether.' Mr Cole has recently returned from his travels, which begs the question, what planet has he been visiting? Australia's policy is to preserve our island continent for the white man, and the view of Japanese statesmen, whether four, forty or four hundred, will not affect us one whit.

He can feel Eliza's anger before she even opens her mouth. 'It's an outrage!' She takes the napkin from her lap and throws it onto the table. 'And to think of all the advertising you've given them over the years!' She is breathing through her mouth, beginning to pant. 'Why, they haven't even given any arguments, they make no actual case. They just strike you down, as if your ideas are ludicrous, as if you were some kind of crackpot!' Her face is mottled red.

Edward lifts a hand to try to calm her. 'It's alright, my dear, don't upset yourself.' He carefully folds the paper closed. 'We've got the ball rolling now, and that's the main thing. It will get people talking about the issue, one way or another.'

Eliza, it seems, has only paused for breath. 'How dare they sneer at you, these ignoramuses, these . . . these philistines! This newspaper's a disgrace—it's not worth the paper it's printed on.'

Edward pours the last of the tea into Eliza's cup. He is also disappointed, though not surprised. Another session spent handing out pamphlets in the Arcade had ended up much like the first. He has even begun to receive some abusive mail, with two rather vicious letters arriving just this morning. Not that Eliza needs to know about that.

'I believe they laughed at me when I advertised for a wife, as well. And that didn't turn out too badly in the end.' He watches her from the corner of his eye. Waiting for the smile he knows will spread across her face.

...

He walks the city streets, the stone paths warm beneath his soles. The sunshine gentle on his face. Beneath the afternoon's calm lies the swell of disappointment. Oh well, oh well, he tells himself, perhaps I should have known. For he remembers when these streets were dirt. When men gambled their futures on a bit of rock. He remembers the sheep being herded down Elizabeth

Street, and the crowds that formed to watch the latest hanging.

In Japan they called him a philosopher, and it bolstered his belief in the power of words. But here, in his city, they see him as a showman, an oddball entertainer with an endless bag of tricks. Who was it that called him a thinking man—Alfred Deakin? The same man who sent him two lines—two!—in response to his latest pamphlet: *The Japanese are a fine race of people, but the government must give priority to the needs of the white man, to protecting his wages and preserving his culture and customs.* The white man so vulnerable, it seems, that he can only prosper on a protected island reserve.

He finds himself on Collins Street, amid the towering sand- and dun-coloured buildings, and the shopfronts with their lavish displays. Low plate-glass windows filled with gold-tipped canes, gloves and cigarette holders. A tram rattles its way up the incline. In a few more steps he will be at Joy's boutique, with the chance of catching Pearl on her way home.

But the boutique door is closed and the lights are off. Edward makes a tunnel of his hands on the glass. He sees the mirrors, dark as jet, and the mannequins, caught in their dreams of moving. He sees the white fleece of his own beard. Sadness rushes in: he has missed Pearl, and perhaps the chance of saying Ruby's name. It seems he is always missing his children lately, passing them on the stairs, or at the table, as they go about their separate, adult lives.

He sees a pale shape moving through the dark interior and takes it for a trick of the light. A reflection, a sunbeam gone astray. Then he hears the workings of the latch.

...

It is a small room, white as an igloo. Twin chandeliers, the size of coconuts, descend from the ceiling. Edward perches himself on a dainty metal chair. The table is white onyx, and set for tea, with a long white rose in a thin vase. Across the table sits Joy. They are alone in a room at the back of the store. Close enough to touch. Edward folds his hands in his lap.

'I think you take milk?' She points to the jug. She wears a large emerald ring and a pale-green shawl. She looks no older than the first time he saw her. He can feel his shoulders, hunched around his ears. Why can't he simply relax? Does he still fear her casting some kind of sexual spell, of trapping him in some way? No—but the memory of this fear is discomfort enough. Joy pours the tea and hands him his cup.

'Pearl mentioned that it's Ruby's birthday,' she says, sitting back and studying his face. Ah, thinks Edward, so Pearl remembers. He has often thought, with only one year between them, that Ruby's death had hit Pearl the hardest. It was impossible to know. Pearl was a mystery, a closed book. She never spoke of her feelings. He had seen her cry only once, as a child: the night Joy left.

'Do you think she was sad?' he asks, leaning forward.

'Oh, I expect so.' She taps her ring on the side of the cup. 'Pearl is always sad.'

Edward digests this. Then, because he doesn't like the idea of Joy knowing his daughter better than he does, he changes topic.

'How's the boutique doing?' He sits back, and the bridge of the chair jabs his spine.

She looks at him without expression. 'Fine. It's doing fine.'

'It must have been awfully expensive.' Edward gazes up at the chandeliers with their stalactite beauty. 'Was it difficult, getting a bank loan?'

'Ah,' she sighs. 'It wasn't easy, raising the money.' The cup hides some movement of her mouth, a smile or a grimace. 'Luckily we've done well enough to justify the outlay.'

They sit there, cocooned by whiteness and silence. As though time might freeze them like fish in a pond. To be discovered in a hundred years. He tells himself, it's time to go.

'I've been lucky, too, with Pearl. She has a real head for business.' Joy traces the edge of her cup with her finger. 'You might do worse than leave the Arcade in her hands some day. Of course, you're probably thinking more of the boys.'

Edward shakes his head. 'No, I've considered all of them.'

Joy looks up quickly. 'And what have you decided?'

'I'm afraid that's more of a family matter.'

Joy's face turns pink, and she shakes her head. 'Oh, Edward, I'm sorry, how rude of me.' Her hands cup her face, the emerald glistening. 'It's no excuse, I know, but I used to feel like part of your family. Well, that was all long ago.'

'It doesn't seem so long ago,' says Edward. 'It feels like only yesterday the girls were in nappies.'

Joy laughs, and Edward feels a warmth spread through him. They lift their cups in unison and drink. The tea is excellent, the porcelain fine and weightless. His shoulders soften, the tension seeps away.

'I heard about your trip to Japan. Was it wonderful?' Joy's eyes are bright with interest.

'Yes. Yes it was.' And he tells her a little about Japan. A country that withdrew from the world for two hundred years, where foreigners were put to death for the crime of trespass.

'I imagine our policies seem rather mild, in that case,' she says, and Edward smiles. In Japan, he thinks, she would have been a geisha.

'I read the *Herald*'s review of your pamphlet.' She bites down on her lip. 'What I don't understand is why you don't take the fight directly to Deakin, if it really means so much to you?'

Edward pulls a rueful face. 'Oh, I sent him one of my pamphlets. He was rather succinct in dismissing it.'

'A pamphlet?' She gives a strange, stifled laugh. 'But you could ruin the man if you chose to.'

Edward shakes his head, his skin aflame. 'No, no, no, it's not the way I do things.'

'But you wouldn't actually have to ruin him. The threat would be enough to persuade him. I have his letters, you know.' Her lips are pale, her tongue works to wet them. 'Just threaten to publish them, and he'll crumble. He wouldn't dare call your bluff. You can take the letters. You and Eliza were my family, when I had no one.'

The offer is vile, repulsive to Edward. He draws back from the table, scraping his chair on the ground. At the same time he's deeply moved; those letters could ruin her, too.

'Joy, listen to me. You've got to destroy those letters. No good could ever come of using them. I could never use them. I can't win by bringing a man to his knees in that way.'

Joy stares at him. 'But if the outcome's the same?'

How could the outcome be the same, he wants to say to her, when every action has a consequence, when we pay for everything in the end?

'I think you'd best destroy the letters. And please, never mention them to me again.'

She looks ready to debate him; her lips are parted, veins stand out on her neck. Then she sinks back, sighing heavily. 'As you wish.'

When Joy offers to lead him out through the alley, Edward declines; he will exit by the street.

...

Edward finds the city with its lights on: hazy orange against an indigo sky. A sea wind blows clean against his face. He lowers his head and walks among the flapping coats as people make their way to restaurants, concerts, theatres. He takes long strides, energised by his talk with Joy, his display of integrity. Bursting with good-will. Approaching the Arcade, he looks up to admire its candy-bright rainbow, gaslit from below.

'Mr Cole, a minute of your time?'

Edward meets the dark, sunken eyes of Juniper Griggs. 'Why, of course, of course. Shall we go in?'

But Griggs shakes his head and beckons Edward away from the entrance. They move down the street until they find a small alcove, a little out of the wind. He reminds Edward of a street urchin, a grown-up Oliver Twist. Something in his plaintive, beaten look. Edward tries to feel some warmth for him, to share with him his expansive good spirits.

'What is it, Griggs? Is there a problem at work, or with one of the other men? Whatever it is, I'm sure we can work it out.'

Griggs shakes his head and lets out a deep sigh. 'I just thought you should know what's being said, is all.'

Edward touches his beard. 'Gossip? You know I won't hear gossip.'

Griggs shrugs. 'It's about your pamphlet. That's why I thought you should know.' He stares at the ground, then quickly up at Edward. His hair, though neatly brushed, is heavily oiled, like something dredged from a barrel. Edward feels his gut turn.

'Alright then, Griggs, what is it? What do they say about the pamphlet?'

Griggs takes his hand from his pocket and straightens up. 'They say that you should be the last man to defend those Orientals.'

'Mmm, and what do they mean by that? I should be the last man?'

Griggs purses his mouth and looks away. A group of youths pass by, laughing and half skipping on the pavement, their faces turned up to the sky.

'They mean because of Vally,' he blurts out, turning back to Edward. His face shines with some deep emotion, his nose permanently skewed by Benson's punch. 'They can't understand why you'd help the Chinese when they made your own son an opium addict.'

Chapter Fifteen

Edward takes the basement stairs with firm steps, although it is dark and difficult to see. He pictures Vally, his mouth falling open in shock and indignation, shaking his head in denial. He will place a gentle hand on Vally's shoulder and promise to take care of it. They will return home. There will be cocoa and, maybe, if the night is chilly, a fire. There will be time then to share their tales of the last five months. Edward will tell him about the arts in Japan, the way theatre is revered and artists held in high esteem. Vally will tell him about the latest plays he has read. There may be talk about his future; the chance, perhaps, to stage some theatre at the Arcade.

At some point, Edward will need to deal with Griggs. He will have to denounce the man as a liar and decide whether to fire him. He has never liked the man, it's true, but that is beside the point; Edward has never fired anyone.

He enters the narrow room with its bare stone walls and smells tobacco heavy on the air. He sees they have built a proper stage. A solid platform against the far wall, with thin, dark curtains either side. Two figures sit at the stage's edge, huddled together, back-lit by a single lamp. He peers at their lowered heads, their dim, familiar shapes. The cold air sends a shiver through him. As he starts to walk towards them, his shoes rapping the floorboards, the men look up.

'Good evening, Golding. Good evening, Robes. Is Vally about?'

Golding wears his rabbit-skin jacket and a fur cap with earflaps. He looks cold. His feet, swinging off the stage, are blue-tinged in their sandals. 'Afraid it's only me and Robes tonight. A couple of miscreants waiting for the muse to strike.'

Robes nods hello. He sits cross-legged in a nest of books and cigarette packets, a pair of tiny gold-rimmed glasses on his nose. 'She's playing hard to get,' he says, picking a flake of ash from his pants.

'I see,' Edward sighs. He had hoped to settle this tonight. He must settle this tonight, his body wound for action now and no chance of getting to sleep. 'I really need to speak to him. Have you any idea where he might be?'

Golding shakes his head and looks away.

Robes runs his hand through pale, thinning hair. 'He doesn't come around here much anymore. We hardly see him.'

'We're in between shows right now . . .' Golding shrugs.

'Alright, gentlemen, if you do happen to see him, will you please tell him I'm looking for him and wish to speak to him at once?'

The men nod, and Edward bows and turns away. The clip of his step so steady and full of purpose when the truth is he has no idea where to go next. The city is large and he doesn't know Vally's habits. He cannot name a single venue where his son might be. He recalls Vally seeing a performance at Her Majesty's Theatre, but that was months ago. Is this something, as a father, he should know?

Climbing the stairs, he feels a twinge in his knee, and he must stop a moment, one hand resting on the icy wall. Come on, he tells himself, you could dig a ditch, row a boat, walk all night if you have to; this is no time for feeling old. It's then he hears his name, echoing up the stairwell, exactly like a scene from the stage. The delayed exit, the last-minute dash from Golding, who sounds breathless, but remains out of sight at the bottom of the stairs.

'Mr Cole? Are you still there?' Followed by a pause. 'You might look for him in Chinatown.'

Something cold burrows into Edward's heart.

...

Edward stands inside the pale wedge of light coming through the window of his dark office. Street light; enough to see by. Falling on the corner of his desk, revealing the thick carving of an elephant's head, the glint of topaz eyes. Enough light to check the time on his clock— ten to eleven—and see the sheen on his black and silver telephone. He doesn't want to make the call, he wants to handle this himself; he just doesn't know where to start.

'Hello, D'Ama speaking.'

'It's Edward. I'm sorry to call—'

'Just a minute.' He hears the sound of coughing, and the muted splash of liquid hitting glass. 'Proceed. And don't bother to apologise, just tell me what you're after.'

Edward rubs the phone's nickel-plated base. 'Where would someone go, in Chinatown, if they wanted to . . . to smoke opium?'

'Well now.' Seconds pass. 'Is this someone a man of means?'

Edward nods, then remembers he must speak. 'Yes, a man of means.'

'Of course, it doesn't automatically rule out the shabbier venues. Sometimes a man will be seeking an experience, a taste of the underworld, in which case there are numerous and ever-shifting dens about the place. But for a man seeking a certain level of style and comfort, there are really only two: China Annie's and Serenity Place.'

'D'Ama?'

'Mmm?'

'I believe I'll need those addresses.'

A shuffling sound travels down the line. 'Give me half an hour and I'll go with you.'

Edward feels forty years of friendship in the offer; the discretion, the gentleness with which it's made. Tears fill his eyes and he is tempted to accept; D'Ama will know exactly what to do. But he also feels a strange and compelling need to face this night alone.

'No, thank you, D'Ama. The addresses will do for now.'

He puts down the phone and quickly locks up his office. He jumps at the sound—*cuckoo, cuckoo, cuckoo*—of his clock striking the hour, the ecstatic bird call dogging his every step.

...

Serenity Place. The name conjures a mossy rock by a small stream, silvery fish and dappled shade. Edward stands in front of the green-painted door wedged inside a row of housefronts. A single Chinese character, made of brass, is nailed to its centre; there is no other sign, no nameplate. He doesn't know why he has chosen this place, or why Golding's words turned him cold. There could be a dozen reasons for Vally to go to Chinatown.

The street is empty, but voices pierce the night, and someone is frying onions. He looks up to see a black strip of sky, a handful of stars. He is alone. No God to call on, or to blame.

A small Chinese man answers his knock with a brief, polite smile. Wordlessly leads him down a corridor lit with red glass lanterns and lined with Persian rugs. Calls him by his name.

'Do I know you, have we met?' asks Edward in alarm.

The man shakes his head. 'You gave my nephew a job. I have seen you at the Arcade. Come.'

The house is long and narrow and orderly. They pass by several doors, each with a brass character nailed to the centre. Edward almost dizzy with the low red light, the heavy-scented air: sweet, floral, musky. He thinks of wild animals, lilies. The man stops before the fourth door and turns to Edward, his smooth skin glowing red. He turns the handle and steps aside, allowing Edward to enter.

Edward's head starts to spin. He grips the cool brass handle and closes his eyes. But he can't turn back now, so he throws the door open with more force than he intends and stumbles across the threshold. The smell is instantly stronger—cloying and sweet, but with a bitterness he can taste.

And there he finds Vally. Lying, serene, on a gold velvet chaise longue. His eyes closed, a half-smile on his lips, like a child pretending to sleep. His lips and cheeks rosy, and his hair falling across one eye. Edward tries to take it all in. He sees a long flute-like instrument resting on a low table; a sort of pipe, he supposes. There are two other men here—white, well dressed—lying on day beds. No one speaks, or stirs, or turns to look at Edward. He seems to lack presence, a figure in a dream. He feels he could scream and bother no one. He could tear the room apart. He has no plan. His only plan has been to find Vally.

His walk across the room—on thick green carpet—is soundless and dreamlike. It seems to take some time. For he can observe the silk hangings on the walls: waterfalls and misty mountains. He can see the soft gold reflection of the chaise longue in the black lacquered screen. He can think, too, about his failures as a father. He has not prepared them well enough, he has been distracted, blind. He feels the drag downward, the lead weight of guilt. He thinks of explorers leading their parties through the desert to their deaths. How heavy their step; no wonder they cannot make base camp.

He stands over his son. All he wants is to see him whole again. To see him restored, in body and spirit. He puts a hand on his shoulder and shakes him.

Vally's eyes open: specks of pupil on cornflower blue. He frowns up at Edward. 'Pa?'

'Get up now, Vally, I'm taking you home.'

He shakes his head. He closes his eyes, the skin beneath them livid. 'Not now. Later. I'll come later. Leave me be.'

Something surges in Edward, a momentary blood-rush, and he bends and grips Vally beneath the arms. Vally mumbles, keeps his eyes shut, but does not resist. Edward tries to hoist him to his feet. The weight of him!

Like something dead. He has to let go and catch his breath. He bends his knees and tries another grip, deeper into the armpits, the damp hollows of his shirt. Then he lifts. Feels the upward movement, the body rocking towards him. He's got him, he's got him now—but what—what is *this*? He drops him on the lounge and staggers back. What he felt was not his son, but the cold, dead body of Lucky Cho.

And the memories pour out of him like ants from a nest.

There is the swampy, muck-bottomed mine. He holds Lucky Cho across his shoulder. Cold and heavy as a slab of ice. He tries to push, to heave him over the rim and back to the surface. His muscles shuddering, and the vomit rising in his throat. The sound—a sickening splat—as he drops the body back into the mud. Smell of faeces and rotten eggs. Like hell, thinks Edward, the sulphur pit. It dawns on him, eventually, to seek some help.

He scrambles out of the shaft and heads towards the nearest men. A couple of miners with mud-caked beards and bad teeth. Please, he tells them, his friend is dead, he needs their help. The Chinaman, says one, and they both shake their heads. They will not touch a Chinaman, not even a dead one.

He indulges a swift fantasy: their skulls, cracked with his shovel.

Soon he is back in the pit. Crying now, and yelling, his muscles pumped with rage. *He will show them all!* His strength doubling every second. He pushes, pulls and drags the body to the surface, tearing fabric, skin: the dead flesh thick beneath his nails. They rest now, side by side, in the yellow dawn. Edward turns his head and throws up whiskey, bile.

He will show them what? Lucky Cho is still dead. He has drowned in a foot of water. A foot. Worse than drowning in an ocean, or a raging torrent. Worse, that is, for Edward who might have saved him. He could not have saved a man from drowning in an ocean—he is a poor swimmer, and that's a fact. But a man drowning in a puddle? All he had to do was go and look.

For they had been drinking in the night, a celebration of their first real find: that glorious two-ounce nugget. They had not gone easy on the bottle. Too many toasts were required: to their luck and their health and their friendship, to their future, to the rain and to the mud. When Lucky Cho had left the campfire, saying he would be back in a minute, Edward had begun to drift and drowse. He knew that time was passing, and that he ought to look for his friend; the camp was dangerous, they would always watch one another's back. But Edward was warm and safe, blissful by the campfire, and soon he slept, or simply passed out. When he woke at dawn, the first thing he saw was the brown cocoon of his friend's empty swag.

He knew, even then, what he had done.

By the time he was lying on the rocky ground coughing bile beside his dead friend, he knew this much: he was a drunk, a fool, a failure. He was a thousand miles from home. His only friend was dead, he'd good as killed him. Guilt like acid seared his heart.

But it was not long after that he got to his knees to search Lucky Cho's pockets for the nugget. Held it in his ripped and bloody palm. And decided there was no point burying that. Or the money pouch, strapped to his dead friend's chest. The nugget and the money more than enough to set up the lemonade stall, the enterprise from which all his ventures flowed. The root of all his wealth.

Finally, as the sun broke like an egg on the horizon, two strangers approached and offered to help Edward bury the body.

Now Edward finds himself staggering through Chinatown, gripping Vally around the waist to hold him upright. The narrow streets are crowded, bodies press against them, and Edward shouts to make way, to let them pass. Vally takes a step or two, then seems to forget. Sweat rolls down Edward's back and chest. It is only half a mile; somehow they make it home.

...

When D'Ama takes the call his voice is warm and clear, free of any sleepiness or surprise. There is nothing more to be done for now, he tells Edward, Vally will sleep it off. In the morning, after locking Vally in, he should go and see a doctor D'Ama knows. He will need to think about leaving someone with Vally at all times. For as the drug leaves his system, things will get unpleasant: vomiting, cramping, night sweats. Not to mention Vally's own behaviour—the begging and pleading, the lying and the stealing. The addict's only thought is to relieve his pain. There is even a chance he might become violent.

Edward sits at his desk, head in his hands. How has it come to this? What new despair is this? He hasn't felt such blackness since Ruby died, such guilt since Lucky Cho. What should he have done? Hit him with a cane, made him go to church or get a job? Insisted that he work at the Arcade? Will someone tell him what he should have done? He believed that all a child needed was good food, love and freedom to move in the world; clearly he has got it terribly wrong. He believed in peace and happiness for the world, but his own son, given everything, does not know peace or happiness. He has given jobs to the Chinese and they have ruined his son.

And wasn't it Lucky Cho who had given Edward his first taste of whiskey? What is it with these people—this cursed, contemptible race—bringing ruin upon them all! And Edward, like a dupe, a dunce, so busy singing their praises. Championing their cause! Working to make it easier for them to come here and spread their foul influence.

Out of nowhere, sobs tear through him. Harsh, barking sounds. Tears darkening the jade and rolling off the mother-of-pearl. His throat so tight it burns. Edward thumps the desk with his fist until it numbs.

He presses one eye deep against his palm. Feels the curve of facial bone, solid beneath the flesh, and tries to net a single clear thought.

One thing he knows is what draws Vally to the drug. The promise of connection. The feeling that you could understand the world, your fellow man, and in turn be understood. Or that is how it had seemed to Edward, when he drank. A fine impulse, when you think about it that way.

He also knows what it takes to give it up. The soul-clenching will. And now he sighs and rubs his face. Vally. His impatient, funny, sensitive Vally. Of his many gifts, a strong will is not one of them. Born weak of will and then handed a life of privilege and ease. Edward's guilt, his incompetence, could not be plainer. What has he ever given Vally that might help him now? His failure so enormous it almost crushes him.

This is not helping. He has to try to think.

Vally is twenty-three years old. At his age, Edward had left England—home and family—far behind. He had crossed the world. He had known religion and its comforts, and given them up. He had worked five different jobs to stay alive. What he learned was this: in the end, with or without the bottle, there is only the self.

His poor, privileged, doomed son.

Edward feels his mouth twitch and tremble through his hand.

In the morning he must tell Eliza. What? That nothing can be done?

Perhaps they could all go away together. He drops his hand and straightens up a little. What's to stop them moving to the countryside? The mythic calm of Mount Macedon, or a tidy farm at Romsey. They could start an orchard and eat sweet apples straight from the tree. Or they could go on a voyage. They could go to England with its glorious theatres: Covent Garden, St James', the Theatre Royal. They could go to museums, buy up books by the ton, eat a hot pie in the street.

He would need to see to the Arcade, of course. Owens would be useful there. As for the campaign, he could drop it and no one would care.

A magpie warbles; dawn is near. His throat is parched and raw. He uses his sleeve to rub the desk dry. Lays down his head and sleeps.

...

Eliza, to his surprise, does not fall apart when he tells her. Instead, she seems to swell, to grow giant with maternal powers, formidable.

'I *knew* there was something!' She clicks her tongue and shakes her head and starts to pace the room. 'Why, he hasn't been himself at all. He barely eats with us, doesn't touch the piano. And, of course, he missed your welcome-home party—*most* out of character. Oh, Edward!' She stops, flushed with sleep and resolution, flannel nightgown twisting. 'We must try everything, every cure, every remedy, until we find the one that works. We cannot lose him to this, this . . . I will *not* lose another child!'

Edward looks on, stunned by the force of her will. No note of self-pity or self-blame. Just the drive to act and to restore. Her eyes are brilliant, crystalline, in the shafts of morning light.

'Where is he now, what's to be done?' she continues, barely taking breath.

'Well, he's asleep in the guest room. There's a doctor, someone D'Ama mentioned, however . . .'

'Then you should go at once. I'll sit with Vally until you return.'

Edward pulls the coarse strands of his beard. 'Hmm. At once, yes. The thing is . . . this could all take some time. We are going to need help watching over him. I was thinking of asking Benson to come and assist us.'

Eliza chews her lip, head tilted right. 'You trust Benson, don't you?'

'Yes.'

She tosses her head and moves to the dresser, looking back at Edward through the carved mirror. 'Then please, go now and ask him. Tell him I will be most grateful.'

Benson agrees at once. He suggests they involve Simon Gabriel, setting up a twenty-four-hour watch between the three of them. He tells Edward that Simon Gabriel is tougher than he looks.

'He once worked at an asylum for the insane. In Lisbon. You should ask him someday to show you the scar on his stomach.'

...

As Edward walks towards the tea salon, he is gripped by a craving for tea. The monkey-picked oolong, an ordinary black—he doesn't care, he wants that minor lift. His shoulders and neck ache from sleeping at his desk, his mouth feels like an ashpit. He has already reached the red-curtained doorway before a thought stops him dead: he cannot face the tea salon today. He turns and takes the stairs up to his office, his legs shaky and slow. Wondering: which of the waiters has that uncle at the opium den? The baby-faced kid with the fringe falling in his eyes? Or the tall fellow, the one with acne like crushed berries spread across his face?

He stops at his office for money and a briefcase; no doubt a lot of money will be spent. Lotions and potions and holy intervention—and what will be the point? Can a bottle of pills impart strength of character? Can an elixir succeed where Edward has failed? The very idea is an insult. But the doctor has D'Ama's approval, which makes him worth a visit.

He unlocks the desk drawer and thumbs through a slim stack of money with tapered white fingers that barely seem his own. Everything has a separate, foreign quality. The rustle of the banknotes is menacing and loud. A shaft of light through the window almost blinding. He reaches under his desk for his briefcase. Lays it on his lap. Only to find it stuffed full of pamphlets. *The Better Side of the Chinese Character* jammed in at every angle, even sticking out the bag's hinged sides. He throws up his hands, curses the heavens. Then he opens the case and grabs pamphlets by the handful, dumping them onto the desk.

...

Edward cannot take his eyes from the gold-plated tooth-pick hanging from the doctor's neck. Gently swinging from its golden chain. If he uses it just once, he thinks, I will stand up and walk out the door. What kind of man needs a gold device to scrape the food from his teeth? What if it's not plated at all, but solid?

'Coca leaves, morphine, patent medicines. A variety of herbs. The latest in hydropathic treatment. Not to mention gold cures, hypnosis . . .'

The doctor's voice is soft and monotone. Edward is steeped in gloom. The longer the list of cures, the worse it grows. Surely, if one of them actually worked the others would be made redundant? He stares at the row of gilt-framed certificates, the polished-walnut shelves. The topmost shelf beyond human reach and no ladder in sight. What is kept up there—the hopeless cases, the files of those beyond cure? He looks back at the desk, the Tiffany lamp with its leadlight colour, pure as any cathedral window. A stack of leather volumes, a pile of papers tamed by a paperweight: a bronze statue of a horse. And is assailed by a sudden memory of Ruby and Vally riding a pony. They cannot be aged more than six and eight. Ruby is ecstatic, wide-mouthed, her head pressing back into her brother's shoulder. Vally is smiling. Not for any love of horses, but indulgently, looking down at his sister. His arm circling her waist. And it comes back to him now how Vally doted on Ruby. Playing dolls with her, and dress-ups, even running a comb through her glossy black hair. Edward had almost forgotten.

'I have to tell you, none of these will work,' says the doctor, his voice suddenly emphatic and stern.

Edward looks up, unsure of how much he's missed. He strokes his beard and makes an effort to look attentive.

'The cures. They do not address the most fundamental problem of the addict.' The doctor reaches into a deep drawer. He takes out a wooden tongue depressor and holds it upright on the desk. Then he moves his hand away and the stick falls flat. 'Relapse.' He raises an eyebrow, as though impressed by his own demonstration. 'Giving up the drug, while difficult, is not impossible. Most will manage for a week, a month, a year. Then comes the relapse, and one must start all over.' He takes the stick, stands it on its end and lets it fall again.

'Are you telling me he can't be helped?' Edward is suddenly clammy, his collar too tight around his neck. Relieved and appalled to have his own opinion confirmed.

The doctor pushes out his lips, making a high-pitched, tiny bird sound. He spreads his fingers on the desk. 'You must be prepared to try and fail, to try and fail again. Then, maybe, he has a chance.' He peers at Edward, something warmer, less definitive creeping into his voice. 'It doesn't sound like much, I know. But this is rare advice. Most people will try to sell you something. What I'm giving you is the only thing I know to have worked.'

Edward emerges into clear, soft sunshine. He stares at the elm trees, startled by the sudden green. As he takes the stone steps down to the street, pigeons flap their wings and rise up a moment. He stands on Collins Street, so that people must step around him, giving him impatient looks. He is gripped by a deep impulse. He should, he knows, turn right and head for home, and Vally. But he finds himself drawn, almost magnetically, to the left; he can't resist the feeling there is something that needs doing first.

...

The man behind the desk smothers a laugh behind his fleshy hand.

'Ah, I'm afraid that is just not possible. The prime minister sees no one without an appointment. He is a very busy man. If you'd like to leave your details I can pass them on, and he may contact you to arrange an appointment. But you cannot, eh, simply walk into Parliament House for a chat. No.' The thought seems to amuse the young man greatly; even his ears have turned pink.

'I'm sure that's true. But if you could please let him know that E.W. Cole is here to see him? If he says he hasn't the time I will certainly understand. But I'd appreciate your asking him.'

The young man looks at Edward, black bell-topper in hand. He grins uncertainly, tipping back on the legs of his chair. 'Alright. What shall I say it's in regard to?'

Edward stares blankly at the youth. But his mouth seems to move of its own accord. 'Regarding some letters that may be of interest to him.'

...

Edward is taken through a wide corridor of murky portraits. The young man has become brisk, business-like. He stops outside a heavy oak-panelled door and knocks twice. 'The prime minister will see you now,' he says, and turns on his heel.

Inside a large corner office with double arched windows and gold and olive décor, his old friend Deakin rises to greet him. Coming out from behind a massive desk, hand outstretched. A well-cut suit on his lean frame. The same beetle-black eyes. But his skin looks unhealthy, pale as wax.

'Edward. This is a surprise!' His eyebrows lifted and no smile. The two men shake hands.

'Thank you for seeing me, Alfred, I know you're busy.'

'That's fine. Take a seat.'

'No, no. I won't trouble you for long.'

Deakin leans back into the desk with arms folded. From the windows, Edward can see a small courtyard, the green tangle of ferns and palms, silver threads of water from a concrete fountain. A restful view.

'I've come to speak with you about the White Australia Policy.'

Deakin presses a hand against his mouth. 'I see. I did read your pamphlet. I believe I wrote you about it.'

'Yes.' Edward nods. 'Yes, I got your . . . note.' He glances at the floor. Deakin's shoes are black and highly polished, a cameo of Edward's face in each. 'You claim to bear the Chinese no ill will, and I believe you. But I wanted, felt I must, in fact, come and tell you that even facilitating or using the hatred of others is a grave mistake.'

Deakin offers a tense smile. 'I'll consider myself warned.'

Edward winces at the bitter tone. The days of their free and easy banter long gone.

'You're a fair and decent man. I always thought of you as a visionary, someone who could see the bigger picture. Can't you see our future lies with Asia—with the world? We cannot retreat from it and not do damage to ourselves. I know you want what's best for your country. So, for your country's sake, I beg of you, reconsider your position on this.'

'Or what?' His voice catches and he coughs to clear it. 'Say it, Edward. Reconsider, or what?'

'Or you must live with the consequences. As we all must.'

A muscle twitches in Deakin's cheek. He raises his hands and covers his face for a moment. 'And the letters? You have them here?'

Edward unlatches the briefcase. He reaches into a side pocket and holds three envelopes out to Deakin. They both stare at Deakin's trembling hands. At the trouble it gives him, drawing a letter from its envelope.

'What on earth . . . is this? What are you showing me?'

'Some rather nasty correspondence, I'm afraid, in relation to my White Australia pamphlets. Profanity, abuse, threats against me and my family.'

Deakin quickly scans the half-page of script. 'It's appalling. Truly. But why bring these to me?'

Why indeed? Because last night he felt how quickly fear, and hurt, and guilt could turn to hate. And how that hatred tarnished everything. And because the person you are is a choice you make, over and over.

But he cannot say all this to Deakin.

'I wanted to show you what "unity" and "common purpose" really look like. I'm no scholar, but they look remarkably like hatred to me.'

Deakin carefully tucks the letter back into its envelope. He hands the letters to Edward. Then he rubs his hands as if to brush crumbs from them. He conjures up a slow, deliberate smile. 'A few fanatics, no doubt. Every country has them. You don't expect me to change government policy over a handful of letters?'

Edward slips the letters into his bag. 'No, I don't know what I was expecting. I just knew I had to try. That was important. But I know you're busy, and I'm in rather a hurry myself . . .'

Deakin walks him to the door. 'Well. We must get together sometime. Give my regards to your family.'

...

Edward takes the route through the book department. It is the best time to see it: people carrying their paper parcels, people reading or strolling through, many with smiles, and all whitewashed by the strong afternoon sun. The pure, clean white of heaven, as he would picture it as a boy. For the second time that day, he simply stops and lets everyone walk around him. Tipping his head back to gaze at the roof. All that space, the creamy light, giving him a sense of openness and possibility. It always has; he's glad to find it still does.

...

He stands in the corridor with Simon Gabriel and Eliza. They are talking in sickroom whispers, a huddled conference, disjointed and brief. It makes him think of Ruby, that terrible night, the looks passed between doctor, husband, wife.

'You've no idea how sorry he is!' Eliza takes hold of Edward, just above the wrist. 'What did the doctor say?'

'Oh, he's hopeful of a recovery. Quite hopeful.' He pats her cool, bare hand. 'But first we must act to relieve any signs of suffering.'

'The cramps have just come on,' says Simon Gabriel. Something soothing in his mild, melodic voice. The skin on his face is partially black, splotched as cowhide. 'Should I go fetch him some liniment?'

'Yes,' says Edward. 'If you wouldn't mind. Eliza, I think you had better get some rest. I'll go and run him a bath.'

...

Vally lies in the bathtub, as naked and vulnerable as he has ever seen a grown man. Thin, and shivering, despite the water's heat. Damp strands of hair across his face and eyes.

'I'm sorry, Pa.'

'I know.'

Edward watches as he curls and uncurls his body, trying to find relief. Knuckles white on the tub's edge. Edward feels an urge to sing to him, something calming and wordless, but he is not the singing type. His narrow hips, the length of his legs, like Edward's own. The same knobby knees.

The water grows cool and Edward adds more hot. Steam marbles the air. He bends to wipe the hair from Vally's face with a soft towel. Vally begins to make a low humming sound. 'I'm going to be sick.'

Edward holds a basin to him. He expels some yellowish water. He lays his head against the tub and groans.

Edward sits in a hard, straight-backed chair, the basin and towel at hand. There'll be no more thoughts of country farms and foreign travel. He doesn't want to leave the Arcade again. They will fight this here among family and friends. It's better that way. He looks at Vally, his heart swelling, enormous. Never has he felt more love for any child.

Vally thrashes like a dolphin beached in shallows, soaking Edward through his shirtfront and lap. Edward, grateful for this small discomfort. Tensing, as Vally tenses, every muscle on call.

'It's like ropeburn,' says Vally. 'Ropeburn on the inside. Please make it stop.'

Edward swallows. 'I can't. But I'll stay here with you, I'll be here through it all.' He stands up, sits back down again. 'Try to remember that it will pass.'

Vally twists his head from side to side, his face screwed tight. He mutters and pounds the side of the tub with his fist. Then he laughs. 'Not a patch on the old man,' he says.

Edward fears it's the beginning of delirium. 'What was that? What are you saying there?'

Vally laughs again. 'Just what people have always said. He's not a patch on the old Cole. And they're right.'

But where, where can he have heard such a thing?

'Vally,' he says. With no idea what comes next. Just the feeling of holding some broken creature; one wrong move might damage it more. 'Vally, I want to tell you something I've never told anyone. Something that happened when I was on the goldfields.'

Really? Will he really tell that story? After fifty years of absolute, guilt-sealed silence? His pores open, all at once, drenching him. He sees that Vally has grown quite still. Only his foot moves—*sloop, sloop*—in and out of the water.

Of course he will tell it. Who in the world will ever need that story the way Vally now needs it? The story of a man who made bad choices, terrible mistakes, and still went on to live a good life.

'Well,' says Vally. 'I'm listening.'

Chapter Sixteen

EARLSBRAE HALL, DECEMBER 1918

Edward opens his eyes to see an old man staring down at him. Parchment-white skin, eyes pale but bright. He tries to call out, to say he hasn't any gold, but the words lack shape, his tongue pasted to his mouth. *Ar-gagne-gole!* He turns his head, half frantic. Sees the carved-oak bed-post in place of dust, flies, men. The pressed-tin ceiling in place of open sky. Decades fall into place like tumblers in a lock. A flash of relief—this is not the goldfields!—followed by the sadness, familiar and almost tender, that is coiled, snail-like, in the regions of his heart. For his wife is dead and he is old, old. His body doesn't work. They say he had a stroke, his entire left side made grudging, uncooperative. What did they expect? That he should walk around whole when he had lost his wife, lost half of himself?

Well, he didn't want to live in the city flat, that sad museum. Not as visitor to their old happiness. So he bought a country mansion and watched their jaws drop.

Told them to each choose a room, to visit often, bring their husbands, wives. Told them he would recuperate there, raise monkeys, garden.

But what has happened to his mirrors? He reaches out a hand and slowly, carefully angles them back into place. There. That's better. Now he can see his marigolds, his pansies and the odd small bird that comes to forage in the rich soil.

By the time he descends the staircase he is dressed for the evening meal: his favourite top hat with the grey silk band, and a tailcoat only slightly worn in the collar and cuffs. In the kitchen he finds food for the animals, left there by cook. She likes to say she is no zookeeper, no farmer's wife, and that her last employer had a brother with a knighthood. Edward loves to feed the animals. To see life sustained by this simple act. He likes the way Alfred gives his hand a cursory lick as he drops the meat into the bowl.

Tonight he is later than usual. Alfred and the marmosets are lined up by the door, waiting. Eyes gleaming in the eucalypt dusk. Edward hears crickets making their racket in the grass and the thin whine of a mosquito. He lowers himself to touch soft marmoset fur. Alfred nudges his way to Edward's hand, his coat rough and coarse beside the marmosets'.

Edward leans against a fluted column to watch them eat. Listens to the snorts and grunts and smacking sounds. Such contentment in seeing animals be themselves. Without the expectations, the disappointments, of our human dealings. All in all, he has been lucky. There was Linda's disastrous first marriage to a bounder, a seeker of Edward's fortune. But he went away quietly enough, after some prompting. The poor girl's embarrassment equal to her heartache. But she will be alright, now that she is married to a fine older fellow. All of them married, except for Pearl. Vally has been lucky with Mathilde. A headstrong girl, she has stuck by him through several long and sordid battles with old demons. Lying, staying away nights, telling her he was at Earlsbrae. A bad patch, after Eliza's death. The last time, Edward had paid for his stay at a scandalously expensive sanatorium, to give the girl, all of them, a rest. Perhaps it had even done some good; he has been well now for almost a year.

A frog starts up, making its noise like rubber on tin. Other frogs join in, their voices bouncing across the lawn. A star appears in the deepening, darkening sky.

Perhaps his children, too, feel disappointment. That he is growing old—dying—like any old man. That is how it seems to him at times.

He hides from them how much he misses Eliza. Shielding them from his loneliest self.

He hears the squeak of a handle, a hinge, and a soft-soled step.

'Pa? Are you still out there? Come inside, before your food gets cold.'

Eddy's voice. Kind. But, it seems to Edward, edged with disappointment.

...

For some reason they eat in grand style every night, with the kind of silverware a count might expect if he were to drop by. There is a fork for eating escargot, and one for taking the flesh from crabs. There is a tablecloth of Japanese indigo. They have never eaten crab as far as Edward remembers. Most nights they eat chicken. In fact, the grand style does not extend to the food itself. Tonight the chicken is being served in a sticky orange sauce, which is remarkable for its absence of aroma and taste, and also for its adhesive properties. It has put Edward in a contemplative mood. Is it really worth the effort of unsticking the chicken from the plate, only to have it stick to the roof of one's mouth?

'You seem a little quiet, Pa,' says Pearl. Edward is surprised that any of them can speak.

'Maybe his visitors have tired him . . . ?' says Belle, Eddy's wife. Edward has noticed her words are like long-distance runners, the last few often failing to cross the line. Sometimes she doesn't say the last word at all, but simply mouths it.

'Well, he certainly slept for long enough this afternoon,' says Vally, spooning chicken into his mouth and reaching for his goblet. Ah, thinks Edward, so that's how one eats it. No chewing, wash it straight down the gullet. And hope it doesn't stick on the way.

'It was kind of a surprise, seeing Joy Endicott come by. She was here only last month.' Eddy hunches his shoulders, and smiles.

'Yes, all very suspicious if you ask me,' says Vally, wagging his fork.

Pearl turns to look at her brother. 'What do you mean? Joy and Pa are old friends. Why do you say it's suspicious?' Pearl's shirt is high-collared, buttoned to the chin. Each button forms a tiny gold lion's head.

Vally holds up his hands, eyebrows raised. 'Let's just say that while Pa is deciding on certain matters, he may be susceptible to . . . outside influence.'

Belle gulps a mouthful of food and turns, wide-eyed, to Eddy.

'Vally, I rather think that's enough. We don't need to discuss this at the table.' Eddy stares at the tablecloth as he speaks, two dabs of colour showing high on his cheeks.

'Do you think it would be too much trouble,' says Edward, and they all turn to stare as though a potted palm had suddenly spoken, 'to ask cook to prepare something other than chicken tomorrow?'

Pearl frowns and tilts her head. 'I thought chicken was your favourite?'

Edward unfolds his napkin and dabs at his mouth. 'Yes, you could be forgiven for thinking that. But in actual fact I like it no more or less than any other food. Perhaps a little less, after tonight.'

He sounds cranky to his own ears. Strange how he often sounds disagreeable; he doesn't mean to be. Belle is right, he must be tired. Not used to having three visitors in one day.

...

Joy had been the first, and she had come in a motor car. A long white motor car. The sound of it had brought Alfred trotting over the grass for a closer look, with Edward shuffling behind him. She wore a summer dress and an oversized peach hat. She removed a long glove and bent to scratch Alfred behind the ears.

They had taken tea in the gazebo, where the roof was fringed with grapevine. Joy removed her hat and Edward realised she no longer looked ageless. Fine lines wandered from her lips and eyes, her forehead gently creased. He thought ageing suited her. For the first time since he'd known her she no longer looked like she was mourning.

He had thought about Joy a lot in the years since moving to Earlsbrae, where she visited him every six months or so. The visits had started after Eliza died, and for a while his children had speculated that he might remarry. Edward had found this amusing; Joy had found it almost alarming.

'Good God, I have money and freedom. What would I do with a husband?'

They spoke about marriage and death and grief; it was amazing all the topics he could broach with her. He told her that, at eighty-six, he had outlived too many people, and it was hard on him.

'This is what it's like: we are all gathered together in a small lifeboat, out at sea. A wave comes along and sweeps away one person. Then a shark leaps up and snatches another. And all I can do is sit there and wait my turn. There is no hope of rescue. Only more sharks and more waves.' He blushed, embarrassed at the bleakness of it. But Joy had pursed her lips and asked, What then? Heaven, afterlife, or nothing?

Well, he thought he had given up on heaven, along with his bible. But he has never lost the feeling that Ruby *exists* somewhere, warm and happy. And he believes, against all reason, that he will see Eliza again.

Joy said she could believe that, too. Not heaven, but something, a reunion of souls.

And it was a warm thought between them. They sat in silence, bees shimmying through the grapevine.

Then she told him she was thinking of retiring. She was fifty-five and very rich. She could start an art collection, become a patroness, a fairy godmother for young and struggling artists. She told him that she would like Pearl to take over the city boutique, and that one day it would all be hers.

'I thought I should check with you first, in case you had other plans for her.'

He told her it sounded perfect. Pearl loved the boutique and, after seventeen years there, she would run it beautifully.

He did not tell her that he thought the Arcade would not long outlive him. That was another grief he was keeping to himself.

...

It saddens him now, that his sons suspect Joy of plotting and scheming to take the Arcade away from them. Though it's partly his own fault for leaving them guessing. The more they question him, the more tight-lipped he becomes, not wanting to encourage behaviour that is clannish or possessive. The Arcade is not a birthright, as some of his children seem to believe, and not necessarily a boon, either; in the wrong hands it would be nothing but a burden.

'Maybe we could have crab tomorrow,' says Edward, raising his eyebrows. 'Crab in a sticky orange sauce.' Belle giggles. Pearl and her brothers look away from him, puzzled.

...

They do not question him about his second visitor. No one could suspect that poor soul of plotting anything. He had come an hour after Joy, in a dark car with a driver. Edward had not seen him for fifteen years, though he had heard of the terrible way his mind was wasting. Forcing him to abandon politics and then public life. Was it true he could read no more than a page at a time, remember no more than a paragraph?

They had sat together under the verandah, facing out onto the rainbow flowerbed, Deakin's skin loose and grey in the midday sun. Deakin whistled to the bulldog, and it came and settled at his feet. 'Good dog,' he said, and stroked its broad back. 'What's his name?'

Edward paused, tapping a finger on his knee. 'Alfred.'

Deakin gave a start and was silent a moment. Then he said—some of the old humour returning to his voice—'You named your dog *Alfred*?'

Edward shrugged, and his beard parted to reveal a grin. 'I also have a monkey named Quong Tart. It makes me feel I'm surrounded by old friends.'

Were they old friends? Deakin wanted to know, it was the reason he had come. The past weighed on him. Conversations from years ago rolled out in his head like radio plays. He did not sleep well. He often thought about Joy.

'I treated her badly, Edward. Turned my back on her overnight, to protect my reputation. But she was no angel. She . . . she bewitched me, I think. Why did I ever think so much of her?'

Edward said that she certainly had her good points. She was intelligent, generous, loyal.

'You know, she faked everything she saw at the séances,' said Deakin. He had taken off his jacket and was sweating, his shirt soaked at the armpits. 'She used them to gain money, or influence over people. Vulnerable people, like Eliza.'

Edward shook his head. 'Whatever happened at those séances . . . that's all in the past. Eliza saw the good in Joy, and that's why they were friends. Forget all that now, Alfred, leave it be.'

But for Deakin it was only the past that was real and immediate; the present was grey and faded.

'We haven't seen each other all these years. I thought you disapproved of me, because of the policy, and the mess with Joy.'

Edward was speechless. For how long would he carry this around, like some malformed twin, wanting it exposed, punished? The man was clearly in a bad way. What did he hope to gain here?

'I want to know how things stand between us,' said Deakin.

Edward touched his beard, and a long white strand came away with his finger. 'I thought you did your best. You pursued your vision for this country, and you gave it everything you had. I am proud to have known you.'

Deakin opened his mouth and a low groan emerged. Tears clouded his eyes.

...

'Maybe we could have salmon tomorrow. I'll talk to cook about it,' says Pearl without conviction, frowning at the half-eaten chicken on her plate. She prods the bird with her fork. She is very thin, thinks Edward. A challenge, like running the boutique, is just what she needs.

'Eddy doesn't eat salmon,' says Belle, glancing at her husband. 'He finds it . . .' She mouths a word: fishy. Edward has become a good lip-reader. People think that, because he is old, he must be deaf as well. They shout to be heard, and when they want to keep something secret they simply whisper it. Edward has found it useful not to correct them.

'Is there something special you would like?' asks Eddy, turning to his father. 'You hardly eat at all lately.'

Edward does not remember hunger. It is hard for him to imagine it now, that pressing, primal urge to fill the belly. Not that he has forgotten those lean and desperate years; he remembers *being* hungry. But the precise sensation eludes him. Instead, he experiences whims, fleeting desires. Most often for apples, crisp and juicy apples; he keeps some in a basket by his bed. Sometimes for foods he has not eaten in years: mallee fowl, or the Yorkshire pudding he ate as a child. The cravings can be sudden, intense, and for a moment they seem the key to everything: health, longevity, happiness.

'Peas,' says Edward. 'And not the kind from a can.'

...

When D'Ama came, it was late in the day. A thick heat had settled over everything. They sat in a courtyard out the back, beneath the shade of the house and a large fig tree. Figs lay squashed and bird-pecked around them. They saw no birds in that heat. The marmosets did not move from their place in the bushes and Alfred was dozing somewhere; they were alone.

'The children tell me not to come out in this heat. But I love it, always have.'

'You mustn't let them boss you around,' said D'Ama, glancing up at the shuttered windows. 'You are the grand patriarch, after all.' He gestured at the house, at the grounds. 'All this belongs to you, not them. Not yet.'

But Edward only shrugged. What does he care for the day-to-day now? What plagues him is the Arcade, and what will become of it. There is no one to run it the way it needs to be run: with single-minded and incorruptible vision. It could make money for years to come, prospering, but without purpose.

D'Ama filled his pipe. His hands were steady and his eyes clear. His suit, a pinstripe, seemed a little out of date. 'Ah, so you're worried about your legacy. What small trace of you will live on after you're gone?' He struck a match and it flared blue-gold; the air around it shimmered. Smoke rose but barely drifted.

D'Ama pushed back his chair. 'Who knows how the world will remember us? We can't all be Shakespeare, Columbus or Darwin.' D'Ama drew on his pipe, then pointed it at Edward. 'But don't worry, Edward, Melbourne will remember you. Who else do they have? Burke and Wills? The Kelly gang?' And he had crossed his legs and laughed his dry, smoky laugh.

Then they had talked about greatness and science and the war, which had just ended. D'Ama said the war had been inevitable. He thought there would always be wars, because that was the nature of men. Edward disagreed. Progress was the destiny of man, and progress would lead to peace. Without corruption or hunger or fanaticism there would be no need for wars, he argued; but the truth was the war had been a shock to him, and a terrible disappointment. It was a failure of reason, a triumph of tribalism, a mistake that must be learned from. D'Ama had said, Well, there will always be mistakes, that's part of human nature, too.

They had talked for several hours, but when Edward invited D'Ama to stay for dinner, he had shuddered visibly.

'Oh no, Edward. You can't complain to me about your cook all afternoon and then expect me to eat her food. Thank you, no, I think I'll go now. But why is it I always come to see you these days? When are you going to visit me?'

Edward had promised that he'd visit soon. But he could not for the life of him recall having mentioned his cook.

...

'Well, of course we won't just feed him peas. But he can have peas and the salmon, and maybe a cucumber salad,' says Pearl, folding her napkin and placing it beside her plate. A print of red lips, perfect on the white linen.

'I don't believe you told us the reason for Joy's visit,' says Vally, tossing his napkin onto the table.

Joy's visit. He had promised not to mention the boutique to Pearl just yet. Why do they bother him with these questions? Why don't they ask him about Deakin, showing up out of the blue after all these years? Or about D'Ama, who has been dead since 1905?

'She came to check on my health. To see if I was eating enough chicken,' Edward says.

...

Edward lies on his back waiting for sleep. He has never slept easily, has always risen early. He used to work his pie stall till the dawn, and tend to the children when they were sick, and he knows midnight in the gulf before it sounds. Now he sleeps no more than four hours a night. The hours pass in reading or remembering. Books form a tower by his bed, their paper markers like small white flags. Reading is a search, he thinks, a treasure hunt. His hunting turned to ransacking, with half-read books on every mantle, every sideboard. He keeps a lamp on in his room, he has his sheets changed every second day. He cannot stand the graininess. As if he is coming apart in those sheets, piece by tiny piece.

Drifting into sleep he returns again and again to the Murray. As though his drifting, any drifting, will always be defined by that river. He hears magpies and the creak of the boat and Beaver with his lazy l's. The wide, flat crack of Beaver's shotgun. Ants trek across his skin, explore the humid ranges of his neck and shoulders. Dragonflies hover, their frantic wings sheer and opal-tinged.

The stench of those old mining boots! Musk and peat and mildew. The trick of rubbing them with cooked-up eucalyptus.

The smell of lightning, like bicarbonate of soda.

The scrubbed-wood smell of the mission church. His back sore from all that sitting, and Beaver hunched and nodding off beside him. The blackness of Aborigines in borrowed clothes. One man dressed in hat and waistcoat, nothing more. His quiet dignity. While the reverend clutched his collar in shame at this minor defeat in front of other white men.

Oh, Beaver. He always believed they would meet again. But he has lived a lifetime—sixty-three years—without seeing that gap-toothed grin. He should have sought him out. The truth is—and it surprises him now—they were tired of one another by journey's end. Beaver's ceaseless humming, like someone taking a file to Edward's brain. And Edward, spitting out a mouthful of stringy possum, had sparked a rage in Beaver, who screamed at him to hunt his own food if his tastes were so particular. Apologies and appeasement followed. But those final weeks were silent and strained, held together by a wary civility. Cabin fever after months in their tiny boat—he sees that now. At the time, it felt like failure.

Perhaps he could still find a way to track him down, send him a letter.

Then he sees the grass stain on Eliza's dress. The one she was married in. The raised grain of fabric stained darker. She didn't mind. She said, 'It's only fresh, clean grass.'

Sunrise in the fernery. Its soft light the pale green of apple flesh.

Chapter Seventeen

EARLSBRAE HALL, JANUARY 1919

The lawyer walks across the black and white tessellated tiles. There is no need to knock; a woman servant opens the door as he approaches. Large potted ferns and birds of paradise brush against his pants as he crosses parquetry the colour of clean-poured ale.

'You can leave your hat right here,' she says.

The lawyer gazes up at the massive, shabby polar bear. There is no hatstand. He pauses. 'On the bear?'

She smiles at him. Her face is narrow, hatched with wrinkles. 'Go ahead. He don't mind.' She folds her arms, waiting to show him through to the back of the house.

...

When it seems everyone has arrived, about a dozen people, he decides to make a start. No one tells him to; they have barely said a word to him. They are his father's clients and he doesn't know them well. Perhaps they were expecting someone older.

As he reads, his eyes flick over the tops of his glasses to check the faces before him. He does this partly to see if his words are being followed, and partly out of interest. He loves to watch the faces of people made rich. To see the first unmediated flush of feeling cross their faces. Mostly he sees relief, satisfaction, awe.

Not today. This family looks as lost as children left by the roadside.

Ada Belinda twists a damp handkerchief in her lap. Ivy Diamond sits on the carpet, embracing a small bulldog. They have a watery composure, the air of people who have recently cried. Valentine holds his hands against his chin in prayer position, fingertips covering his mouth.

There is enough money and property to allow them all to live well, in some style, for the rest of their lives. This is what he has just told them. It is the part of his job he most enjoys.

Not today. Today he might as well be reading the shipping news to a group of desert dwellers. He takes a sip from his water.

'As you may be aware, this comprises the bulk of the estate, apart from a few small gifts and bequests which I will read out presently. Are there any questions so far?'

Nobody speaks. Valentine turns to gaze out the window. Pearl sits with her arms crossed and pressed to her stomach. No one bothers to look at the lawyer. Except for a small evil-looking monkey, which appraises him with glittering eyes. They had insisted on bringing the monkeys inside. They were family pets, they said, and would not bite. But the lawyer knows that jungle animals can never be trusted. He sits with his back to the wall.

'Alright then, on with the proceedings,' he says, shuffling the papers in his lap. The sound, to his ears, as loud as autumn leaves crunched underfoot. He reads out the names of a dozen people remembered in the will in some small way. Octavus Benson, Simon Gabriel, Nathaniel Owens, Mrs Quong Tart. His voice, precise and nasal, is muffled by the thick carpet.

'Now I will read out the section of the will entitled "Legacies".' His shirt is clammy, sticking to his back and armpits, his body cooked with embarrassment. He resists an urge to fan himself with legal documents. There is no way to avoid reading the complete will. He knows, for he has checked.

'I must warn you that what I'm about to read is altogether unorthodox, if not totally unprecedented.' He is surprised to see an effect, finally, upon his listeners. Ivy Diamond throws her head back and laughs, startling the dog. Edward grins, and Ada Belinda raises her tear-stained face.

The lawyer clears his throat.

> To Ada Belinda, my lovely Linda, I leave you my empathy and love of books. We named you ABC in honour of the alphabet, and I see that we were prophetic. Remember, books are never destinations, they are adventures, so have as many of them as you can.
>
> To Edward William, Eddy, my namesake, I leave you decency and a sense of honour. With these you will always do what is right for yourself and for others. You will have the love and trust of those around you, as I have had the love and trust of those around me.
>
> To Valentine Frances, Vally, named for the saint of love, I leave you my imagination and self-belief.

Use them to accomplish what your heart desires, they are a powerful force. Make sure it is really what your heart desires.

To Pearl Adelia, my shining jewel, I leave you my determination and courage. Live the life you want, and if they call you eccentric, take it as a compliment. If they don't, ask yourself what you are doing wrong.

To Ivy Diamond, my baby girl, I leave you good will and a happy disposition. The world is a grand place; go and have a wonderful time in it.

Goodbye, children. Live your dreams. Think of me in rainbows.

Edward William Cole

The lawyer feels the heat move into his neck and face. He imagines them a glowing, adolescent red. But the people in the room look almost happy. Ada Belinda has tucked her handkerchief away. The colour has returned to Pearl's lips and cheeks; she is instantly, strikingly beautiful. The lawyer, already overheated, averts his gaze. He looks at Octavus Benson and Simon Gabriel, side by side in their high-polish shoes, turning shy smiles to one another. It has gone, the lawyer concedes, as well as could be expected. He takes his glasses from his nose and rubs them with a cloth.

A monkey, hidden beneath a chair, chatters to himself.

'The final section refers to the maintenance and running of Cole's Book Arcade. In the earlier section I spoke of the division of the real estate. This section refers only to the business—in particular, to the appointment of three trustees who will jointly run the business together and will draw a salary for their efforts, commensurate with current managerial salaries. The trustees are named as follows: Ada Belinda Cole, Octavus Benson and Simon Gabriel.'

The faces before him look so startled that the lawyer scans the room, certain the monkeys are finally up to something. But the room appears orderly and, finding nothing amiss, he concludes that his words have taken them aback. Simon Gabriel lets his mouth hang open— a perfect pantomime of surprise—and turns to Octavus Benson as if to speak. But Benson is leaning forward, hands on knees, blowing the air from his mouth in one long breath. Ada Belinda looks straight ahead. Fingers pressed to her reddening cheeks as though to stop the colour spreading. The others stare openly at the three trustees.

The lawyer gathers his papers together, his damp hands leaving small, clear traces on the pages. What's the matter with these people? They receive their 'legacies' without so much as blinking, and then this ordinary business arrangement leaves them agape. He shakes his head. His task, at least, is done. He picks up his briefcase, nodding to Eddy and Pearl who are seated closest to him, and hurries from the room.

It's not until he reaches the front lawn, with its palm trees, bees and wistful smell of roses, that the lawyer slows his step. Pushing his glasses back up the bridge of his nose, somewhat embarrassed by how nervous the household made him. It isn't always easy dealing with people in their grief, and this family was certainly on the peculiar side. He allows himself a wry smile. Already he is turning the morning to anecdote, something to share with his colleagues over lunch. Making sure not to leave out the polar bear.

'Please, wait a moment!' The voice comes from behind him and the lawyer breaks into a fresh sweat. He turns to find Octavus Benson barrelling down the drive towards him. He seems agitated, wagging his large head from side to side. 'Did you hear the one about the woman, the black man and the thief?' he mutters, and starts to laugh a little wildly.

The lawyer feels his mouth go dry. Is the man a lunatic? Should he make a dash for his car? But Benson rubs his face and seems to collect himself. He drops his shoulders as though to minimise his substantial bulk, and clasps his hands together. 'I'm sorry to chase after you,' he says. 'But you left so suddenly, and I have a question about the will.'

The lawyer peers closely at his watch. 'I'm afraid I only have a minute. I must get to another appointment.' His voice thin and uncertain to his own ears.

'I wanted to ask, did he say anything to you about why he chose us?' Benson spreads his palms. 'The trustees, I mean.'

The lawyer frowns. 'Mr Cole was actually my father's client. If he said anything, it would have been to him. You could speak to my father, only he isn't too well right now.'

'I'm sorry to hear that,' says Benson. They smile awkwardly at one another. Then Benson turns and walks back towards the house.

Epilogue

MELBOURNE ZOO, ROYAL PARK, 1929

By the time Fletcher reaches the gate, his boots crunching gravel, he has been listening to the animals for half a mile or more. Birds, lions, monkeys—as well as Gracie, his eight thousand-pound Indian elephant. The sound: a sonic montage, discordant and enthralling, as essential to his dawning day as sunrise. The animals are always restless in the mornings, before their feed. Or is it, Fletcher wonders, that they dream each night of jungle, boundless savannah, sculpted desert, and so wake each day to the strangeness of their world?

He nods and smiles at the other keepers as he makes his way to Gracie's enclosure. Everyone is friendly, but the animals come first. The time for coffee and small talk is later, just before they open the heavy iron gates. As usual, Gracie is waiting for him. Her trunk sways a casual hello, but her dark eyes are fixed on Fletcher as he hauls out the hay and vegetables she will eat by the pound. He breathes in the hay, sweet and wholesome against the elephant's swampy odour.

As he works, he tells Gracie about the day ahead. His voice is low and rhythmic; the elephant has good ears. He tells her that the morning's chill will soon give way to a fine autumn day. She is no longer young and feels the cold in her bones, her knees and swollen ankles. He tells her that already, as they speak, there are people leaving their houses and making their way to the zoo to see her. That she is a fine, strong elephant, and that most of them have never seen an elephant before. Some of them are children who will want to ride on her back, and who will have stayed awake all night just thinking about this. The elephant sways and twitches her long ears.

After she has eaten she moves close to him, allowing him to stroke her trunk and look into her eyes, which are small, like chips of amber in her walnut hide. He feels the complex play of muscles beneath the skin. Fletcher checks on her water and her straw and, waving goodbye, goes to join the other keepers for their morning tea.

He sugars his tea, three spoonfuls, and listens to the talk around him. There are two conversations going at once, both about football. When asked which team he favours, he always says the Tigers. Not because he knows one team from another, but because tigers are a wonderful animal, proud and stealthy.

'Dished out some punishment,' says one, a man named Levin, and by this Fletcher deduces that the Tigers have won another game.

He smiles and pushes the hair from his eyes. 'We taught 'em a lesson,' he replies, having heard this said.

This leaves Fletcher free to stare out the window at the tall ghost gum with cockatoos in its upper branches. Above, the sky is pale and cloud-streaked.

He tries to picture the heat and colour and chaos of India.

He has read that the towns smell so pungently of spice they can be detected from several miles away, and that you cannot walk the streets for all the crowding of cows and water buffalo. But it is the jungle that he longs to see, with real wild elephants, and tigers hiding in its dense heart.

It is for this that he saves his money, forsaking games of football, and beer—which is easy—as well as the geographic magazines and tobacco he once bought every week. It is not that he doesn't love his job, the zoo and Gracie, but that somehow it seems these things are a dress rehearsal for what awaits him.

He keeps a jar of cloves by his bed, to accustom himself to exotic smells.

He drains the tea, savouring the last sweet drops, and leaves the tea room with the other men. He goes in search of Ted.

Lately, the demand for elephant rides has been growing. The children form sprawling queues where they jostle and push one another. It would be good to have an extra pair of hands around. Fletcher cannot supervise the rides and the queuing children both; he must keep his eye on Gracie, to see she does not become tired or irritated. An eight thousand-pound elephant in a bad mood is no one's friend.

He finds Ted, the young assistant keeper, cleaning out the aviary floor. It's a mug's job, the kind they give you when you start. Fletcher smiles to see it. It reminds him of his apprenticeship, nearly twenty years ago, and gives him a warm feeling in his chest. He remembers how it felt to have a job, the respect of others and a little money in his pocket for the first time, and the way he would fall asleep, head knocking against the window, on the train ride home.

Ted looks up and flashes his teeth in a grimace. 'Little buggers poop a lot,' he says.

Fletcher nods. 'Try cleaning up after an elephant.'

Ted laughs and wipes his brow. He is young, with golden hair and biscuit-coloured skin. He moves easily, picking up his tools and locking the gates behind him. 'Don't count on any help from me today,' he says. 'We got monkeys coming in at ten, a pile of them.' He shrugs. 'I guess they'll want me for the whole day.'

Fletcher scratches his head. He is disappointed, but doesn't like to show it. 'What sort of monkeys?'

Ted shakes his head. He holds the bucket away from his body, swinging it by the handle. 'I don't know, a mixed bunch. Come from some arcade closed down in Bourke Street.'

Fletcher stares. Of course, he has read about the closure of Cole's Book Arcade. Yet it doesn't seem that long ago that he was twelve, sitting in a sun-drenched chair and looking through *The Jungle Book*.

He opens his mouth to tell Ted. Ted moved down from Brisbane last year and wouldn't know of Cole's. Fletcher often fills him in on things: the death of Squizzy Taylor, the invention of a lie-detector machine. But this, he realises, he has no words for. He could tell him about the books and the fernery and Wonderland. But how to put into words the feeling that it gave you: that possibilities abounded, that the world was wide and that you yourself were capable, adventurous, destined? And if he found the words, what meaning would they hold for someone who has Luna Park and the pictures every weekend?

Fletcher rocks back on his heels. 'I used to go to that arcade. Quite a place, in its day.'

And Ted walks off with his great bouncing steps to meet the monkeys. Perhaps the same ones that Fletcher used to stare at, bug-eyed, for hours at a time.

As he stands there the aviary birds grow loud and restive, their calls increasing to fever-pitch. He is puzzled for a moment, shading his eyes and squinting up at the iron cage. Then he sees the cockatoo, a free bird, which has perched itself outside the aviary bars. Grey-tongued: a molten bead inside its beak. Talking up its freedom, or playing it down, or whatever it is that free birds talk about.

...and finally thanks to the extraordinary children's author Edward Ogilvie, whose story inspired this work of memoir... and me in so many ways...

Acknowledgements

Thank you to everyone who helped bring this book into the world: Judith Lukin-Amundsen and Melanie Ostell for their generous advice on early drafts; Ali Lavau and Catherine Taylor for their editorial guidance and insights; the dedicated team at Allen & Unwin, especially Annette Barlow, Clara Finlay and Renee Senogles; Lisa White for her charming cover; *The Australian* and Vogel's for their support of new writing; the ASA mentorship program; the residencies that gave me time and space to write: the Katharine Susannah Prichard Writers-in-Residence program and the Writing at Rosebank Fellowship; Bronwyn Eastman for a flexible and book-friendly workplace; Patrick O'Brien for showing me the magic of Cole's Book Arcade; my family, the Langs and the Buteras, and especially Mum and Dad, for a lifetime of love and support.

A special thank-you to Gerard Butera, for everything—not least his belief in me, this book and the value of art in our lives.

And finally, thanks to the extraordinar͟ ͟ ͟e
Edward Cole, whose story inspired this work ͟ ͟ ͟n,
and me, in so many ways.